Realms Of The Fae 2
Marked By The Hunt

Realms Of The Fae 2
Marked By The Hunt

Avril Sabine

Cracked Acorn Productions
Australia

Realms Of The Fae 2: Marked By The Hunt

Published by

Cracked Acorn Productions

PO Box 1365

Gympie, Queensland 4570

Australia

978-1-925131-57-4 (Kindle)

978-1-925941-23-4 (EPUB)

978-1-925131-58-1 (Print)

Genre: Young Adult Urban Fantasy

Copyright 2016 © Avril Sabine

Cover design by Caitlyn Petersen

*For Mum, who's always there for me no
matter what else is going on in her life. No
words are adequate to convey how I feel, so all
I can say is thank you.*

When Quinn's sister disappears she follows her, ending up in the realms of the Fae. Stuck in a strange world and constantly surrounded by danger, she has to figure out how to rescue her sister and return home, while trying not to catch the attention of a vindictive Fae. Somehow she needs to do all of that as well as avoid the Wild Hunt, a pack of Fae and Demi Fae and their overly large wolves, which spend their nights hunting those marked to die. Quinn isn't sure she's up to the challenge. She fears no human would be.

*

This story was written by an Australian author using Australian spelling.

Name Pronunciation

Like many names there is more than one way to pronounce the following ones. These are the pronunciations used in this story.

Kaeder (kay-der)

Mairwin (mare-win)

Baenen (bay-nen)

Gwyl (gwill)

Derwyn (der-win)

Tamek (tam-eck)

Darci (dah-see)

Arnall (are-nell)

Maya (may-ah)

Chapter One

Quinn could think of no way to change her mum's mind. That didn't mean she was about to give up. "But Mum–"

"I told you last week your father and I are going out tonight. If you don't take your sister with you, then you can't go." Her mum half turned away.

"It's the school holidays. Of course I want to spend them with my friends. I've been looking forward to this all week." She'd made plans with Daisy when she'd stayed with her during the first three days of the school holidays.

"You knew before you went to Daisy's grandparents that we needed you to babysit." She held up her hand when Quinn opened her mouth to speak. "Enough. I need to finish getting ready or we'll be late." She strode from the lounge room.

Recognising the finality of her mum's tone Quinn

didn't bother following, sending a glare in Marley's direction instead. At fifteen, her sister was two years younger than her, but nearly as tall. Where she had murky green eyes, her sister's were the clearest green. Her sister's brown hair also had perfect auburn highlights. When she'd recently tried to do something similar to her own brown hair, it had ended up making all her hair a dark plum colour. It didn't look bad, but it hadn't been what she'd planned to do.

Marley rose from the lounge chair. "Are we going to the dam, or staying home?" She had a hopeful expression on her face.

Quinn wanted to say no, but who knew when she'd next get the chance to go swimming in the dam during a full moon. Daisy had mentioned several times when she'd stayed with her Saturday, Sunday and Monday that she had to go swimming in her grandparents dam during a full moon. That it was like swimming in a pool of silver. It probably wasn't, because Daisy had a tendency to exaggerate, but she wanted to find out for herself.

Marley's hopeful expression faded. "Please, Quinn."

"I should say no since you nearly killed Buddy."

"How was I supposed to know he'd eat the biscuits, plastic bag and all? I didn't even give them to him. He got them off the kitchen bench himself. It's not my fault he's not very smart. You should have got a cat. They're smarter than dogs."

She opened her mouth to defend her dog. He wasn't very pretty, she had no idea what breed he was, he had a boring name, but she hadn't been able to resist his sad eyes when she'd seen an ad for him. His last owner had died and he'd needed a new home in a hurry. His deep brown eyes had stared at her out of the photo, begging to be loved.

There was no time to argue. Not if she wanted to go to the farm with Daisy, Ted and Scout. "Don't you dare hassle Scout."

"I never hassle him. He's the one who always talks to me."

"That's because he's being polite. You're the one that rambles."

"Did he say something?"

"Of course he didn't. He's too polite for that. But I know him." In fact, she'd known him nearly her entire life. As well as Daisy and her twin brother Ted. The four of them had been best friends since they were toddlers, all living in the same street, only several houses separating them.

"Can we go?"

She paused a moment before nodding. "But if you

annoy anyone…" She let her words trail off rather than trying to figure out a threat.

"I won't. Promise." The last word was flung over Marley's shoulder as she hurried from the room. "I won't be long. Don't leave without me."

She stared after her sister, sighing. How was she ever going to get Scout's attention when Marley was hanging around monopolising him? She had no idea, but guessed she better get ready and send a text to Daisy so they could pick her up.

It didn't take long to put on swimmers, pulling a pair of jeans and a t-shirt over them. After shoving a few things in an overnight bag she spent a few minutes with Buddy, who still hadn't bounced back from his vet trip. Since it was only Sunday she supposed it hadn't been that long. He was sure to be fully recovered in another few days.

By the time Ted hit the horn out the front, Marley was waiting in the lounge room for her. She wore a skirt and far too much make up, her overnight bag at her feet. Before Quinn had the chance to warn her sister away from Scout again, her parents entered the room.

"I want you both home by lunch tomorrow." Her mum kissed first her cheek, then Marley's.

Quinn nodded. There wasn't any point in staying

longer since she'd have Marley with her. "Sure." She returned her dad's hug as he said goodbye.

"See you, Mum, Dad." Marley picked up her bag and headed for the door. Opening it, she grinned at Scout who had his hand raised to knock. "Hi, Scout."

Quinn wanted to push Marley out of the way so she could be the one to receive Scout's smile. Instead, she said goodbye to her parents and headed for the door, her grip tightening on the handle of her overnight bag. It was so unfair. Marley had barely spoken to Scout until this year. "Are we going or standing around all night?" She slid her feet into the sneakers she'd left by the front door.

Scout turned his grin towards Quinn. "Going." He looked past Quinn to her parents. "See you."

Quinn trailed behind Scout and Marley, enough light cast from the streetlight for her gaze to roam across his narrow frame. Ted had called him Scout back when they'd first started school and his favourite phrase had been 'we should check that out'. Nothing had changed. He still liked to 'scout' out new places and explore. There were times when she envied his tendency to go off for days at a time exploring. Most times she remembered the disaster her own attempt at exploring had been and her envy soon died.

Once the overnight bags were in the boot, Quinn

got in the front seat, wishing it wasn't her turn. Marley was likely to take sitting next to Scout as an invitation to talk to him the entire drive. After buckling up, she faced Daisy who was seated behind Ted, unusually silent. "What's wrong?"

Daisy gestured towards her brother. "He's the reason Paul won't date me. Actually, both of them are." She looked past Marley to include Scout in her glare.

Quinn frowned. "That doesn't make sense."

"He heard about the last one." Scout grinned.

"Oh." Quinn shared a sympathetic look with Daisy. Although she did understand why they'd gone after the last one. He'd cheated on Daisy and Ted was as protective of his sister as she was of him.

"What could he expect?" Scout asked. "You and Quinn are like sisters. Of course I'm going to look out for you."

"Exactly," Ted said.

Quinn's heart plummeted. Sister was the last thing she wanted to be.

"What about me?" Marley asked.

"Did you want me to think of you as a sister?" Scout asked.

Marley giggled.

Quinn interrupted before her sister could come up

with a more sickening reply. "Will we get to the farm early enough to see the moon reflected in the dam?"

"Yep. We'll arrive exactly on time. The moon will be directly overhead. We calculated it to make sure," Daisy said.

"I calculated it," Ted corrected.

"I helped," Daisy argued.

"Do you think you and Ted can go back to your stony silence, Daisy? I'm going to have a sleep. Might as well since we've got an hour to kill," Scout said. "Ouch. No need to hit me."

Quinn grinned at her friend, who looked like she was having a difficult time not returning the grin. Facing forward, she got more comfortable. Maybe Scout had the right idea. If she slept through the hour it took to get to Daisy and Ted's grandparent's farm, she'd manage to stay up a lot later once they arrived.

It didn't work. She tried to sleep, but thoughts of Scout sitting in the back with Marley kept interrupting. Did he really think of her as a sister? Closing her eyes, she tried not to think about it. The thought kept intruding. What made him prefer Marley? And after his last comment to her sister, it was pretty obvious he did. She tended to giggle around him. An annoying giggle that managed to sound not only fake, but nervous. How could he prefer that?

Still trying to figure it out, she fell asleep, not waking until the engine was silent. Blinking sleepily, she looked towards Ted, who chose that moment to open his door. Squeezing her eyes shut she reached for the overhead light, turning it off while mentally agreeing with the grumbles coming from the back seat.

"I don't see what you lot have to complain about." Ted got out of the car. "You didn't have to stay awake." He peered back into the car. "And all of you snore."

Daisy flung her door open. "I do not."

Quinn got out of the car more slowly, smiling as she listened to Daisy and Ted's good-natured arguing. The smile faded when she glanced in the back to see Marley half sprawled over Scout, who was gently waking her. She hurried after Daisy and Ted. Nothing was the same when Marley was with them. Normally it would have been the four of them walking together, joking.

Trying to take her mind off Marley and Scout, who she could now hear following her, she looked around at her surroundings. Ted had parked in the paddock near the dam. There was only a short distance to the side of the dam that rose up high enough to make a good jumping platform.

Reaching the top, she stood beside Daisy and Ted, staring at the moon reflected in the still water below. It looked amazing. Daisy had been right. This was something she needed to do. They'd gone swimming each night she'd stayed at the start of the holidays, but those nights were lame in comparison. Although they hadn't seemed so at the time.

Marley came to a stop beside Quinn, Scout on her other side. "Are we planning to go in, or are we going to stand and stare all night?"

Quinn fought the urge to push her sister in. Her hands curled into fists as she barely managed to control them.

"I don't see you rushing to get in," Scout teased Marley.

Marley tugged off her skirt and top, tossing them to the side as she kicked off her sneakers. "I guess I'm going first." Raising her hands above her head, she dived into the water. Her body slid through the centre of the reflection of the moon, barely making a ripple.

Quinn waited for her sister to surface. The water remained still. She took a step forward, nearly at the edge. Marley better not be playing a joke on them.

"Where is she?" Scout's voice reflected the worry Quinn felt.

"Is it possible to hold your breath that long?" Ted asked.

Daisy grabbed Quinn's arm. "I'm going to throttle your sister when she surfaces. This isn't funny."

When the water remained smooth, fear curled through her stomach. She tugged her arm from Daisy, ignoring her comment to let someone else go. Not bothering to remove her shoes or clothes, she dived off the bank. Aiming for the reflection of the moon, she slid through it, the water colder than she'd expected. Is that what had happened to Marley? Had the cold caused her to cramp? Her hands brushed the bottom of the dam, the depth of the water making it impossible for her to see.

Twisting and turning in the water she tried to find her sister. When her breath burned in her lungs, she swam to the surface, hoping to find her there. Breaking the surface, she tread water as she wiped the drips from her eyes. Her mouth dropped open and she wiped at her eyes again. The scene before her remained the same.

Chapter Two

She was no longer in the dam. Looking around, she had no idea where she was. Somehow she'd ended up in the middle of a forest edged lake, the only similarity being a reflection of the moon in the water. But even that was different. This moon was several days off full. She continued to tread water, trying to figure out what was going on. What had happened to the dam? And the rise of dirt Daisy, Ted and Scout had stood on. Most important of all, where was Marley?

Not knowing what else to do, Quinn swam for the shore. She was only halfway there when a shout rang out across the lake. That had been her sister. She tried to swim faster.

"No! I'm not going with you. Anyway, I'm too young to work in a nightclub. Let me go," Marley shouted.

Quinn was now close enough to the edge of the lake to see the shadowy figure of her sister under the trees and a tall thin person who had to be over six feet. She didn't know whether to shout out a warning or try and take him by surprise.

"Masquerade isn't any old nightclub. You accepted the favour, you must pay the price. Why did you come to this realm if you weren't looking to pay early? You had until the end of your human year before I came to collect the debt. So why did you call me to you?"

"I don't know how to return home. I want you to take me back."

"I told you to call me when you're ready. Before the last day of the year. I'm not a… what do you call them in your world? Taxi."

"I didn't plan to come here. I was swimming with my sister and her friends. You have to take me home. They'll be worried."

"Swimming?"

"Yes. Let me go."

The man holding onto Marley laughed. "It's a full moon, isn't it?"

"What's that got to do with anything?"

The man laughed once more. "Absolutely everything. But that isn't my problem. Time to repay the favour." He threw Marley over his shoulder and strode through the trees.

Marley stayed still for a few seconds before she began kicking and screaming.

Quinn tried to swim faster, but she was already going as fast as possible. By the time she reached the edge of the lake, she could no longer see or hear Marley. She dropped to the grass, shivering. Wrapping her arms around herself, she tried to think what to do. Where were they? Hearing a noise behind her, she rose to her feet to face it, wishing she had something to defend herself with.

A shadowy figure came to a stop, hands raised, palms towards her. "It's okay. I'm human. Like you."

She took a step back from him. It was okay? Her sister had been kidnapped, she had no idea where she was and who started a conversation with a comment like that? She eyed his broad shoulders, wishing there was more light to see him clearer. "What would you be other than human?"

"Fae."

"Fae? You mean like fairies and elves?" She took another step away. Could she outrun him?

"Yeah." He lowered one hand and held out the other. "I'm Gideon."

He must think her an idiot. There was no way

she was getting close enough to shake his hand. "I'm Quinn." She waited for the usual comment people made. It was annoying having to explain that her name wasn't a boy's name. Her parents had chosen to give her and her sister unisex names.

"I guess you'll be going to Masquerade."

It took her a second to register his comment since she hadn't been expecting it. Then it took her a few more seconds to make sense of it. "The man who kidnapped my sister mentioned that name."

Gideon nodded. "I heard."

"You heard?" When he nodded again, she demanded, "Then why didn't you help her? Why did you let him take her away like that?"

It was Gideon who took a step back this time. "He's Demi Fae."

The way he'd spoken the words made it seem like that was all the explanation she needed. But it wasn't. "You could have done something."

"I was nearly that clueless when I first ended up here. I only wish I hadn't thought it was far too crazy and researched more when I had the chance."

"I don't have time for this." She half turned away from him, unwilling to turn her back on a stranger. Particularly one that was taller and probably stronger than her. She had to find her sister. As annoying as she was and even though she'd nearly killed her dog and was chasing after the boy she liked, she couldn't desert her.

Gideon reached for her, grabbing hold of her wrist. "Shh. Can you hear them?"

She started to pull away from him, freezing when she heard the barely discernible howling of dogs in the distance. "What is it?"

"The Wild Hunt."

She stared at him, wishing there weren't so many shadows to hide his expression. "This is not happening." She slowly shook her head. "These are all myths." Fae, Demi Fae, Wild Hunt. They were all words from fairytales. He was clearly crazy. She didn't know exactly what was going on, but she did know her sister was in trouble. "I have to go." She tried to pull out of his grip.

His hand tightened around her wrist. "They might not hurt you, but if they do catch you they're going to ask if you've seen me. And there's no reason for you to risk your life by lying to them." He drew her towards the lake.

She struggled to escape. "Let me go." Her words brought to mind her sister's pleas. "You don't understand." Her sister was getting further away and she had no idea how to find her.

"I'm going to Masquerade Nightclub. If you hide with me, I'll take you there."

Again she froze. She needed to find her sister, but the sounds of the Hunt growing closer made her want to run. Gideon's grip on her wrist added to the feeling she'd had ever since her sister had failed to surface in the dam.

"Look, I know I'm a stranger. But I'm desperate here. I'm not about to let them catch me. Please, what could it hurt to hide until they're gone?"

She let him tug her closer to the water. She had no idea. With how close the sounds were growing, she'd better figure it out fast. She took another couple of steps forward when he continued to tug on her wrist. "Are you sure you know where my sister was taken?"

He nodded. "I've been making my way there for the past month."

She couldn't risk not finding out if he knew. Her sister needed help and she had no idea where to find her. "Okay." She followed him into the water, trying to ignore the fear rising in her. The situation was strange, she didn't trust Gideon, but she couldn't understand why she was so scared. A little scared was to be expected, but not the rapidly increasing fear she was feeling.

Gideon continued to hold her wrist tightly. "When

they get close you need to stay completely still and not make a sound." He stopped once the water was up to his chest and finally let go of her wrist.

She watched as he half removed the black backpack, she hadn't noticed he was wearing, and take two narrow tubes from it. "What are you doing?" Her body was tense and she wanted to run. Remaining where she was took a ridiculous amount of effort.

He put his backpack on again and held out one of the tubes. "It's a hollow reed. When the Hunt is close we need to stay beneath the water. It's the only way to be absolutely certain they don't pick up your scent. You really don't want to be marked by the Hunt too."

She wanted to ask him more questions, but the sound of the Hunt had grown louder and the urge to run became impossible to ignore. Still clutching the reed, she started to turn away. Mindless fear swamped her and the only thought she had was escape.

Gideon grabbed her hand and wrapped her fingers around the thick chain necklace at his neck. "Don't run. Never run. They will chase." Continuing to hold her hand around the necklace, he raised the reed to his lips and sank beneath the water, tugging her with him.

The fear receded the moment her hand wrapped

around the necklace and she was able to think again. She mirrored his actions, sinking beneath the surface of the water. It took her a moment to get the hang of breathing through the reed. The sound of the Hunt was loud, even beneath the water. She tried to resist, but curiosity got the better of her and she rose enough to peer above the water. Fear raced through her and she froze. Gideon dragged her down and she was relieved he did. She'd seen more than enough.

There was no way she wanted to come face-to-face with the creatures travelling away from her. They'd carried a mixture of weapons. Swords, spears, axes, bows. And they'd all been mounted on horses with wolves running with them. Impossibly large wolves with sharp teeth that looked like they'd make short work of a full grown human. They hadn't scared her as much as the creatures riding on the horses. The one that had led the pack had a rack of antlers rising from his head, his torso bare and showing wiry muscles. He'd been the least frightening. The assorted creatures travelling with him had struck fear into her. There'd been spider like people with multiple legs, clinging to the backs of horses. Amongst them had been extremely large horses with even larger creatures that looked square and solid and mountainous, lower incisors protruding over their upper lips. And there'd been others. Numerous creatures of various shapes, sizes and colours.

When the sounds of the Hunt had faded into the distance, Gideon let her rise. She stared at him, lost for words.

"What did you think you were doing? I told you to stay still."

"What were they? Those creatures. What were they?"

"Fae and Demi Fae. You can always tell a Fae from a human by the ears. They have a slight point to them, even the Fae that are part human. Those ones, the Fae in the Hunt, they live in the Fringes. Outcasts and misfits. Some are looking for a way to return to favour while others love the hunt."

"How do you…" Her voice trailed off. Escape? Stop them? She tried to figure out how to ask what she wanted to know. "You said you were marked by the Hunt. How do you stop being marked?"

"By avoiding them for seven years."

She opened her mouth twice and still nothing came out. She opened it once more. "Seven years?" Her voice sounded like it belonged to a mouse.

"That's why I have to go to Masquerade Nightclub.

It's a sanctuary. A place where even mortal enemies aren't allowed to attack each other."

"How do you know all this?"

"I've been stuck in the realms of the Fae for a month. The Wild Hunt is only active at night. From sunset to sunrise. It's safe to travel during the day."

She closed her eyes, her hand tightening around the reed she held. Why couldn't this have been a dream? A nightmare. But it felt too real. The chill of the water against her skin, the shiver of her body from the light breeze that swirled around her and the echo of the Hunt in her memory.

Chapter Three

Quinn opened her eyes, wishing for daylight so she could see Gideon better. "Why is this happening?"

"What do you mean?"

"Why am I here? How is any of this possible?"

"Your sister made a bargain with the Fae. A Demi Fae to be precise."

"How do you know?"

"I heard them arguing before you arrived. I was hiding amongst the trees near the water's edge. From what I can figure out, she was taking your dog for a walk and he was sick. She was talking to him, wishing she could understand him so she could figure out what was wrong. Your sister was worried about what you'd say when you came home and found him sick. Kaeder noticed her and offered to tell her what your dog had to say if she agreed to owe him a favour in exchange."

"Kaeder?"

"The owner of Masquerade Nightclub. He collects humans for his staff. So he's often in our world adding to his collection."

"Well he's not about to collect my sister."

"What are you going to do? Offer yourself in exchange?"

She shook her head, not liking that option either. "There must be something."

"He traps people into owing him favours so he has humans to work in his nightclub. He's not going to want to exchange the favour for anything less than he already has."

She'd figure it out when she got there. "Can we leave now? I want to find my sister."

"We can't move on until daylight. They might come back this way. We have to stay beside water."

"I need to find my sister." She should have pushed Marley in the dam like she'd been tempted to. Should have said no to taking her. Or refused to go to the dam if she was stuck babysitting. If she'd refused to take Marley none of this would have happened. She would have been safe. Her thoughts faltered. Until the end of the year. "If I hadn't followed her, would we have known? Or would she have disappeared without us knowing?"

Gideon shrugged. "That depends on your sister. Only if she managed to get word back to you."

The sound of a wolf howling drew her attention and she stared into the forest. "Did they leave some behind?"

"I doubt it. There are wolves in the forest. Most of them stay away from people, but when they're in a pack…" His voice trailed off.

Quinn was glad. She didn't need graphic details. Her mind was more than capable of coming up with enough gory details on its own without anyone else's help. "Do they only hunt at night too?"

"No."

"Then how are we meant to get to the nightclub?"

"By using a great deal of caution."

That wasn't what she wanted to hear. "How far away is it?"

"It's still a couple of days away by foot."

"I can't take that long to find her." Her teeth were starting to chatter.

"Come on, let's wait on the banks of the lake out of the breeze." He wrapped his fingers around her wrist again and tugged her towards the trees.

She shook free of his grasp, continuing to push through the water. "Stop grabbing me all the time." She sent a glare towards him even though she knew he wouldn't be able to see it. "I need to find my sister. Now."

Gideon pointed to a cluster of trees with some low shrubs at their bases. "That's where I hid when I heard them. It's fairly sheltered."

"Are you listening to me?" She stumbled onto the bank of the lake, stopping to face him.

"Yeah, but I don't think you're listening to me."

"I have to find my sister. She's only fifteen. I was meant to be looking after her tonight."

Gideon remained silent for a moment. "I don't think you understand exactly how dangerous it is here. This is the realms of the Fae. All the rules are different. And nothing like what we're accustomed to. You could be killed because one of the Fae didn't like the way you spoke to them. Or they could torment you for an eternity. Most of the food can't be eaten and something as simple as iron can protect you better than a gun." He held up his necklace before letting it fall back against him. He started to reach for her, but let his arm drop to his side before he came into contact. "Come on. Let's get out of the breeze."

She watched him walk towards the cluster of trees he'd hidden amongst earlier. Her sister needed help. She looked in the direction Kaeder had taken Marley. How was she meant to sit around waiting for daylight when her sister was in trouble? She shivered, wrapping her arms around herself.

"Are you coming?"

She looked in the direction Gideon's voice had come from, unable to see him.

"Daylight's only about two hours away. Two and a half at the most."

With one last look towards where her sister had been taken, she headed for the clump of trees. She nearly tripped over Gideon. When he shifted, she heard a crinkling noise.

"If you sit beside me, I'll share my survival blanket with you. It's dry. All my stuff is stored in resealable plastic bags."

She wanted to say 'no way am I getting that close', but she couldn't stop shivering. She sat down, moving near while still trying to keep some space between them.

Gideon reached out and wrapped an arm around her shoulders, tugging her against him, the survival blanket making crinkling sounds. "I don't bite." He lowered his voice. "Much." There was laughter in his voice.

She wanted to protest his actions, but the warmth of his body and the shelter of the blanket kept her silent. "How did you end up here?"

"The same as you. Through a moon portal. It was absolutely freezing. I guess that's to be expected. Sydney in July isn't exactly summer."

"Wait a minute. You said you've only been here a month. September is nearly over so it couldn't have been July."

"That long already? Dad probably thinks I'm dead." The earlier humour faded from his voice to be replaced by desolation.

"Gideon, it can't have been July."

He remained silent for a moment. "Time doesn't run the same between the human world and here. Haven't you heard all those stories about people who've returned home only to find a hundred years have gone by while they've spent only a short time in the realms of the Fae?"

She felt like she was going to throw up. In a hundred years there'd be no one left alive that she knew. That couldn't happen. Her parents, her friends and Buddy. "No. I can't stay here that long." She started to rise.

Gideon's arm tightened around her and he pulled her back against him. "Don't panic. That'll get you killed."

"Stop grabbing me all the time. I have to go after my sister."

He took hold of her shoulders, forcing her to remain seated, the survival blanket falling away. "Running won't help. Neither will panicking. In this realm most of the time you'll only have yourself to rely on. Favours come with strings. Ones so thick and tangled they trip the unwary."

She stilled. "What do you expect for helping me?" She felt him come closer, his face centimetres from hers.

"To be human."

Several times she replayed his words over in her mind and still they made no sense. "Who?"

"Both of us. I'm not Fae and yet I've spent a month trying to think like one, trying to be one. I have no Fae magic to make any promise to me binding. All I want is to not have to worry about being human with you."

"What's wrong with being human around the Fae?"

"Because then you might find yourself becoming the pet of one for an eternity. With no rights other than what your Fae gives you."

Panic hit again and she struggled to rise, fighting against his grip. "No. I need to go." She had no idea where. Other than she wanted to get her sister and get out of this place. According to her schoolteachers, she wasn't very good at following orders. Becoming the pet of some Fae didn't sound like a good position to be in with a flaw like that.

Gideon's grip tightened on her and he dragged her close. "There's nowhere to run to. And there's no escape. Not if you want your sister back. And even when you find her that doesn't mean you'll be able to leave. Not for both of you."

At his quiet words she froze. She refused to believe. There had to be some way to escape. For both her and her sister. "What did you do?"

His grip on her relaxed. "When?"

"To the Hunt."

"Nothing. It doesn't work like that. Unless you get in their way."

"How does it work?" He was silent for so long she began to think he wasn't going to answer.

"I killed someone. But I don't know if that makes me a murderer since I didn't know helping dad remove the tree would make him die."

"You killed someone?" She didn't like the squeak that had returned to her voice. Clearing her throat, she tried again. "What do you mean?"

His hands remained on her shoulders and his face close to hers. "I was suspended. Again. Apparently teachers don't like it when you make the class laugh at them."

"Isn't that the truth?" She'd been in trouble for that a few times. Never suspended though. "What has that got to do with you killing someone?"

"Dad said if I wasn't at school, I had to help him. He's a tree lopper. Not an arborist. He hates that word. He's Truman the tree man. He loves telling people that. Thinks it's funny. Or cool, or something. Anyway, he usually makes me work for him every Saturday. Reckons that with the amount I eat he can't afford to support me if I don't contribute."

She smiled at the humour in his voice, relaxing as she listened to his deep voice, the shadows continuing to press in around them.

"It was a large old tree with spreading branches and leaf litter nearly ankle deep on the ground underneath. I can still hear the crunch as we walked close to it so Dad could decide on a plan of action. The new owners of the property wanted it gone because the roots were destroying the back fence. They thought two large trees in the one backyard was excessive."

She could almost picture the tree with its spreading branches and the shadowy depths beneath it. He'd said July. Maybe there'd been very few shadows beneath the tree. It might've lost all its leaves for the winter. He remained silent so she spoke. "What happened?"

"After it was cut down, he left me to load all the wood into the trailer. We sell it to a man who sells it on for firewood. He took my ute and I was left with his work truck and trailer. Said he might as well make the most of having the help and get a quote done at another place. I'd nearly finished cleaning up when a man appeared." Again he fell silent.

"Who was he?"

Chapter Four

Gideon's grip momentarily tightened on her shoulders before letting go of her and moving back. "A Dryad. I didn't know that then. He carried another man in his arms. So similar looking they could have been brothers. Dark eyes, hair like sunlight and willowy." He fell silent again for a moment. "How was I supposed to know Dryads even existed? I never would have helped cut down the tree if I'd known. I didn't believe him. I mean, who would? I didn't know what to think. I guess I thought he was crazy. He talked about how I'd cut up the heartwood, making sure his friend would die. Then he threatened me with the Wild Hunt, saying I was marked for them now. That he'd give everything he owned in exchange for them hunting me down and killing me as messily as possible. I stood there like an idiot, not knowing what to say."

Hearing the sadness in his voice, she automatically reached for him and found his hand was tightened into a fist. She uncurled it and held on. "How did you find out it was real?"

"He walked across to the other side of the yard to a tree that matched the one we'd cut down. His pace never faltered as he walked straight towards the trunk and disappeared into it. I have no idea how long I stood there before I crossed the yard and circled the tree, looking for the trick."

"What do you mean he disappeared?"

"Straight into the tree. I even knocked on the trunk, asking him to come back and talk to me. No one answered." He laughed, a self-derisive sound. "I must've looked demented."

"How can he blame you? Dryads don't exist in our world." She cringed at how crazy her own words sounded. "I mean…"

His fingers tightened on hers. "That's what I thought. By the time my dad returned, I'd convinced myself I'd imagined it all. Yet that night at home I spent hours on the internet reading all this crazy stuff about Dryads, the Wild Hunt and the Fae. By the time I'd stumbled to bed in the early hours of the morning, I didn't know what to think. Other than to worry I was losing my mind." He laughed again, the same sound as before.

"How did you end up here?"

"They didn't come for me straight away. Maybe it took the Dryad time to find them. Or convince them or something. I don't know. It was a Friday night when they finally came. I had car troubles so I was stuck walking to a mate's place when I heard them. I couldn't help myself. I ran. Through backyards, over fences, through streets until I was thoroughly lost. The sounds of them kept getting closer and closer. I ran into one backyard and stumbled into a barbecue area. I grabbed a frypan that was sitting on a bench, planning to use it as a weapon. The moment my hand closed over the handle and gripped not just the timber of the cast-iron pan, but the iron as well, the urge to run faded. I was able to think again. I looked around, trying to figure out what to do. In the backyard was a swimming pool, the full moon reflected on the still surface. I had no idea if it would work, but I'd read in several articles about moon portals leading to the realms of the Fae. The type of water didn't matter. All you needed was a full moon or nearly full moon reflected in it. And you have to dive into the centre of the reflection. You couldn't get more full than the one I was staring at and the moon was directly overhead. So I jumped."

"Did they follow you?"

"Not then. It was a couple of days, or should I say nights, before I heard them again. By then I'd traded gear from my backpack as well as the cast-iron pan for an iron necklace. I'd also paid for some information to help me learn how to survive being marked by the Hunt. My best chance is to get a job at Masquerade for the next seven years. Without letting them know I'm wanted by the Hunt. Then I can worry about going home." He fell silent again. "I wish I could tell Dad I'm okay. Who knows how many years will have passed in the human world after I've lived here for seven years."

She had no idea what to say to him. Everything she thought of sounded pathetic. She could only think this was all so messed up. She continued to sit with him, holding his hand, tiredness tugging at her. When she noisily yawned, he drew his hand from hers.

Wrapping his arm around her shoulders, he pulled her close. "We might as well sleep while we can. We've got a long walk ahead of us."

She started to protest him grabbing her again, but didn't bother. It was warmer against his side and he was probably right. Closing her eyes she relaxed against him. One part of her brain was telling her she was crazy to trust an absolute stranger while the other said she was going to need every bit of help she could get. Both parts argued until she fell asleep.

Her dreams were filled with the Wild Hunt. When she heard her name repeated several times, she struggled to escape the nightmare and blinked sleepily as she stared at the boy lying on the grass beside her, half leaning over her, his broad shoulders shading her from the sunlight. He had short, sandy brown hair and deep brown eyes that reminded her of Buddy's. Right down to the sadness in them. He looked like he'd needed a shave several days ago and she opened her mouth to point it out. The night rushed back in on her and she closed her mouth instead. She pressed her hand against his shoulder so she could sit up, her clothes uncomfortably damp.

"You okay? You sounded like you were having a bad dream."

She nodded, not wanting to think about it. "How old are you?"

He smiled fleetingly. "I turned seventeen in February this year. My last year of high school. Supposedly. Although one of my teachers kept threatening to fail me. What about you? "

Her sister's birthday was in February. "I turned seventeen in April." She rose to her feet, trying to ignore the rumble of her stomach. "I have to find my sister."

"I know." He remained seated, rummaging through his backpack.

"You said you'd help me."

"I will." He drew out a resealable plastic bag and opened it, taking out a folded piece of paper.

She stared down at what she guessed was a hand drawn map. None of the symbols on it made sense. "What are you doing?"

"Planning today's path."

She knelt beside him, eyeing all the scribbles. They still made no sense. "Where did you get it?"

"From a human who was feeling homesick and wanting to know how the world had changed since he'd last been there a decade ago." Gideon folded up the map and put it away before rising to his feet. He gestured ahead. "We go that way."

Shaking her head, Quinn stood up and pointed in the direction Marley had been taken. "My sister is that way."

"We go that way eventually, but we need to go a lot further in this direction first. This way also has an orchard. I've got three pears left so we're going this way." He gestured ahead of them again before he rummaged around in his backpack, pulling out two of the pears.

She took the pear Gideon held out to her. "How do you know the human didn't lie?"

"He could have. Unlike the Fae we humans can lie. But I don't think he did." Gideon grinned. "He wanted a lot more from me than a story." He took a bite from his pear, striding off in the direction he'd indicated.

It took her a few seconds to understand. She hurried after him, curious. "You're gay?"

"He certainly was." He grinned at her again. "It was rather flattering considering the looks of some of the other guys there. I don't think I've seen a single ugly Fae. And don't let how skinny they are fool you. Although the dark ones aren't as skinny as the light ones. But they're all far stronger and faster than a human. You wouldn't stand a chance against them in a fight."

"Why would I want to fight them?"

He nodded towards the pear she continued to hold. "Are you going to eat that?"

"Yeah. Why would I want to fight them?" She took a bite of the pear, making sure he knew she wouldn't be giving it back. She was starving.

"You might not want to fight them, but what would you do if one of them was dragging your sister away?"

"Hopefully more than I did this time." Finishing up the pear, she tossed the core into some bushes.

"You want to split the other pear with me?"

She nodded.

Gideon stopped, taking the pear from his backpack and a dagger from a sheath that had been hidden by the long sleeve of his shirt. He cut the pear in half and held one segment out to her.

She stared at the dagger. "Where did you get that?" She doubted he'd have been wandering around the streets of Sydney with it. At least she hoped he hadn't been.

He lowered the dagger to his side. "I'm not going to hurt you." He paused a moment before he spoke again. "Do you want the pear?"

Her gaze darted to the dagger several times before she grabbed the pear and took a few steps away from him.

Gideon walked to the edge of the lake they followed and rinsed off the dagger before returning it to the sheath. He remained crouched at the water's edge, looking up at her. "My wannabe lover gave it to me. He said if I ever managed to survive the Hunt I should come back and see him."

Knowing where he'd got the dagger didn't make her feel any better. "Why did he think you'd need it?" Her gaze was drawn to where it was hidden.

Gideon rose to his feet, taking a step towards her. He stopped when she backed away. "Because the realms of the Fae isn't a safe place. Those of the Wild Hunt aren't the only ones who carry weapons."

She thought of the man, no, the Demi Fae, who'd thrown her sister so effortlessly over his shoulder. "How would something so small be able to protect you from the Fae?"

"It's what it's made of that will protect me from them."

Her gaze was drawn to the necklace she'd held while the Hunt had raced past. "Iron?"

He nodded.

"How does it work? Does it keep them away from you? Like, I don't know, garlic for vampires?"

He chuckled. "If you had enough of it, yeah. It weakens them and, if they remain around it, will eventually cause sickness and death. The amount of iron I have I'd need to come in contact with the Fae for it to do much good. Or at least be standing right next to them. You really don't want to be getting that close to a Fae you're wary of."

"I need some iron."

Gideon slid the ring off his little finger and held it out to her. "The same one who gave me the dagger gave me this ring too."

She stared at it, her hands remaining at her sides. "What are all the strange symbols on it?"

"It says protection. Written in the old Fae language. He said there's magic in that language. Which is why they no longer use it except for creating things like talismans and weapons."

She took the ring, surprised at how warm it felt, and slid it on her middle finger. It was too loose so she tried her first finger. It fit. "He seems to have gone to a lot of effort to help keep you alive. What did you do for him in return?"

Gideon smiled. "He wants me to live long enough to eventually return to him."

"Will you? When it's all over."

Chapter Five

Gideon's smile faded and he stared at her for a moment. "I told him humans don't belong in this world. He said he'd once believed that and no matter how homesick he occasionally gets, he'll never go back." Gideon gestured in the direction they'd been travelling. "Are you ready to go? We need to be by water again before dark. The Hunt never gives up."

Nodding, she twisted the ring on her finger, feeling the word engraved on it. When Gideon moved away from the water's edge, she washed her hands before joining him, keeping plenty of distance between them. Several times she looked towards him, trying to figure him out. She didn't know if she should trust him. He'd already confessed to being a murderer, although like he'd said, she didn't know if it counted.

When she looked towards him again, Gideon met her gaze. "What's wrong?"

She shrugged and shook her head. Then shrugged again. "I don't know. None of this seems possible. It can't be real. And you." She shook her head once more. "I don't understand you. Why are you really helping me?"

"Would it make you feel any better if I gave you the dagger?"

"That's not it. Well, not exactly."

"Are you sure? Because you've kept a pretty big distance between us ever since I took it out. If you're worried I want something else, you can stop. I'm only looking for a friend."

His comment made her think of Scout telling her she was like a sister. If this kept up she'd be starting to wonder if something was seriously wrong with her. "It's everything. The dagger reminded me it's real." She stopped abruptly and faced him when he stopped too. "If all this is real, how are we going to get out of here? Both me and Marley."

"I don't know. You need to find out exactly what your sister promised. The exact terms. Then you can figure out how to work around them. And don't promise anyone anything. Promises are binding around here. They use magic to enforce them."

"You're not making me feel any better. Every single thing you tell me scares me even more."

His lips twisted into a wry smile, fading almost immediately. "Sorry. I wasn't trying to make you feel better. I was trying to make sure you didn't get trapped here. Forever."

She momentarily closed her eyes at the feeling that washed over her at the thought of never being able to return home. She took half a step in his direction. "What can I do? I have no idea what to do."

Gideon started to reach for her, then lowered his arm. "Yeah, you do. You need to get to Masquerade Nightclub. When you get there, you can figure out what needs to be done next."

She stared at him, glad she didn't have to make the journey alone. "How long have you been on your own?"

"I've spoken to exactly three people since I've been in the realms of the Fae. Other than you. Two humans and one Fae."

"Three people in one month? That's it?"

Gideon nodded, the wry smile returning to his lips. "Now do you understand why I was so happy to see you? You're not only human, but you're from my world. And an Aussie too from the way you and your sister spoke."

"Yeah. The Sunshine Coast." She hesitated. "You're saying you'd have helped any Australian?"

He laughed. "Probably not. I don't think I'm that nice, or that desperate yet."

His eyes momentarily lost the sad look that reminded her of Buddy. She hoped her parents were taking care of her dog. As she continued to stare at Gideon, she saw the sad look return to his eyes.

"What's wrong?"

"Maybe I should be asking you that. You look sad again."

"It's hard not to be. You made me forget for a few seconds that I'm running for my life." He gestured in the direction they needed to travel. "We're wasting daylight."

She fell in beside him, this time not keeping as much distance between them. As they walked, she checked out her surroundings. They continued to travel along the edge of the lake, a forest beside them. At times it reached down to the lake and they were forced to weave their way through trees. Other times it was well back and she felt nervous walking through the open grassland. She guessed it must've been well after lunch by the time they reached an apple orchard, having left the lake behind. Seeing the ripe fruit, she started to step out of the trees sheltering them.

Gideon grabbed hold of her upper arm and drew her towards him. "Wait. We need to make sure there's no one here."

She pulled out of his grip. "I'm starving. Hurry up and check. I'm also thirsty."

"Don't drink the water from any lake and don't eat the fruit until after we make it safe."

"How do you do that?" It better not take too long because she was desperate for something to eat.

He glanced towards her before returning his gaze to the orchard. "You're not going to like it." He paused. "Come on. I can't see anyone out there."

She hurried after him. "What do you mean? Why aren't I going to like it?"

He took off his backpack and opened it up, holding it out to her. "You hold it, I'll fill it."

She took the backpack. "Gideon. Why aren't I going to like it?"

Reaching up into the tree, he picked several apples before turning and putting them in the backpack. "Because we need to travel to naturally running water and wash them. Like a creek or river." He turned away to collect more.

"What about a drink? When do I get one?"

He put more apples in the backpack. "Same place.

My water bottle is empty or I would have offered you a drink."

He'd been right. She didn't like it. Her stomach grumbled as she watched him put more apples into the backpack. "How far away is it?"

"A few hours." He eyed the amount of apples in the backpack before turning away and collecting several more.

"Hours!" She couldn't help how shrill her voice sounded. "You've got to be kidding me."

After placing several more apples in the backpack, he took it from her. "I wish." He slung the backpack into place. "Come on. I'm hungry too."

"We could run." As little as she liked the idea she liked being hungry less.

"No. We still have further to travel today. We're better off pacing ourselves."

She started to ask him how much further they needed to go, but decided she really didn't want to know. Not yet anyway. She remained silent, trying not to worry about what was ahead of her. It was a fail. All she could think about was Marley and the man who'd taken her. Kaeder. She had no idea how she was going to get her sister back. It wasn't like she could return home without her. She felt guilty thinking of leaving her behind. As annoying as she sometimes was, Marley was still her little sister.

Neither of them had spoken again by the time they reached the creek. Quinn wondered if Gideon had remained silent for the same reason she had. That he was too thirsty to talk. "Is it safe to drink?" She gestured towards the creek.

Nodding, Gideon put his backpack down on the bank and removed two of the apples. He didn't bother to remove his boots before he waded into the water and washed them. "Here. Catch." He threw an apple to her.

She caught it and grinned when he took a bite of his. "Finally." She bit into the apple, savouring the sweetness. Moisture filled her mouth. It didn't take long to finish it and she helped Gideon wash the rest of the apples and fill his water bottle. She took the second apple he handed her and groaned when she saw him put his backpack on. "Already?"

"Yeah. I need to get to safety as soon as possible. The longer it takes, the more chances the Hunt has of catching me."

"I know, but surely a few minutes to sit down wouldn't hurt." She stared at him, hopefully. For a moment she thought he might agree.

He shook his head. "We slept later than I'd planned

this morning." He held her gaze a little longer before walking off.

She stared after him for a moment before sighing and catching up to him. "I don't want them to catch you, but my legs ache and my feet feel like lead." She also didn't want to be alone in a world she had no clue how to survive in.

He glanced towards her. "I'm sorry."

That was the last word spoken between them until the sun sank below the horizon and shadows filled the forest they travelled through, still following the creek. Struggling to see where to step, Quinn stumbled. "Now can we stop for a break?"

"You'll know when it's time to stop."

"How?"

"You'll hear them."

She started to ask who, then realised. "You're waiting for the Hunt before we stop?"

"Sometimes they stay in the area for hours, looking for me."

At his words, she stumbled. How could she face hours of hearing the Hunt? How had he? She didn't want to think about it. Before she could say something, she heard them. Well in the distance, but the sound made a shiver travel through her. "Now can we stop?"

"Shortly." He rummaged in his backpack and drew out a waterproof torch, shining it on the creek. He headed further upstream.

"What are you looking for?"

"Somewhere to hide." He stopped, the beam of light staying still, showing a large boulder in the middle of the creek. "There."

She followed him into the creek, wading out to the boulder, the water making her shiver from the cold. "This is worse than the lake."

"Creeks always are." He knelt in the water, turning off the torch and rummaging in his backpack again.

Quinn remained standing. The last thing she wanted to do was get completely wet, but with how the sound of the Hunt grew closer it didn't look like she'd have a choice. She took the two apples and the hollow reed Gideon held out. "How many reeds do you have?" She took a bite of her apple.

"A few. I didn't want to risk losing one and being without if I couldn't find another reed bed."

"When will we reach Masquerade?"

"Tomorrow afternoon."

The apple halfway to her mouth again, she froze. "Really?"

"Hopefully."

Relief washed over her. She could survive two days.

She'd feared it'd be far longer. "How did you manage a month of this?"

"I didn't cover as much ground at the start. It took me time to find help and then to learn how far I could travel in a day without being away from water. I nearly didn't make it one night."

She wasn't about to ask him to tell her that story when she could hear the Hunt coming. Instead, she ate her apples, glad for the iron ring that kept her from wanting to run away mindlessly. It would be impossible to escape the creatures she'd seen last night. Nothing human could outrun them. She didn't know if anything could.

Chapter Six

By the time the Hunt was close, they'd finished their apples and were lying on the creek bed, their heads leaning against the edge of the boulder that was underwater, reeds allowing them to breathe. Even though she couldn't see anything, she kept her eyes open. If the Hunt was about to find her, she didn't want it to be a surprise.

Gideon reached for her hand and tightened his fingers over hers.

She wished she could speak to him, but settled for squeezing back. The warmth of his hand in hers had her wriggling closer to him, hoping his body was equally warm. It wasn't, but it seemed far warmer than her own and she pressed herself against his side, trying to stop shivering. It was a fail and she continued to shiver as she waited for the Hunt to leave the area.

Gideon's fingers tightened on hers and she started to pull out of his painful grip. Until she saw them. They were on the bank, the wolves sniffing the edges and lifting their heads to howl. Sharp fangs glittered in the flaming torchlight some of the riders held, their horses pawing at the ground. Her own hand tightened on Gideon's, her breath freezing in her lungs.

The leader stared across the creek, his antlers rising from his head, the horse he rode tossing its head. His chest was still bare and the flickering flames from the torches caused light to leap across his skin. Quinn couldn't take her gaze from him. What if he looked down? Would he be able to see them through the racing waters of the creek that frothed and foamed through the rocks?

Her vision of the Hunt was wavy, but distinct enough for her to see far more details than she wished. Lungs burning, her breath came out in a rush and she gulped more air in, trying to remember to breathe only through the reed. How long did the Hunt plan to stay there? She pressed closer to Gideon. What would they do if the Hunt spotted them? Run? How could they outrun such large wolves? They had to be the size of a small pony. Her heart raced at the thought of being brought down by one of them. She could almost feel the teeth tearing into her flesh.

Gideon slid his arm across her waist, pulling her tighter against him.

For once she wasn't tempted to tell him not to grab her. She stared at the wolves as they threw their heads back and howled once more before racing along the bank in the direction her and Gideon had come from that afternoon. Even when the rest of the Hunt followed, she remained pressed against Gideon.

The sounds faded and Gideon sat up, dragging her with him. "Sorry I grabbed you, but I was worried you were about to run. Are you okay?" He let her go.

She took the reed from her mouth. "I don't know." She drew in a shuddering breath. "I want to go home." Her eyes closed at the sound of her voice. When had she last sounded like that? An image came to mind in a rush. She'd been little. Had recently learned to ride a bicycle and graduated to having her training wheels removed. She'd been with Daisy, Ted and Scout. Her and Scout had run into each other and she'd ended up scraping her hands and knees. She'd said the same words then, in exactly the same voice. Scout had looked like he was going to cry. "I want to go home." The words were a whisper this time.

"I know. I do too."

Thoughts of Daisy, Ted and Scout made her feel homesick. "We're not going to make it, are we?" How could they with creatures like that roaming the land?

"Of course we are. I thought the same when I first came here. But it's been a month. Thirty-three days to be exact."

She shivered at the thought of being hunted for so long. How had he stood it? And on his own. Worse, how was he going to survive seven years of being hunted? She doubted she'd be so calm about it. Had he been this calm when he'd first found out?

"We can get out for a while if you want. It'll be warmer on the bank. I can wrap the survival blanket around us to prevent our body heat from escaping."

She let him draw her out of the creek, stumbling over the rocks she couldn't see in the dark. "How did you end up with the survival blanket?"

"I traded for it when I found out I'd have to spend so much time hiding in the water." They reached the bank and he let her go.

She wanted to protest, beg him not to let go. When had she become such a clingy person? She wanted to go home. The person she was here wasn't her.

He rummaged in his backpack until a crinkling

sound was heard over the rustling noises coming from the bag. "Found it. Come over here."

Sitting beside him, she helped him put the blanket around them and leaned against a tree. "I'm so tired."

"You have a sleep and I'll wake you in an hour or so. Then you can keep watch while I sleep."

That sounded like a good plan to her. Particularly the fact it involved staying in one place for more than a few minutes. She didn't know how she was going to manage another day of walking. "Okay." She rested her head against the hard planes of his chest. "You don't mind me using you as a pillow, do you?"

He chuckled softly. "Why would I complain about a beautiful girl snuggling up to me?"

How hadn't he lost his sense of humour? Weariness washed over her now she could no longer hear the Hunt. "I'm not the beautiful one. That's Marley."

"I have no idea what Marley looks like. It was too dark to see her clearly, but I do know what you look like. My statement stands."

She smiled, not stupid enough to argue. He'd find out soon enough. Tomorrow afternoon. A sigh escaped. Would he be like Scout and have eyes only for Marley? Not that he was interested in her anyway. Nor she interested in him. Before she could decide the answer, she sank into sleep, plagued by dreams of the Hunt chasing her. A moment before the antlered Fae caught her in her dream she woke, heart racing.

Blinking, she drew away from Gideon, who was fast asleep. Faint light filled the forest and she realised day was arriving. What had happened to him waking her?

Gideon stirred, his eyes opening and fear momentarily clouding them. "What's wrong?"

"You were meant to wake me."

He smiled wryly. "You were so relaxed I couldn't bring myself to disturb you." Yawning, he stretched. "I didn't mean to fall asleep."

Running her fingers through her hair, she winced at the knots that stopped her progress. She must look a mess. Obviously Gideon had been too long without human company if he thought she was beautiful.

Gideon rummaged through his backpack, drawing out four apples. "We'll make a move once we've eaten."

She wanted to argue. Instead she took the apples and ate them. There was no way she wanted to endure a repeat of last night. She still had no idea how Gideon had survived a month of such nights. They remained silent as they finished eating.

Gideon rose to his feet. "Are you ready?"

"Nearly." She made her way to the creek and

washed her hands and face before having a drink. Her gaze was drawn to the boulder they'd hidden beside. It seemed far too close to the bank. The froth and foam of the water prevented her from seeing beneath the surface.

Gideon came to stand beside her. "They won't be able to catch us after tonight. And you'll be able to see your sister and figure out what you can do to help her." He held out his hand.

Taking it, she rose to her feet, continuing to hold it as she met his gaze. Once again they reminded her of Buddy's. "What if she's no longer there?"

"She will be. That's where Kaeder said he was taking her. Come on." He tugged on her hand, heading in the direction they'd been travelling last night, letting go after a moment.

She walked beside him, remaining silent as the sun slowly rose, not speaking until it was well overhead and they stopped to have lunch. Like the previous meals, it was apples. After their meal they continued on, eventually veering away from the creek once they'd refilled the water bottle. The new direction led them through the forest and onto a dirt road, a wide grass edge bordering it.

Mid afternoon, hearing the sound of horses, Gideon tugged her back into the forest. They hid behind trees and watched a carriage rumble past, drawn by four white horses. They didn't return to the road until the sound was well into the distance and the dust had settled on the road.

Quinn stared down the road as she forced herself to keep plodding along. "Is that really what they use to get around?"

"Modern technology doesn't work here. They also can't use iron, remember? Although they do have metals of their own."

"Oh."

"They use horses and sometimes magic to get to places."

"How does their magic work? Can we learn to use it?"

Gideon shrugged. "I wouldn't have a clue. I do know when it's being used. It smells of nature. Flowers, spices, the ocean, rainforests or other natural things. And they're all different. Like they have their own personal magic signature."

Quinn continued to stare down the road. "What's that?"

"I'm not sure." Gideon walked faster.

Hurrying after him, she tried to keep up until she realised it was the carriage that had passed them. Her steps slowed until she came to a stop. "Gideon? What if it's a trap?"

Gideon stopped several metres ahead, turning to face her. "We have to go this way. The road leads to the start of the Fringes, where Masquerade Nightclub is. We can't risk going into the forest and possibly losing our direction with how thick the trees grow here."

She wanted to argue that staying on the road wasn't a good idea, but what other option was there if the forest was out?

"We could probably stay just inside the tree line."

"Okay." That didn't sound as bad as being out in the open. It was also a good distance from the road because of the large, grassy edges. They reminded her of extremely wide footpaths. The type without a concrete strip running down the centre. She glanced towards the sky as they reached the trees. "Will we have enough time to get there before dark?"

"We should do. It'll be close though."

As they drew near to the carriage she fell silent, not wanting to be noticed. They were nearly past it when a woman called out.

"You two. Over here."

Quinn grabbed hold of Gideon's arm, tugging him back to her when he stepped out of the tree line.

"What are you doing?" She kept her voice low so the woman couldn't hear.

With a half smile, he looked at her hand on his arm.

Remembering her own comments about not grabbing, she let go. "We don't have time for this."

"We need to make time. Never ignore the Fae. Some of them are vindictive." He took hold of her hand and headed towards the carriage.

Chapter Seven

Quinn reluctantly walked at Gideon's side. Reaching the carriage, she stared at the woman who stepped out. She'd never seen anyone so beautiful, not even Marley could compare.

The woman stared down her nose, taller than both of them. Her white blond hair was piled elaborately atop her head, decorated by jewels as blue as her eyes, there was a slight point to her ears and her body was almost painfully slim. "A gold coin each if you can get my carriage back on the road." She waved regally towards the rear wheels, which were stuck in a puddle of mud.

Quinn looked up and down the road, seeing no other puddles. "How did that happen?"

"My brother left in a huff. Of course he had to make one last nuisance of himself before he went. Older brothers can be so sanctimonious sometimes.

What did he expect after delivering lecture upon lecture the entire drive?"

Quinn tried to think of a polite way to say no.

"How about a lift instead?" Gideon asked.

The woman looked horrified. "Let humans ride in my carriage with me?"

"We could ride up front. It looks like you're without a coachman." Gideon gestured towards the area.

"Of course I have no coachman. I tell the horses where I wish to go, and they take me there." She looked from one to the other. "Where is your master?"

"If you could give us a lift to the edge of the Fringes, we wouldn't be late arriving," Gideon said.

"Out of the question. What about one and a half gold coins each?"

"It hardly seems a fair bargain when the two of us are likely to be coated in mud," Gideon said.

Quinn opened her mouth to tell him they should forget about it. Before she had the chance to speak, his hand squeezed hers and she met his gaze. She had no idea what he was silently trying to tell her, but she remembered how he'd held her hand as they lay in the creek waiting for the Hunt to leave. She closed her mouth. He better know what he was doing.

"Very well. Two gold coins each and not a single coin more. It's robbery expecting so much. If I wasn't already late I would have sent for help."

Gideon nodded. "Okay, it's a bargain. You give us two gold coins each and then we push the carriage out of the mud." He held out his hand.

The woman stared at his hand in distaste before she withdrew four small gold coins from a drawstring bag at her wrist and dropped them on his palm.

Gideon pocketed the coins and headed behind the carriage. He placed his hands against the back of it. "If you'd like to have a word with your horses and hop in the carriage, we'll get you unstuck."

Seeing the woman head into the carriage, Quinn hurried around to Gideon's side, placing her hands on the back of the carriage near his. "I hope you know what you're doing," she muttered.

He spoke equally soft. "Me too."

"Onward," the woman called out.

The horses began to move and the carriage creaked and groaned. Quinn pushed against it, closing her eyes as mud sprayed up around them. The carriage jerked forward and Quinn landed face first in the mud, Gideon beside her, the carriage continuing along the road. She glared at him when he laughed, wiping the mud from her face. "I hope you're not expecting us to turn up at Masquerade looking like this."

He staggered to his feet and held out a hand. "There's a river that runs through the Fringes. It passes under the road not far before you reach the start of it. We can wash there."

Taking his hand, she rose to her feet. It better not be far away. Being coated in mud was extremely uncomfortable. "You could have said no to her."

He let go of her hand. "I couldn't. You don't annoy the Fae. Ever. They always retaliate."

"How will we get to Masquerade before dark?"

"We'll have to move faster." He picked up his pace.

She tried to keep up, but her legs ached from yesterday. Gradually he got a little ahead of her and she wondered if she should say something. In the end, she didn't need to.

He matched her speed. "We'll pace ourselves for now and go faster when we're closer to Masquerade."

She doubted it would be possible to go any faster. Not with how much her legs ached and protested the speed she was already forcing them to go. She didn't bother to say anything. He'd find out eventually. She'd never thought of herself as unfit and had a fairly active lifestyle. But it hadn't prepared her for days of walking.

The sun was setting when they reached the river where it passed under the road. Ahead of them loomed the Fringes, a collection of buildings that seemed to have been thrown randomly into place, some of them appearing to defy gravity in the way they'd been constructed. It sprawled across the landscape, taking up as much space as a city. The forest stopped well before the Fringes, an open expanse where very little grew.

"Are you planning to clean yourself?" Gideon stood in the river, washing the mud from his body.

Quinn dragged her gaze away from the Fringes and eased herself into the river. It was as cold as she'd feared. "We should stay here. Hide in the river until morning."

"No." He slid beneath the water to wash mud from his hair.

She waited for him to surface, continuing to rub at the mud that clung to her. "Why not?"

He wiped water from his face. "The water's too clear. They'd spot me immediately."

"We could hide under the bridge."

Gideon shook his head. "It's not safe enough here. It's only about ten minutes from Masquerade and I can't hear the Hunt. We should have plenty of time. Are you finished?"

"Nearly." She slid beneath the icy water, closing her eyes as she ran her fingers through her hair, trying to get rid of the mud. Surfacing, she found Gideon on the riverbank. An uneasiness settled in her stomach. She hoped he was right. The last thing she wanted to do was come face to face with the Hunt. She took the hand he held out to her and let him help her from the river. "I'm ready." Her uneasiness increased at the words. She didn't feel ready.

Gideon kept looking over his shoulder as they travelled the road into the Fringes. The city appeared deserted. "We'll use the money we earned today to buy a human meal at Masquerade. It'll give us a chance to check out the place." He took two of the coins from his pocket, holding them out, another glance behind. "Here."

She hesitated, wishing he'd stop looking over his shoulder. It was making her nervous. "Won't you need them to pay for the meal?"

Shaking his head, he chuckled. "They're solid gold, Quinn. I was surprised she was willing to pay so much even with being late somewhere. The woman must've been from the nobility. They're always wasting money. Either that or she was desperate. Maybe both."

She took the coins and slid them into her pocket.

"How would you know? You said you've only had contact with three people since you've been here."

"Yeah, but I saw a lot during the times I had to hide."

His words sounded final so she dropped the topic even though she wanted to ask what had happened. She focused on trying to keep up with him, unnerved by the way he kept checking behind them. Nothing followed them and she couldn't hear the Hunt. The only sounds were their feet against the cobblestone road that the dirt road had become when they'd entered the Fringes. Her legs ached and she wanted to ask him to slow down, but knew it wasn't safe. She wanted to be at Masquerade well before she could hear the sounds of the Hunt.

"Look. There it is, at the end of the road."

Her gaze travelled to the building Gideon pointed at. It was three stories high with two balconies across the front of both the upper floors and a rooftop garden that was dotted with trees, shrubs and many coloured lights. Two large lanterns hung at the front door with stained glass panels throwing fragments of various coloured light on the ground around them. A timber sign hung above the door and the word 'Masquerade' was written in gold, excessive curls in the lettering. The front door was closed and laughter drifted down from the rooftop garden. It didn't look like any nightclub she'd seen.

Her gaze remained on the closed door. "Will they let us in? Do they have an age requirement like they do in our country?"

"No. I don't think the realms of the Fae have many rules. Not those sort of rules anyway."

Movement to the right of the building drew her attention. Uneasiness turned into panic and she clutched at Gideon's hand. "It's him. Gideon, we have to run." She started to turn away from the building, dragging her gaze from the antlered figure coming out of the narrow alley that ran along the side of the building, leading a dark coloured horse.

Gideon wouldn't let her. He spoke in a whisper. "Don't run. Even on foot he'd capture us. He's alone, no wolves to track me down. Keep walking and try not to catch his attention."

The door of Masquerade came closer. Her grip on Gideon's hand tightened. Her gaze travelled from the door to the leader of the Wild Hunt and back again. Where was his pack? His wolves? Why was he alone, with only his horse?

"Stop looking at him," Gideon whispered.

She couldn't help it. He was only a few metres away. Soon they'd have to pass him so they could reach the door. His head turned in their direction and his gaze met hers. They were a green brighter than her sister's. If it hadn't been for Gideon holding her hand and keeping her moving, she would have frozen in place. The momentary relief she felt when she was no longer pinned by his gaze, vanished. She saw recognition in his eyes when his gaze shifted to Gideon.

"Run." Gideon dragged her along beside him.

Her feet seemed to tangle and she crashed to the cobblestone road, her hand dragged from Gideon's. She wanted to protest when he turned back to help her. The leader of the Hunt was too close. Scrambling to her feet, she waved Gideon on, a shiver running through her when the leader stopped, threw back his head and howled.

The eerie sound was echoed by wolves that seemed far closer than Quinn would have liked.

"Hurry up." Gideon grabbed her arm, dragging her with him towards the door.

Behind her she heard the pound of feet. Her gaze remained fixed on the door and she almost crossed her fingers when the thought occurred to her that it might be locked. The door was close enough she could see the individual nails holding together the numerous planks of timber it was made from.

Gideon's hand was dragged from hers and she spun to see the leader held him.

Gideon fought to escape. "I didn't know. How was I supposed to know any of you lot existed?" There was fear and desperation in his tone, which mirrored the expression on his face.

"Do you think I care?" The deep voice of the leader cut through Gideon's protests.

Quinn barrelled into him, mentally calling herself an idiot, hitting out at him with the hand she'd slipped the iron ring onto. He staggered back, recoiling from the iron. His grip on Gideon was broken and she stumbled to a halt, grabbing hold of Gideon's hand before the leader could regain his balance. They pelted for the door, Gideon opening it. Bursting inside, they spun to face the doorway.

Chapter Eight

The leader ducked his head so he could enter the foyer. "Your money will eventually run out and you'll be forced to leave." His finger was pointed at Gideon.

When the finger aimed in her direction, Quinn barely managed not to take a step back. Her breath froze in her lungs when his gaze caught and held hers, the green gaze pinning her in place.

"You have been marked by the Hunt. You shouldn't have interfered. The moment you leave sanctuary we'll track you down and make you regret tonight's actions." He lowered his hand, his gaze still holding her in place.

Light-headedness struck Quinn and she forced herself to breathe before she passed out. This couldn't be happening.

"What are you doing in here, Gwyl? You know

you're not allowed at Masquerade after dark. I thought you'd already left."

Quinn spun to see a young woman standing in a doorway behind a counter. Her hands were on her hips and her dark brown hair, streaked with various colours, was pulled back from her face to show her ears were human. Which made Quinn wonder how it was possible for her to have black butterfly wings rising from her back. A sound behind her had her facing the front door. She turned in time to see Gwyl duck his head and slam the front door behind him.

"Are you two meant to be here?"

Quinn faced the young woman again, her mind empty of all useful thoughts. How was she supposed to answer that? What if the woman threw them out for Gwyl to capture?

Gideon held up a gold coin. "We're looking for a human meal each."

The woman eyed them up and down. "And you couldn't have dried yourselves before turning up?"

"We've been visiting friends." Gideon dropped the coin onto her palm.

She sighed. "I'll put you in the tiled area we keep for Mermaids, Naiads and other water people." She half turned away. "I'm Darci."

Quinn followed Darci down a hallway, her gaze

fixed on the wings that were obviously a part of her. How had she gained wings? Was it some kind of magic? Was she part Fae? She looked towards Gideon, whose gaze also seemed firmly fixed on the wings. From his expression, it didn't look like he knew anything about them either.

He glanced towards her, a question in his eyes.

She slightly shook her head, not about to speak while they had an audience. They stepped into a room and she looked around. It seemed like a typical human restaurant, if you didn't take into account the strange and varied creatures at the many tables. Human waiters wandered amongst them, serving trays held high. The humans were as strange as the creatures, some even stranger. She wasn't sure if the vines and flowers decorating some of them were part of them or decorations. Others appeared to have animal parts like wings and horns growing from their bodies.

"Here you go." Darci waved towards a table set on a tiled floor, several drains in the floor amongst the handful of tables.

"Thank you." Quinn sat across from Gideon at the two person table.

"Would you like a menu or do you want the human special of the day?" Darci asked.

"The special will be fine," Gideon said.

Quinn waited for Darci to walk away before she spoke. "What if I didn't want the special?"

"Do you want me to call her back?"

"No. But I don't like people ordering for me."

Gideon shifted his chair closer to her, the feet scraping on the tiles. "Sorry." He lowered his voice. "I wanted to get rid of her so I could talk to you." He reached for her hand, clasping it in both of his. "I'm so sorry. I didn't mean to get you marked by the Hunt."

"I don't want to talk about it." Or think about it. She pushed the thoughts away, afraid she'd run screaming if she let herself dwell on them. Seven years! How was she going to survive in this place for seven years? Not thinking about it was obviously a fail.

"If there's anything I can do to make-"

"Please. I can't talk about it right now." She met his gaze, wishing they didn't look so much like Buddy's. She wasn't certain, but it was possible they looked sadder than usual. She drew her hand from his. "All I want to do is find my sister." She left unspoken the words she wanted to say. It looked like there'd be no going home for her. Not for seven years. The last two words echoed in her mind, like a death knell.

"Have you seen her?"

She shook her head, her gaze travelling around the room again. Not a single human looked familiar. "What if he's taken her somewhere else?"

"There's more than the restaurant. Besides a rooftop garden, there's also a bar. She could be in either of those places. And there's a day shift."

"How am I meant to find out if she's here?"

"I don't know, but we'll figure something out."

Like the plan to get here before dark? She clamped her teeth down on the words before they escaped. She was the one who'd chosen to help him even though she'd known it was a stupid idea. She was still trying to figure out what crazy impulse had caused her to do something so stupid. Maybe she'd been trying to repay the help he'd tried to give her when she'd fallen.

A boy, holding a tray, arrived at their table and placed drinks in front of them. "I'm Oscar, your waiter for the evening."

He looked far too young to be working here and she was tempted to ask him his age, but guessed that wouldn't be polite. "What is the drink?"

"Apple cider. It's made from the apples of a local orchard. It comes with the day's special."

She held the cup to her nose, breathing in the sharp scent. "Ahh, okay." It felt odd to be served an alcoholic beverage without being asked to provide identification. And not only that, but to be served by someone who looked younger than her.

"Is there anything else I can get you?" Oscar looked from Gideon to Quinn.

She shook her head.

"We're right, thanks," Gideon said.

"I'll be back with your meal when it's ready." Oscar gave them a nod before moving onto a nearby table.

"It's alcoholic." She gestured towards her drink.

Gideon grinned. "I told you they didn't seem to have many rules around here."

"Is it safe to drink?"

"Yeah. I was told that as long as I let them know I want human food, they won't serve me any Fae food that'll cause me to be trapped here. Being a sanctuary means they can't do that."

She took a cautious sip of her drink. When nothing happened, she took a larger mouthful. "It doesn't taste very strong."

"That doesn't always mean anything."

She placed the cup on the table. "I suppose." Once again she glanced around the dining room. Where was her sister?

"Are you okay?"

She held his gaze for a moment. "I don't know." It felt odd sitting here so calmly when her world had fallen apart. She pushed that thought from her, unable to think about it right now. The words 'seven years' continued to echo in the back of her mind. She really wished they'd stop. "How long do you think seven years in the realms of the Fae will take in the human world?"

"I don't know. Apparently there's no set time. Sometimes it races ahead, sometimes it nearly keeps pace. But I reckon it'd have to be at least ten to twenty years. Maybe more."

Buddy wouldn't live that long. The poor dog was going to think he was jinxed. She was the second owner to abandon him. She doubted he'd understand someone leaving him because they'd died. How could you explain something like that to an animal that couldn't understand you?

"What are you thinking of?"

"My dog."

"What's he like?"

"I haven't had him long." She told him about the ad, but didn't mention how his eyes reminded her of Buddy's. By the time she'd finished telling him about her sister nearly killing her dog, their food had arrived. She stared at the roast meal in front of her, the smells making her mouth water. "Are you sure it's okay to eat this?"

"Absolutely." Gideon picked up his cutlery. "This place would soon lose its sanctuary status if it started trapping humans here with Fae food."

"Are you sure it isn't only a sanctuary for Fae?"

His hand swept the room in a gesture. "Look around. There's more than Fae in here."

She had another look, her mouth dropping open when she saw her sister at the far side of the room, holding a tray and wearing a dress that seemed to float around her as she moved. She half rose from her seat.

Gideon dragged her back down. "What are you doing?"

"That's Marley."

"Where?"

She pointed out her sister.

"Don't do anything stupid."

She glared at him. It was a little too late for that warning. "That's my sister."

"I know, but racing over there and making a scene will only get you thrown out. Gwyl is outside hunting. Do you really want to end up out in the dark while you're marked by the Hunt?"

She gripped the edge of the table, trying to remain seated. "I can't leave her here."

"I know."

Wanting to argue that he didn't know, she met his deep brown eyes. Sadness filled them. She supposed he did. Reaching across the small distance separating them, she took his hand. "There has to be a better way than waiting seven years. And does it have to be seven years here or can it be seven years in our world?"

"Seven years in whatever world they hunt you in. This is the only place I know where we'd be safe from them. Nowhere else offers sanctuary."

She thought of something she'd learned in history. "Aren't churches meant to be a sanctuary?"

His lips twisted into a wry smile. "I thought of that. I've got a feeling the only thing trying to stay in a church would do is have them calling our parents to collect us. Or the police." He nodded towards the food. "Eat up while it's hot. We'll probably be back to apples tomorrow."

She had a mouthful. Nausea rose and she barely managed to swallow the food. How could she eat when her sister was here, needing help? There had to be something she could do. Placing her cutlery on the table, she looked in the direction where her sister had been. She was gone. Once again she half rose from the table.

Gideon tugged her back into her seat. "People are going to start thinking I'm terrible company."

"I can't see her."

"She went out that door at the back of the room the waiters have been using. Only a couple of minutes ago."

She pulled her arm from his grip. "Will you stop grabbing me all the time?"

"Then stop trying to go running into trouble."

Glaring at him, she couldn't prevent the words that came tumbling out. "Like earlier?"

Chapter Nine

Gideon nodded slowly. "Yeah. You should have let him take me. You barely know me. I'm not worth losing a decade or two over."

Her glare faded and she reached for him again, holding his hand. "How could I leave you to him after you'd stopped to help me? You're not a murderer. Not even accidentally. "

His wry smile made an appearance. "I did think at one stage that I might be considered a hired killer. After all we were paid to cut down the tree."

She reluctantly smiled, thoughts of her sister causing it to disappear nearly as quickly as it had arrived. "Not even that. They should let the world know they exist. Or remain in the realms of the Fae where people would know not to cut down their trees."

"Thank you." He squeezed her hand before letting

it go. "Now have your dinner. I was serious when I said we're back to eating apples tomorrow. Especially if we don't manage to get a job here. The handful of coins we have aren't going to last us seven years." He picked up his cutlery again and began eating.

She tried to eat. Each mouthful was an effort. She spent more time watching the doorway for her sister than eating. But she didn't see her. The only person she recognised coming through the door was Oscar.

He headed towards their table, his tray held high. "Is the meal satisfactory? Can I get you anything else? A napkin perhaps?" He put a folded linen cloth beside Quinn's plate. "You might want to place it on your lap to catch any spills." He looked between Quinn and the napkin several times before turning away from the table and heading to another one.

She stared after him, trying to figure out what was going on. "That was odd."

"Very." Gideon watched Oscar too.

Not knowing what else to do, Quinn picked up the napkin and placed it on her lap. Unfolding it, she stared at the piece of paper that had been hidden within the material.

"What's wrong?"

Shaking her head, she looked at Oscar. The boy was walking towards the staff door. She watched him go, hoping to catch a glimpse of her sister when he opened it. No one was there and the door closed again.

"Quinn?"

She stared at Gideon, not sure what to say to him. Unable to think of anything, she opened the piece of paper. Blinking, she tried not to give into the tears seeing her sister's handwriting brought. 'Meet me at the stables at sunrise. Marley!' The exclamation mark had a love heart instead of a dot, like her sister always used.

"Quinn?"

She met his gaze again. "She knows I'm here." Keeping her hand below the table, she handed him the note.

After he read it Gideon returned the letter to her, smiling. "See, no need to panic. You'll see her soon."

"I have no idea how to find the stables." She also had nowhere to put the letter. Her clothes were damp and the ink would run if she put it in her pocket.

"We'll figure it out."

"I hope so."

"Now do you think you can eat your dinner?" He grinned. "It tastes a lot better than apples. Or pears."

She returned his grin. "Yeah. I think so." Picking up her fork, she had a mouthful, relieved it didn't make her feel ill. She'd finally get to see her sister and hopefully figure out a way for her to return home. Then she'd work on her own problem. Her sister's problem better not be anywhere near as bad as hers.

Once they'd both finished eating, Quinn looked around the room. "What do we do now?"

"It's probably too early to head to the stables."

Before she could agree with him Oscar returned, placing several silver coins on the table. "Your change from the meals. If you wish, I can show you where the bar is."

She turned to Gideon. He shrugged, collecting the coins off the table. She faced Oscar. "I guess." Not knowing what else to do with it, she slid the note into her pocket before rising to her feet. She supposed it didn't really matter if the writing ran, she already knew what it said.

"This way."

They followed Oscar, winding their way through the tables and back into the hallway. They took another door and found themselves in a dimly lit room with music playing, a bar running the length of the far wall, lights glittering and shining off glasses hung in racks above it. Several humans poured drinks while others carried them to the patrons seated around the outside of the room, the centre taken up with a crowded dance floor.

Oscar found them an empty table and started to leave.

Quinn reached for him, her hand stopping before she made contact. "Wait." She fell silent until he faced her. "Where are the stables?"

"I'll return to show you the way when I finish for the evening. About an hour before sunrise." He walked away before Quinn had the chance to thank him.

She stared after him. "What are we meant to do now?"

Gideon gestured towards the bar and the crowded dance floor. "Looks like dancing or drinking are the only choices."

"You dance?"

He grinned. "I've been known to let myself be talked into dancing every now and then."

The tone of his voice made her wonder what joke she was missing. Mentally shrugging, she ran through the options. Staring at each other across the table wouldn't help sunrise arrive any sooner. "How about now? Want to dance?"

"Sure, why not?" Rising to his feet, Gideon held out his hand.

Taking it, she rose to her own feet and walked with him to the crowded floor. She'd barely managed to face him when the song ended and a slow one began. Around them many of the people did what she guessed was a waltz, a handful standing wrapped in each other's arms and swaying on the spot. "Maybe this wasn't such a good idea."

"Of course it was." He continued to hold her hand, his other going to her waist and drawing her closer. "Anyone can slow dance." He grinned.

"Gideon…" She started to draw away from him.

His grin faded. "One dance. I'll show you how to waltz."

She snapped her mouth shut the moment she realised she was staring at him open mouthed. "You can waltz?"

"My mum was a dance instructor."

"Was?"

"She was in a bad car accident and hasn't been able to dance since."

"I'm sorry."

"Don't be. She found other things she enjoyed doing more. Now watch where I put my feet and you do the same. Like there's a piece of string joining our toes together."

She tried to mimic his steps, but found herself

stepping on his toes an excessive amount of times and saying 'I'm sorry' nearly continuously. After three slow songs, she was almost relieved when the next one had a faster beat. "I hope you don't plan to teach me how to dance to this song. I'd probably end up breaking your toes at this pace."

Gideon chuckled. "You weren't that bad. I've certainly danced with worse. Mum used to make me partner some of the new students if there wasn't an even number in the class. Until I was fourteen. That's when she had the accident."

"Oh." She had no idea what to say. "Do you think it's much longer until sunrise?"

"I have no idea." He glanced towards their table, which was still empty. "Do you want to sit down for a bit?"

"Yeah."

He kept hold of her hand as they weaved their way through the crowd and headed back to the table. "Do you want a drink?"

"I'm right." She sat across from him, trying to think of something to say. "Do you have any brothers or sisters?"

"Only me." The sadness returned to his eyes. "Dad will be devastated."

"What about your mum?"

"She hasn't lived with us for a couple of years. She's been backpacking around the world. Apparently nearly dying made her realise there were things she needed to do. Being with us wasn't one of them."

"I'm sorry." She struggled to think of something else to say. Maybe they should have kept dancing.

"What about you? Any other siblings other than Marley?"

"No. Our parents will be frantic." She thought of her friends. "Daisy, Ted and Scout were already getting worried when Marley didn't surface straight away. I can't imagine how panicked they were when I disappeared too. And Buddy." She couldn't stop thinking of his sad eyes. It didn't help when she was staring into Gideon's equally sad ones. "I've probably traumatised him for life. He was starting to get used to me when I disappeared. You should have seen how happy he was when I came home after being away for three days."

"I'm sure your parents will take care of him."

"I know they will, but it's not the same."

"Where were you when your sister was looking after him?"

She told him about staying at Daisy and Ted's grandparent's farm. About swimming and horse riding and helping with the cattle. She listened as he talked about some of his own holidays. Several had been flying out to whatever location his mum was currently in and living like a local in out of the way places with few amenities. She laughed as he wryly told her about some of his less than pleasant experiences.

Quinn was so caught up in the conversation that it was a surprise to see Oscar stop at their table. "It's nearly sunrise?"

Oscar nodded. "An hour away. Did you still want me to show you to the stables?"

Quinn rose to her feet. "Yes." Uneasiness returned and she dreaded talking to Marley. What if there was nothing she could do? What would happen if they were both stuck here?

Oscar led them back into the hallway, through the restaurant and out the staff door. Quinn's gaze darted everywhere. Other than the waiters, nothing appeared to be out of the ordinary. It was similar to any kitchen that could be found in a typical restaurant in her world. Stepping outside, she feared she was no longer in sanctuary.

She stopped by the door, trying to see into the shadows at the sides of the cobblestone courtyard where the lanterns didn't reach. "Oscar, wait." When he stopped and faced her, she continued speaking. "Is it safe out here? Is it still–"

"Masquerade Nightclub," Gideon interrupted.

"It's all part of Masquerade." Oscar pointed to the far side of the courtyard, which was about ten metres away. "The stables are there. You can wait out here or inside." He stepped past Quinn and into the kitchen.

She stared at the closed door. "I thought he was going to show us inside the stables." She turned to Gideon. "Why did you interrupt me before? When I was about to ask him if it's considered sanctuary out here too."

"Because we don't want anyone to realise we need sanctuary. Kaeder might expect us to pay."

"Wouldn't Darci already know?"

Gideon shook his head. "She came out after Gwyl said you are marked." He half turned and gestured towards the stables. "Want to wait inside?"

Chapter Ten

Before Quinn had a chance to answer, a Fae came out of a door further along the building and strode towards the stables. His hair was as pale as his skin, drawn back to show his slightly pointed ears, and he was dressed in clothes that made her think of medieval lords. "I don't know." She watched as the Fae entered the stables.

"What if your sister is already in there? She might have got away early."

Quinn took a deep breath, trying to convince herself to walk towards the stables. She couldn't help thinking about the Fae they'd met yesterday afternoon. What if the one in the stables was as arrogant as she'd been? "All right." She slowly walked towards the entrance, the smell of horses reaching her before she arrived.

Gideon remained at her side. "We'll figure it out. Don't worry about it."

She felt like asking him if he was kidding. Of course she was going to worry. She stepped into the warmth of the stables, lanterns hanging at intervals along a long wide corridor, stalls opening onto it along both sides. In some of them, horses hung their heads over the door of the stall, watching them. At the far end was a closed door in the middle of the wall.

The Fae who'd entered had been pacing. He turned to face them. "About time. Saddle my horse." He tossed a silver disk to her before striding outside.

Staring at the numbered disk she held, she tried to figure out what she was meant to do with it. "Are all Fae so arrogant?"

Gideon chuckled. "Pretty much. At least most of the nobility seem to be."

"How can you tell if they're part of the nobility?"

"They're arrogant?"

She gave him a look, clearly telling him she wasn't amused. Looking at the number again, she walked to the closest horse. On the door of the stall was an indent with a number. They didn't match. Several stalls along she found the matching number and pressed the disk into the indent. The latch of the stall clicked open and she held out her hand to the white horse, speaking softly as she entered the stall.

He didn't seem to be bothered by her presence. She found his tack hanging up high on the far wall of the stall and had to stretch to get it down. It didn't take her long to saddle him and she was glad of all the lessons Daisy had given her years ago. She led the horse past Gideon and to the Fae who waited out the front.

The Fae took the reins from her and swung up into the saddle, tossing her a silver coin before riding towards the side of the building and into the alley. She stared at the coin, having no idea how much she'd been paid.

Gideon joined her in the courtyard. "I wonder where the person is who normally saddles the horses."

"I don't know, but they missed out on their tip." She held the coin up. "Although I wouldn't have a clue if I was paid the right amount."

"Here comes another one." Gideon gestured towards the Fae who stepped out of the far door and headed towards the stables. "Come on." He grabbed her arm and tugged her inside. "Try greeting him. He might give you a couple of coins if you don't keep him waiting."

She slid the silver coin into the pocket with the

note and gold coins, smiling at the dark haired Fae who walked in the door. "Can I help you?"

He flipped a disk to her. "Tell her she'll get apples when we return home, but only if she behaves." He stepped outside.

"Okay." She drew the word out, sharing a look with Gideon who shrugged slightly.

"Don't look at me. I don't know much about their horses. I thought only people with the ability to talk to animals could make them understand, but I'd do what he said. This world is extremely odd."

She couldn't argue that statement. Taking another look at the disk, she strode to the correct stall, Gideon at her side. She pressed the disk into the indent and eyed the large black mare waiting in the stall. "I was told to warn you that you'll only be given apples, when you get home, if you behave."

The horse tossed her head, snorting.

"Does that mean you're going to behave?"

The horse shook her head.

"That doesn't look promising." She continued to remain outside the stall.

"Do you want a hand?" Gideon asked. "Not that I've had anything to do with horses."

"It's okay." She held out her hand to the horse. "Please. I'd really appreciate it if you behaved." She remained still for nearly a minute before the horse nudged her fingers. "All right. Let's get you saddled so you can go home to those apples." She remained wary, but the horse stood patiently. It wasn't until they were about to step outside that the horse nipped her shoulder. Not hard enough to hurt. Stopping, she stared up at the horse. "Really? That's you behaving?" When the horse snorted, she couldn't help smiling. "Okay. Fine." She reached up to pat the horse, but the mare pulled away, trotting through the doorway.

The Fae picked up the trailing reins. "Did she behave?"

Quinn couldn't shake the feeling that the look the horse was giving her dared her to tell on her. In the end, she met the Fae's dark eyes. "She didn't hurt me, if that's what you were worried about."

The Fae grinned. "A diplomat. Fascinating." He tossed her two silver coins before swinging into the saddle and heading for the alley.

"Why do I feel like I've missed something?" Quinn asked Gideon who'd come to stand beside her.

"I thought the same."

"I hope it's nothing to worry about."

Before Gideon had a chance to comment two Fae and a person that had pale skin with a hint of green, arrived. They were kept busy for a while as other Fae and Demi Fae asked for their horses. Quinn saddled the horses and Gideon took them to their owners. By the time things had quietened, they'd earned a handful of coins each.

"Maybe we should ask to work in the stables." Gideon pocketed his share of the coins.

Quinn heard Marley's voice and any answer she might have given him disappeared from her mind. She was about to rush out to her sister when she heard another voice.

"I can't wait to meet this person you believe can solve all your problems."

"Is that Darci?" Quinn tried to place the voice.

"I think so," Gideon said.

"You wait and see. She will be able to help me," Marley said. "She always knows what to do." Marley stepped into the stables, Darci at her side, her wings no longer visible.

"If it isn't the girl who's been swimming with the water folk." Darci eyed her up and down. "You don't look like a rescuing party to me. More like one in need of rescue."

Quinn wasn't about to tell her how close to the truth her words actually were. Instead she covered the last steps between her and her sister and hugged her tightly. "You okay?"

"How did you find me? I nearly dropped my tray when I saw you sitting in the restaurant."

She pulled away from her sister, not sure how to answer. "Marley, this is Gideon."

Gideon came forward with a smile. "Hi."

"Wow. Your eyes are exactly like Buddy's," Marley said.

"Marley!"

"Well they are."

"So. You don't tell people they look like a dog." She glared at her sister.

Gideon chuckled. "After hearing all about him I don't know if I should take that as a compliment or an insult." Even though he was smiling, the sadness didn't leave his eyes.

Quinn returned to his side, reaching for his hand, squeezing it reassuringly. "Neither. Your eyes nearly always look sad. Buddy's do too."

"Sounds like your sister isn't the only one who thinks that."

A smile slowly formed and she wasn't sure if she should agree or disagree.

Marley stepped forward, tugging on Quinn's free hand. "Are we going home now?"

"This I've got to see," Darci said.

Quinn wanted to ask Darci what had happened

to her wings, but she needed to focus. She let go of Gideon's hand to stare at her sister. "What did you promise him?"

"The very thing he gave her," Darci said.

Quinn tried not to feel annoyed. "Well, Marley?"

"I didn't realise he could make me stay here. I was going to tell him bad luck. He should have got the agreement in writing or something."

"What did you agree to?" She felt like shaking her sister.

"I was worried about Buddy. He lay there whimpering and I thought I'd killed him. I wished I could understand him. I'm pretty sure I said that out loud, but I'm not certain now. I know I spoke out loud when I told him it'd be easier if he could speak."

"Marley. Get to the point."

"Kaeder can understand animals. He told me what was wrong with Buddy in exchange for me working for him in his nightclub for as long as Buddy remained alive in the human world. I would forfeit what I'd gained if I didn't honour the bargain. I had until the end of the year to sort everything out and move to the realms of the Fae."

"You want me to kill my dog!"

"No! Well…" Marley looked away.

"That's not going to happen." She drew her hand

from Marley's grip, sending a slight smile to Gideon when he rested his hand on her shoulder.

"I told you she wouldn't be able to help," Darci said.

"I-" She broke off as a solution occurred to her. "Are you sure that's exactly what he said? The exact words?"

Marley nodded.

"Quinn, no." Gideon stepped closer and lowered his voice. "Have you forgotten?"

She met his gaze, seeing a warning mixed with the sadness in his eyes. There was nothing she could tell him, no assurances she could make. She hadn't forgotten. She looked to Darci. "Is there any way to return to the human world other than at night and through a moon portal?"

Darci shrugged. "Many of the Fae can travel to our world, but they'd want something in return. It's not a problem though. There's a full moon in two nights."

She was tempted to tell Darci that was the problem. Night.

"You're going to kill Buddy?" Marley stared at her. "Really?"

"No."

"But-"

She interrupted her sister. "I've got it all under

control as long as you don't make a promise to anyone else."

Kaeder strode into the stables. "You're not one of my staff."

Chapter Eleven

Quinn would have stepped back at the dagger sharp gaze directed towards her if Gideon hadn't been in the way. Kaeder's face was angular, there was the slightest point to his ears, his closely cropped hair was a sandy blond and his eyes ice blue. "I'm looking for work." She glanced towards Gideon. "We're looking for work."

"Where's the boy who's meant to be here?" Kaeder turned to Darci.

"Why are you looking at me? How am I meant to know where he is? I manage the inside staff," Darci said.

"This is inside."

"No, you have to go outside to get to it, so technically, you have to take care of this area," Darci said. "Don't go thinking you can con more work out of me."

Kaeder turned his back on Darci. "Boy! Where are you, boy?"

"It's Mike," Darci said.

"How can I be expected to remember all your names? You each look the same to me," Kaeder grumbled.

"Even me?" Darci raised an eyebrow.

Kaeder smiled. "You are always an exception. To every rule."

Darci inclined her head before turning away from him. "Mike!"

A gangly boy staggered out of one of the end stalls, rubbing his eyes. "Wha-" His eyes widened when he saw Kaeder. "Sir."

"You're fired." Kaeder turned his accusing finger from Mike to Quinn. "You're hired."

"I only work nights."

"Food and lodging in exchange for working nights." Kaeder took her hand and shook it. "Done." The smell of damp wool filled the air as he let go of her hand.

When Quinn was about to ask what the smell was she caught Darci's eye, who mouthed the word 'no' at her. The opportunity was lost when Kaeder started to leave and Gideon rushed after him, asking for a job.

"I only need one person in the stables of a night.

I already have a boy who takes care of things here during the day." Kaeder didn't slow his steps.

Quinn continued to stand where she was, dazed by how quickly everything had changed. She watched as Gideon followed Kaeder out the door, talking about other jobs that might be available.

"Does that mean you're stuck here too?" Marley asked.

"Only for as long as she wants food and lodging," Darci said.

Mike, who'd stood with his mouth gaping nearly the entire time, closed it with a snap. "What am I meant to do?"

"Report to the cook. You're back on kitchen duties," Darci said.

"But I hate working in the kitchen," Mike wailed.

"You should have thought about that before you slept on the job." Darci's hands went to her hips. "Inside. Now."

Mike went, grumbling under his breath.

Quinn waited until Mike was out of hearing before she spoke to Darci. "Is there any way to return here without needing to use a moon portal?"

"Find a way to make one of the Fae indebted to you and ask them to take you there and back again. But why would either of you want to return to the human world? It's nothing compared to this place. Even here in the Fringes, with all the outcasts and misfits, it's a million times better than home."

She doubted it would be possible to find a Fae to help her. "Are there any other ways?"

"There are a few natural portals. Through caves, certain types of bridge reflections and things like that. I could give you a list of some of them within a few hours of your home. I don't know all of them, but I hear things working here at Masquerade."

Quinn nearly agreed. But no one did anything for nothing around here. "What do you want in exchange?"

"That you don't take off without warning. I need to make sure there's someone to take care of the stables while you're gone. It's not meant to be my area, but Kaeder will blame me anyway," Darci said.

"Okay."

Darci grinned. "Excellent." She pointed to the far end of the stables. "There's a small room at the end, on the right, you can sleep in. The bathroom is straight ahead or you can use the one on the top floor near the staff rooms in the main building. You can take your meals in the kitchen. Nothing fancy, but it will be human food."

Her stomach rumbled and Darci laughed. Quinn

smiled, feeling a little more in control of everything. "Breakfast would be good."

Darci nodded. "Come on then." Darci headed out the door.

She started to follow, but Marley grabbed hold of her arm, drawing her back. "What?"

"You can't be planning to stay here. Why do you need a job?"

"I need somewhere to stay while I wait for the full moon."

"So we aren't staying? We're going home?"

She couldn't bring herself to tell Marley. Not yet. "Don't worry about anything. I'll have to leave you here for a bit, but I know what to do so you can go home."

Marley wrapped her arms around Quinn. "I knew you'd figure it out. The moment I saw you I knew you'd fix everything."

Darci put her head back in the doorway. "Are you two coming?"

She pulled away from Marley. "Yeah." Trailing behind Darci, she tried to figure out how to tell her sister that she was staying behind. Her and Buddy. No words came to mind, other than panicked, disjointed ones. They wouldn't help, only have Marley panicking too.

Stepping into the kitchen, she found it to be as busy as earlier. It seemed like the place never slept. She sat at a small table in one corner that Darci waved her to. Marley joined her and they sat silently, waiting for breakfast.

The meal was also silent and Quinn was glad. There were a lot of topics she wanted to avoid discussing with her sister. Particularly the one about her plans and how they'd both get home. When the meal was over, she escaped to the stables, wondering where Gideon was. Why couldn't she be interested in someone like him rather than Scout, who obviously wasn't interested in her at all? Not that Gideon seemed to be interested in her either.

Reaching the stables, she found several new horses in stalls and wondered who'd put them away. Was the day person already on duty? A glance around showed she was alone. If he was, she had no idea where he was. She stopped at the stall of one of the horses, a blood bay. "Aren't you beautiful?"

The horse tossed its head, holding it high as if it completely agreed with that statement.

Unable to open the stall door without the disk, she leaned over it to be able to stroke the horse's neck. "My best friend has a horse with a coat nearly as dark a red as yours. Well, it's actually her grandparents' horse, but she uses it when she visits them." She smiled, shaking her head slightly. "I really hope you can understand me and not only whoever owns you. I was going to say that'd make me feel a little less crazy than talking to myself. But I actually think it would make me feel crazier." She sighed, continuing to stroke the horse's neck. "I used to want a horse a few years ago. One as beautiful as you. But I'm glad now I didn't get one. Then I'd have left two pets behind."

"Get away from my horse."

She spun to see Gwyl step inside. She started to raise her hand to press it against her heart, barely managing to stop before she did so. "What are you doing here?" Surely he couldn't capture her here. This place was meant to be safe. And it was day. Didn't he only hunt at night?

"The very question I'd planned to ask you."

"I work here." She raised her chin, making sure her shoulders were straight. There was no way she was going to cower before him. "How about you?"

Gwyl flipped a silver disk towards her. "Saddle my horse."

She caught the disk and pressed it into the indent. The stall door clicked open. She nearly sympathised with the horse, but speaking those words out loud wouldn't have been a good idea.

Several times while she was saddling the horse, she glanced towards Gwyl, wishing he hadn't stayed to watch her. All the other Fae had waited out the front. Including the handful of Demi Fae who'd come in. Why did he have to stand there with eyes narrowed, as if expecting her to do something to his horse? As if she'd harm an innocent creature. The moment the horse was saddled, she held out the reins to him.

"Bring her here."

Her teeth clenched together on the disagreement that wanted to escape. She had no idea what was allowed and if she could refuse such a basic request. Continuing to hold out her hand, the reins in it, she took a couple of steps forward. He didn't reach out and take the reins until she was nearly standing on his feet. Another step and she would have been.

"You can't stay here forever. I wonder what Kaeder would have to say if he knew one of his staff was wanted by the Wild Hunt."

She pressed her lips together on the plea that nearly escaped. She doubted it'd make a difference, only have him speaking with Kaeder sooner. She refused to look away from his clear green eyes. Holding his gaze meant she noticed when the look changed from anger to anticipation.

"Here." He held out an autumn leaf to her.

She automatically took it.

"Call me when you're ready for the hunt. I think you might actually be a worthy challenge." He strode for the door, leading his horse.

She closed her hand over the leaf, tightening it into a fist. "How am I meant to do that?"

He glanced over his shoulder only long enough to speak. "Whisper my name against the leaf." He stepped outside.

She watched him until he was out of sight, her heart pounding at the thought of being hunted by him and his wolves. When she could no longer see him, she opened her hand and stared down at the leaf. It wasn't crushed into fragments like she'd expected. Whatever it was, it wasn't a typical fragile autumn leaf. Uneasiness curled through her and she was tempted to throw it away. Instead she put it in her pocket with the note and coins.

Feeling exhausted and not knowing what else to do, she headed for the room at the far end of the stables. She was nearly halfway there when Gideon called out her name and she turned around.

Chapter Twelve

Gideon strode towards Quinn, grinning. The iron necklace was in his hand. "Can you look after this for me? I'll be working evenings in the bar. Kaeder said this much iron would scare his customers away. It was difficult enough to convince him to let me keep the dagger. He was a bit suspicious at first. Wanted to know why so many humans had turned up looking for work. Like two is a great number or something. Anyway I told him there wasn't many other ways to earn a living in the realms of the Fae for humans. Not without becoming the pet of some Fae."

She took the necklace, surprised by how heavy it was. "What did he say to that?"

"There's always ways to earn money when you're capable of lying."

"Like what?"

Gideon shrugged. "Who knows, but whatever it is, it won't keep me out of the way of the Hunt."

"He's given you a room?"

"Yeah. How about you? Did he give you somewhere to sleep?"

She gestured towards the three doors at the far end. Darci had offered the room to her, but she guessed it was pretty much the same thing. "I was about to head to bed when you came in."

He reached for her, resting his hand on her shoulder. "I want to thank you for everything. When Gwyl grabbed me yesterday I thought it was all over. I've never been more terrified in my life. Not even when the Hunt first came after me. I'm sorry you got caught up in it."

She had no idea what to say. 'You're welcome' certainly didn't fit in this situation. "I don't suppose you know of any way I can return home without needing to wait until night and a full moon."

"I'll keep an ear out for you. And let me know if there's anything else I can do to help." He reached for her hand, holding it lightly. "Even if I didn't owe you, you're my friend so I'd help you out anyway." Smiling slightly he let go of her hand, starting to turn away. "I'll let you get some sleep. I could do with some too. It'll be nice to sleep somewhere dry for a change."

She nodded.

He paused. "Are you okay?"

She nearly told him about her encounter with Gwyl, but what could he do? "Yeah. Tired."

"Get some sleep then. I'll see you later."

Again she nodded and this time when he turned away he kept walking. A sigh escaped. She had no idea what to do. Waiting for the full moon didn't seem like a good plan. Gwyl's clear green eyes came to mind. Not when she had the leader of the Wild Hunt eager to track her down. Hopefully Gideon would learn some other way and she wouldn't need to use a moon portal. Or be away from Sanctuary at night. Yawning, she headed to the far end of the stables. Her body ached, was exhausted from all the walking and she was nearly asleep on her feet.

After using the toilet and washing her face, too tired to shower, she stared at herself in the bathroom mirror. She barely recognised herself. The wild eyed girl who stared back at her, hair a tangled mess and the dark plum dye almost gone from the amount of time she'd been spending in the water, seemed like another person. No wonder Darci had thought she'd needed rescuing. Too tired to care, she headed to her room.

Pausing in the doorway of her new room, she eyed the tiny space. A narrow bed was pushed against one wall and a small window was hidden behind a thick, black curtain that shifted slightly in the breeze. At the foot of the bed was a chest and the bed was unmade, sheets and blanket lying in a rumpled heap at the end of the mattress. Looking inside the chest she found clean linen and stripped the bed. Leaving the iron chain on the chest, she threw a sheet over the top of the mattress. Not bothering to make it properly, she kicked off her sneakers before she dropped onto it, falling instantly asleep.

Pounding on her door woke her and she stumbled groggily from bed, slipping her feet into her sneakers she'd tripped over. "Yeah?" The room was pitch black and she ran into the door, her hand patting the timber as she tried to find the handle.

"Your shift is in half an hour."

It was much later than she'd planned to sleep. Obviously she'd been more tired than she'd thought. Swinging the door open, she stared at the boy she guessed must be day shift. "Ahh, thanks?" He was shorter than her and wiry, black hair cropped close to his head, brown eyes without a single hint of sadness and he had a faint accent she couldn't place.

"I thought you might want to eat first." He looked her up and down, a grin forming. "You're a nice change from Mike." He held out his hand. "I'm Finch."

Taking his hand, she returned his smile. "Quinn."

"Interesting name. The last Quinn I knew was male."

She drew her hand from his, the comment familiar. "Yeah, I hear that a lot." She paused. "Yours is interesting too."

He laughed. "Yeah, apparently I earned it. If you want to hear about interesting names, you should ask Darci about hers."

"Okay." She said the word cautiously, not sure if she should ask Darci since he had a gleam of mischief in his eyes.

"I'd better let you go eat. Early evening and before dawn are pretty busy around here." He looked her up and down again. "You sure you can handle it on your own?"

She looked him up and down the same as he'd done to her. "How do you manage on your own? Isn't the tack placed a little high up for you?"

He laughed. "Fair enough. I keep forgetting all

about that woman's movement thing you ended up having back home."

"When did you leave our world?"

"Late eighteen hundreds. But I've been back a few times since. London doesn't look the same. Last time I went back I had no idea where I ended up. I think it was one of the colonies."

She stared at him speechlessly. "You don't sound like you're from that era." Not that she knew exactly how someone should sound from then, but his words seemed far too modern.

Finch laughed. "They couldn't understand me in the beginning. Had a right hard time trying to make myself understood."

"You're so young." She blurted the words out, then reddened when he laughed again.

"It's Fae food. If you don't want to leave then you eat their food and can live forever. It's the magic in it. You can't go back after that. Not for more than a day or two. Other food becomes dust. Unless of course you have magic of your own. Then you can eat what you like. And live as long as the Fae. Are you planning on staying?"

She shrugged, words beyond her. She wanted to ask him endless questions, but guessed she better have something to eat before she had to start work. "I'll have lunch, ahh, dinner so you can finish up work for the day."

Finch stepped out of the doorway. "It's not the work I mind. All I ever wanted was to work with horses. It's their owners that give a person a right hard time. I like chatting to all my four legged friends."

"You can talk to horses?"

"That's what got me here. I wanted to talk to animals. Much better than people." He grinned. "Although you're all right. Not full of demands like some." He nodded his head in farewell before he sauntered down the corridor, absently patting one of the horses that put its head past the stall door as he walked by.

She watched as he vaulted over one of the stall doors, taking a brush from a hook at the back of the stall and running it over a black horse. If that was the only way to get into a stall when the owner had the disk she doubted she'd be spending any time brushing horses. She stood there nearly a minute before she remembered she was meant to be having dinner and headed for the exit. Her head was full of all she'd learned and she had no idea what to think about most of it.

Stepping outside, she found day had almost ended. Before she could cross the courtyard, Gwyl and the

Fae woman they'd helped on the road came out of Masquerade's main building. She froze, unable to take her gaze from Gwyl. The woman stopped halfway across the courtyard, reaching up to rest her palm against his cheek. The words she spoke were too soft for Quinn to hear.

Gwyl shook his head, stepping away from her.

The woman followed. "Please, Gwyl. Let my brother go. Your pack is large enough you wouldn't miss one person."

"It doesn't work like that." He turned away from the woman, stopping when he saw Quinn. His eyes narrowed and he strode towards her, ignoring the woman who called after him.

Quinn tried to make herself move out of the doorway, but it was like she was glued in place. She held his gaze, unable to look away and wondered if this was how a rabbit felt when caught in the headlights of an oncoming vehicle.

Reaching her, Gwyl stopped. "Are you ready for the Hunt? I'll give you an hour. Do you think you can outrun me?"

She knew she couldn't. "How fair would that be when you have a horse and I'm on foot?" The steadiness of her voice surprised her.

A gleam entered his eyes. "I'll leave her here. You

and me. I need no help to hunt. You won't be able to win, no matter what advantage I give you. No one can. You might outlast the rest, but in the end it won't be you who wins."

She knew the moment the sun set. The gleam in his eyes became a predatory glitter. Fear raced through her and she tightened her hand that wore the iron ring. She should have worn the necklace. "Maybe I'll be an exception." He came close enough that her vision was nearly completely filled by his eyes. Her heart sped up and she fought the urge to run. In the distance she heard wolves howl and there was a pawing in the stables behind her.

He breathed in deep, like an animal scenting prey. "I'll know the moment you leave sanctuary. You won't need to call me." He held her gaze a moment longer before he shifted her to the side and entered the stables.

Quinn nearly gave into the weakness in her legs to collapse on the ground. Until she noticed the Fae woman watched her. Keeping upright, she returned the stare. The woman looked away first, her gaze drawn to the doorway beside Quinn. Wanting to know what the Fae saw, she started to turn.

Chapter Thirteen

Gwyl burst from the stables, riding low over his horse, his antlers either side of the mare's neck. As soon as he was in the open, he threw back his head and howled. The answering cries sounded closer and Quinn felt goosebumps rise on her arms. She wanted to run into the stables and hide in her room. She refused to allow herself. Somehow she had to get not only Marley, but also herself back to the human world, before it became completely impossible and they were both stuck here forever. If she managed to live that long. She thought of the leaf in her pocket as she crossed the courtyard.

"What is he to you?" the Fae woman demanded.

Only snarky replies came to mind, the nicest being 'how is that your concern'. She played it safe and remained silent, her gaze on the door ahead of her.

"I'm talking to you, human."

She'd nearly reached the door, only a few more steps.

"Mairwin! What's taking you so long?"

Quinn looked over her shoulder to see who had called out. It was another fair-haired Fae. He looked similar to Mairwin.

"He said no. That I'm wasting my time," Mairwin said.

"What are we going to do?"

"Return in the morning when he finishes hunting." Mairwin strode towards the alley, the man hurrying after her. "I refuse to take no for an answer."

Quinn watched them go, wondering what was going on and who Mairwin and the Fae with her were. She shook her head slightly. There were enough problems of her own to worry about without wondering about those belonging to others. She entered the main building, stopping when her sister nearly ran into her.

Marley grinned, holding up a cloth wrapped parcel. "I was bringing you roast beef sandwiches."

"Thanks." She took the parcel from her sister, surprised to find it was warm. The kitchen was filled with strangers and a glance around showed her the only one she knew was Mike. If the glare he sent in her direction was any indication, he didn't like her. It wasn't her fault she'd been given his job. She hadn't encouraged him to sleep instead of work. "I guess I better get back to the stables." She motioned towards the door.

"I'll see you after work."

"Okay." She turned towards the door.

"Quinn."

She looked over her shoulder at her sister.

"Thanks for coming after me. I was so scared until you came here."

She was getting sick of never knowing what to say. "Try and stay out of trouble." The moment she saw her sister's expression, she knew they hadn't been the right words. "Sorry, but I was worried when you went through the moon portal. We stood there waiting for you to surface for ages. Then I followed. I saw Kaeder throw you over his shoulder and take you with him."

"I didn't expect any of this. None of it seemed real. Even when he told me what Buddy said. I thought he was probably a vet or something."

She nodded. "I'll see you in the morning." When Marley nodded, she returned to the stables, nodding to Finch when he asked if she could take over. He left with a wave over his shoulder and she sat, leaning up against an empty stall, and unwrapped the still warm parcel.

Slices of freshly cooked roast beef were in the middle of thick slices of bread, a dark gravy soaking into them. Her mouth watered and she ate quickly, finishing a moment before a Fae arrived with a horse for her to unsaddle and put in a stall. She took the reins and gave him a silver disk in exchange.

The first part of the night was busy, like Finch had warned. Things were quiet when Finch returned. He headed to his room that was opposite hers, a mumbled goodnight as he stumbled past her, the smell of alcohol and perfume trailing in his wake. The stables weren't busy again until dawn approached and numerous Fae returned to collect their horses and leave. A handful of others arrived and Quinn learned that some of the Fae rented rooms at Masquerade for various lengths of time. There were even some who never left, unable to step out of sanctuary. She knew how they felt.

Marley arrived a little before sunrise and chatted to her whenever she had a few minutes between fetching horses. She half listened to her sister.

"You should have seen him."

"Who?"

"I already told you. Your boyfriend. Gideon."

"He's not my boyfriend."

"Are you sure? I thought he was with the way you were holding his hand yesterday."

She didn't bother explaining it hadn't been like that. It had been more about comfort or reassurance. "He's not my boyfriend."

"If you say so. Anyway, he's amazing. I was working in the bar last night and a Fae woman was complaining that her friend she was dancing with was useless. That he'd broken every toe with how he trampled all over her. She was getting really shrill."

A slight smile formed as she remembered how she'd trampled Gideon's feet. He'd probably empathised with the woman.

"Someone went to fetch Kaeder. We all thought she was going to make a major scene. Gideon crossed the room and held out his hand, asking her if she wished to dance. He was utterly amazing. They glided around the floor and everyone stepped back to watch. They'd all been watching her anyway. Even the musicians had stopped playing. They started up again when Gideon and the woman danced. It was like watching one of those old time dance competitions on TV. I've never seen anything like it before."

"His mum was a dance instructor."

"Really? Well he had the Fae lining up to dance with him. The women and the men. Kaeder stood in the doorway rubbing his hands. You could almost see him thinking of some way to turn Gideon's skills to his advantage."

It sounded like Gideon would be fine. Now she only had to solve her and Marley's problems. "I'm going home tomorrow. To sort things out so you can get away from here. I'll leave a bit before sunset." She needed to find somewhere to hide until the moon was high enough she could use a moon portal to return home. She dreaded the thought of lying in cold water for hours.

Marley fell silent for a moment. "You will come back, won't you?"

Surprised at how young Marley sounded, she reached for her sister, wrapping an arm around her shoulders. "Of course I will. Didn't I come after you even though you didn't expect it?"

Marley rested her head on Quinn's shoulder. "I didn't know what to do when he brought me here. Darci told me not to carry on, that this place was better than our world, but I don't think things were good for her back in our world. I want to go home. I really don't want to stay here. I miss everyone."

"Don't worry about it. I've got it all under control."

If she could avoid being caught by Gwyl. As if thinking of him had conjured him, Gwyl entered the stables, leading his horse. She pulled away from Marley, keeping her voice low. "Go back to the main building. I don't want you around him."

"The leader of the Wild Hunt? He's not so bad. Darci said he sometimes rents a room here."

"Please, Marley. Go inside. I'll see you tonight before I start work."

"Okay." Her sister left, dragging her feet.

Quinn waited until they were alone before she approached Gwyl, collecting a disk from the door of the stall the mare had been in earlier. She held it out to him. He stood there, watching her for a moment before he took it and handed over the reins. He continued to watch her and, when she gave up on him leaving, she turned away and led the mare to the stall. She hated having to turn her back on him, but she couldn't stand there all day waiting for him to leave when it looked like he wasn't about to.

While she unsaddled the horse, she kept glancing towards Gwyl. He remained in place, watching her tend to his horse. She wished he'd go. It was unnerving having him watch her every action. It began to annoy her and instead of leaving the stall once the tack was hung up, she took down the brush and ran it over the mare. Maybe he'd get sick of watching and leave. It didn't take her long to figure out her plan was a fail. By the time she'd finished brushing the horse she wanted to say something to him. She remained silent, not wanting him to know how much him remaining there annoyed her.

Leaving the stall, she closed the door, stopping outside it to meet his gaze. He'd lost the glitter in his eyes and the menacing feel that made her want to run when she looked at him. "Was there something else you wanted?"

"Have a look in the courtyard and tell me what you can see."

She was tempted to tell him no. After a moment, she walked to the door, giving him a wide berth. Mairwin paced back and forth, alone. She watched her for a moment before she stepped away from the doorway. "Mairwin is out there."

"Tell me when she leaves."

"I can't. I have other things to do." Like figure out a way to go through a moon portal tonight without being caught by him.

He crossed the space between them.

She held her ground, only after reminding herself she was in sanctuary. "Your horse has been unsaddled. That's all I needed to do." An idea occurred to her.

"Unless of course you want to give me a couple of days reprieve in exchange."

"There is no reprieve once the hunt has begun. All I can offer is to let you go and give you a head start the first time I catch you. We can toy with our prey, but there's only one way to end the hunt. Someone must win."

"Five times."

"You would haggle with the Hunt?"

She almost laughed at his tone of incredulity. "I will haggle with anyone if it will get me what I need."

"My first offer stands. No more than once."

She wanted to continue trying to haggle, but could hear the finality in his tone. He wasn't about to offer more, no matter how much she wished he would. "Done."

The scent of rich earth rose up around them and Gwyl gestured towards the doorway. "Check for me again."

She stepped outside, her gaze drawn to Mairwin. She didn't have the time to wait all day if the woman happened to be persistent. "If you're hoping to see Gwyl again, you're too late."

"He's gone already?"

She started to say yes, but changed her mind at

the thought of Gwyl listening to what she might say. "You missed the chance to talk to him."

"Do you know where he went?"

"I'm not his keeper. I doubt he tells anyone where he goes."

Mairwin sent one more look towards the stables, her lips thinning, before she silently left.

Chapter Fourteen

Quinn felt the heat of Gwyl behind her and she turned, taking a step away from him. No wonder he didn't wear a shirt with the heat coming off his body. She met his clear green eyes. "Don't forget you have to let me go if you ever catch me."

"It is only once and the promise can't be broken. Don't you understand how Fae magic works?"

"No."

"Then why would you come to this realm when you don't understand one of the most common talents?"

"I came to fetch someone home." She tried to decipher the look in his eyes at her words.

"Have they joined the Hunt?"

She shook her head. "No. I can't imagine her ever wanting to. Actually, I don't understand why anyone wants to join."

"Revenge."

She wanted to run at the harshness in his voice when he spoke the word. It was only a flicker of emotion in the depths of his eyes that held her in place. "You regret it?" Her voice was soft, the words spoken before she had time to think better of it.

"Why would I regret something I sought?" He moved her aside and strode towards the main building, entering the far door.

It took her a moment to realise he hadn't really answered her question. Gideon's words came back to her. The Fae couldn't lie. She started to head towards the main building then remembered how Finch had woken her. With one last look at the door Gwyl had disappeared in, she strode inside to knock on Finch's door. "Finch? You ready to take over?"

There were several crashing noises behind the door before Finch opened it, yawning. "I haven't eaten."

"I was about to get breakfast. I could bring you something back."

Finch's eyes lit up. "You'd do that for me?"

She hadn't thought it was that big a deal, but what did she know? "Sure."

Suspicion crept into Finch's eyes. "What do you expect in exchange?"

She nearly said nothing. "Information. There's so much I don't know about this realm."

Finch grinned. "That's no hardship. I've got loads of information. Especially after working in the stables all these years. The things you hear around here."

"Okay. It's a deal." She took the hand Finch held out and shook it.

"Tell the cook I'll have my usual breakfast."

"Okay." She turned away, hurrying through the stables before any Fae could arrive. There were things she needed to do. She'd much rather sleep, but didn't want to risk sleeping in like yesterday. This way Finch would wake her when it was time to begin work. Quinn stepped into the kitchen at the same time as Darci entered it from the restaurant.

"You." Darci pointed at Marley who was rising from the table in the corner. "Serve Gwyl."

"No." Quinn hurried forward, taking hold of her sister's arm and drawing her behind, as if to shield her with her body. "I don't want her anywhere near him."

"You don't get to make that decision. I do." Darci's hands went to her hips. "Understand?"

"He's not safe."

"This is a sanctuary. Nothing will happen to her here. Besides, he's not as bad as the last Gwyl."

Quinn frowned. "What? What do you mean the last Gwyl?"

"It's the title of the leader of the Hunt. No one ever knows their name, not even they do."

"What happened to the last Gwyl?" If something happened to this one, would that mean she'd be free from the Hunt?

Darci shrugged, her hands still on her hips. "All I know is the last Gwyl still lives in the Fringes."

She stared at Darci, trying to make sense of it all. "Where in the Fringes?"

"Near the pit. You don't want to go there. It's the worst part of the Fringes."

Darci was wrong. She did want to go there. He might have the information she needed to escape the Hunt. "I don't care if this one isn't as bad as the last one, I don't want Marley near him."

The cook stepped forward with a plate of food. "Then who's going to deliver this to him?"

Quinn took the plate. "I will." She walked towards Darci, who remained in the doorway. She held the young woman's gaze until she gave a single nod and stepped out of the way. Quinn tried to ignore the uneasiness in her stomach as she entered the restaurant. There was only a handful of people scattered around the room so it was easy to spot Gwyl with his antlers rising from his head.

He turned his head and looked directly at her.

It was an effort to cross the room while pinned by his gaze. Placing the plate in front of him, she took a step back from the table. "Is there anything else you need?" The words sounded like something a waiter would say.

Gwyl held her gaze a moment longer before shaking his head and looking at the food in front of him. "This is all I require for now."

She stared at him a moment longer, surprised he sounded fatigued. When he looked towards her again, she turned away and headed for the kitchen. How had he become the leader of the Wild Hunt? And would it change anything if he was no longer the leader? She needed to find out. Entering the kitchen, she turned to the cook. "Finch wants his usual breakfast and I'll have a human meal, please."

"Everyone wants something," the cook muttered, turning away and preparing two plates.

Ignoring the comment, Quinn turned to Darci. "I leave tomorrow night."

"For how long?"

She shrugged. "I'm not sure. It depends on how hard it is to get to a portal in the human world."

Darci drew a folded piece of paper from a pocket and held it out to her. "This is the most logical one. It's a few hours from where you live and only half a day's walk from here in this realm."

She took the paper and slid it into a pocket of her jeans, wishing she had another change of clothes. She'd have to ask her sister where she'd got her different outfits from. There better not have been any promises involved. "Thank you."

"I wouldn't thank me yet. You'll come out near a Troll village. Try and avoid them. They don't like humans very much." Darci turned to Marley. "You can help clean up the rooms that were vacated this morning and then you're off duty until sunset." She headed back into the restaurant before anyone could say another word.

The cook held up two plates. "Food's ready."

Quinn took the plates. "Thank you." She turned to her sister. "I'll see you before I start work tonight."

"When will I get to go home, Quinn?"

"Soon." She wanted to remind her sister to stay out of trouble, but held back the words. "Be careful." She headed for the door, relieved when Marley opened it for her.

The moment she came into the stables Finch

grabbed his plate from her. "I was about to come after you."

"Darci was in the kitchen giving out orders."

Finch grinned. "She likes to do that. Don't blame her though. Things go wrong and she's the first one Kaeder points a finger at."

She settled beside him on the floor in front of an empty stall. "I kind of got that impression when I met Kaeder. Sorry I took so long to bring you breakfast."

"It wasn't that much a hardship. I'd rather stay here. I managed to get a couple of horses brushed. That's something you can do during the quiet times of an evening."

Quinn shook her head. "I doubt I could leap over the stalls like you do."

Finch laughed, eyeing off her legs. "Now that I'd like to see, but it's not the only way into a stall. There's a master disk hanging on a hook on the far wall, near the bathroom door."

"Thanks." She ate her food as she tried to think how to word the questions she needed to ask. "Do you know anything about the last Gwyl?"

"That's someone I avoided as much as possible. He was a right hard man to deal with. I was almost glad when he broke the curse and we got a new one. I don't think the new one was with them long before he became leader of the Wild Hunt."

"How do they choose their leaders?"

Finch shrugged. "I don't know."

"How do I find the pit?"

Finch stopped with his food halfway to his mouth, gaping. He lowered the food. "You don't want to go there. It's like a rabbit warren. You get lost in there and you're not coming out. Half the Fae living there are mad from iron sickness."

"I need to talk to the last Gwyl."

"You don't need to go into the pit for that. He lives in a shack just outside it. But you don't want to visit him. He doesn't like anyone. Humans or Fae."

"I need to ask him some questions."

Finch finished his breakfast and set his plate aside. "He won't go answering anything for free. He'll want something. Not gold, something else."

"Like what?"

Finch shrugged. "A favour. Don't offer an open ended one. He could ask anything of you. And he'd be the sort who would."

"How do I find out what he wants?"

"Ask him." Finch grinned. "That usually works."

"Can you draw me a map of how to find his place?"

Nodding, Finch patted his pockets and only came up with a pencil.

Quinn drew the note from her pocket and left it folded. She listened as Finch explained the directions he drew, taking the paper from him when he was finished. "Thanks."

"You'll be back before it's your turn to take over?"

"Yeah. I'll be back well before then." She couldn't be out after dark. If she was out that long, then something had gone terribly wrong.

Finch got to his feet, leaving the plate on the floor. "I won't cover for you if you're late." He gestured towards the plate. "And you can take that back to the kitchen or it was pointless me getting out of going over there for breakfast."

She watched as he headed to one of the stalls and vaulted over the door, murmuring to the horse before taking down a brush. She sat there for several minutes, thinking over everything. By the time she rose to her feet, she still had no clearer idea of what to do. But she wasn't about to let that stop her. She needed information and this was the only way to get it.

Stacking the plates she started to head for the door, changing her mind and going to her room first. Taking the iron chain, she slipped it over her head.

Hopefully those already sick from iron would be less likely to come near her.

She tucked the necklace under her shirt before taking the plates back to the kitchen. She'd nearly escaped when Gideon came into the room, heading straight for her. The smile that was forming in greeting faded when he took her arm and ushered her outside.

Chapter Fifteen

Quinn pulled away from Gideon. "Stop grabbing me." She got a proper look at him. "You've shaved." She could see why the human who'd helped him had been interested.

He ignored her comment. "I need to talk to you." He glanced around. "Alone."

"What's wrong?"

"I have to get a tattoo if I want to work here long term."

"What for?"

"Decoration. That's what Darci's wings are. A tattoo with Fae magic in the ink. When they're not on display, they're a tattoo on her back."

That explained one of her questions. Sadly one of the unimportant ones. "What's the problem?"

He glanced around again, dropping his voice even lower. "I don't do well with needles."

"How bad are you exactly?"

His lips twisted into a wry smile. "I've been known to pass out at the sight of them." He grasped her shoulder. "They can't find out. There are ones who'd use it against me. The weak don't survive in this realm."

She rested a hand on his. "Tell Kaeder you need time to think about what sort of tat you want. That it's not something you can choose in a single day."

"Then what? I can't keep telling him that forever."

Quinn was surprised by the panic she could hear in his voice. She hadn't heard it any of the times the Hunt had been close. Only when Gwyl had caught him. "It'll give you time to figure out another plan."

"I can't go through with a tattoo. I really can't."

She tightened her hand over his. "It's okay. We'll sort something out."

Gideon drew away, turning his back on her. "I thought everything would be good once I arrived here. That's what I kept telling myself. I had to get here and everything would be fine. They wouldn't be able to get me."

She had no idea how to comfort him. Everything she thought of sounded lame. "I'm going further into the Fringes today."

He spun to face her. "Are you crazy? I've heard

stories about what it's like further in. You don't want to go in there."

"I have to. I'm going home tomorrow night. I need to sort things out so my sister can leave."

"Do you want me to come with you?"

She was tempted to say yes. Going further into the Fringes on her own sounded like a really bad idea. "No. But I wanted you to know in case something happened. I'm going to see the last Gwyl."

"What do you mean?"

She explained everything she'd learned about the Wild Hunt.

"Let me come with you. Maybe there's a way I can get them to stop hunting me. Then I won't have to stay here and get a tattoo."

"I was hoping you'd look out for my sister."

"And what about me? Am I meant to remain here for seven years instead of trying to figure something else out?"

She started to speak, but a Fae came into the courtyard, heading for the stables. She waited until he stepped through the doorway before she spoke again. "I'll see what I can find out for you, but I really need someone to keep an eye on Marley. If I'm going to go to all this trouble I want to know she's not going to be caught up in something else."

"Is that it? You'll only help me if I watch your sister?"

She couldn't believe what a mess she was making of it. "No. I'd help you anyway. I'm not Fae. I'm human."

"Sorry. I can't stop thinking about needles. What am I going to do?"

Reaching for him, she rested her hand on his shoulder. "I know you'll figure something out. Didn't you make it here? On your own." She watched as the tension eased from his body.

"You're right." He ran a hand across his face. "I'm so tired."

"Get some sleep. I'll be back later." Sleep would be nice, but there was too much for her to do first.

"Take care out there. I'd miss you if something happened to you. You're the only friend I have here."

Always a friend, never anything more. She pushed that thought aside. She didn't want to be anything more to Gideon. Thoughts of Scout crept in. If she couldn't figure out a way to return home in far less than seven years Scout would have lived part of his life before she saw him again. "You be careful too. Just because it's sanctuary, doesn't mean there's no dangers." An image of Gwyl sitting in the dining room came to mind. She drew away from Gideon. "I better go before it gets too late."

He walked with her to the start of the alley. When she was partway down it, she glanced over her shoulder and saw he stood there watching her walk away. She faced ahead, refusing to think about Gideon or Marley left behind at Masquerade. They were safe there. They had to be safe there. Taking either of them with her would be crazy, even though the thought of going on her own made her heart race and uneasiness fill her body.

Bringing to mind the directions Finch had given her, she headed for the river, following it further into the Fringes. It was murky this far in and she hoped she never needed to hide in this part of the river. Who knew what might be living in it. She kept close to the shadows of the buildings, feeling like someone watched her. It took all her effort not to keep checking over her shoulder. She didn't want to appear nervous. She strained to hear any sounds that might be threatening, even though she had no idea how to tell them apart from the noises that were non-threatening. It took her far longer to reach her destination than she liked. But she guessed more than a minute in this area was enough to make her nervous.

Standing in front of the last Gwyl's shack, she stared at the dilapidated, two-storey building. What was she doing here? How had she thought she might be able to sort this out? Taking a deep breath, she knocked on the door. Silence greeted her. Should she knock again? This time she couldn't resist checking over her shoulder. Had that been someone peering at her around the corner of a building? The streets in the Fringes were narrow and the tall buildings created all sorts of shadows suitable for hiding in. She couldn't help thinking about some of the strange creatures she'd seen at Masquerade.

Forcing her hand to rise, she knocked again. This time she heard noises inside and hoped it meant the last Gwyl was home. When the door swung open, and a man glared at her, she nearly stepped back. She guessed he was a dark Fae with his long black hair, drawn back to show slightly pointed ears, and his more solid build. "Are you the last Gwyl?"

"I don't go by that name." His gaze dropped to the necklace she wore before meeting her eyes again. "Who are you that you've come to my door wearing so much iron?"

"I have questions a-"

"Did you think to threaten them from me with your iron?"

She shook her head, automatically taking a step away from him. "No, I was going to ask you what you needed."

"What sort of questions?"

They tumbled through her mind, an endless list of things she needed to know. "I want you to tell me about the Wild Hunt."

His jaw tightened as he took a step towards her, his hands curling into fists. "I never talk about those days."

"I don't-" She broke off at the sounds of banging and clattering coming from two buildings away.

He pointed in the direction of the noise. "That. You want questions answered, you get rid of that."

Why couldn't his favour have been simple? "What name do you go by now?"

"The one I was born with."

A sigh nearly escaped. She held out her hand, the one without the ring. "I'm Quinn."

He didn't take her hand. "Derwyn." His glare remained firmly in place. "If you're trying out that old human saying, it won't work. Not around here."

"What saying?"

"The one about catching critters with honey instead of vinegar."

"Oh. You can catch more flies with honey than

with vinegar." She hadn't heard the phrase in years. "That wasn't what I was trying." She didn't have a clue what she'd been trying to do. Noises from the building two over caught her attention. "What's happening over there?"

"She's doing it deliberately." Derwyn scowled in the direction of the noises. "At all hours. Day and night. If she thinks I'm the one moving on, she's wrong. She'll be doing the moving."

"But what's she doing?"

"Making noises. Isn't that obvious?"

She barely managed not to point out people usually had a reason for making noises. She doubted Derwyn would appreciate the comment. Not with how sharp his tone was. "Have you asked her to stop?"

He took a step forward, looming over her. "Of course I asked her to stop. Do you take me for an idiot?"

She didn't know if she should retreat or hold her ground. Her hand went to the iron necklace. She'd expected him to keep more distance with all the iron she was wearing.

"You're going to use that against me?"

"Of course not. I-"

"You want to use it against the wood Fae?"

"Well…" She struggled to think of a way she could help him.

"Hide it near her bed. She isn't going to want to stay here if she gets iron sickness and can't figure out why. Make sure you hide it so she can't find it."

Quinn eyed the noisy building. Gideon had only mentioned dark and light Fae. "What's a wood Fae?"

"Like Gwyl is."

An image of his piercing green eyes came to mind. There was so much she didn't know about this realm and its inhabitants. So much she needed to learn. "Won't it make her crazy?"

"She's already crazy."

"But the iron would–"

"She's not stupid. When she starts to get sick she'll move. She's being deliberately annoying."

"How would I get it in her house while she's at home?" Maybe he was using this as a way to get rid of her, not his neighbour.

"I'll distract her and you go in the back. Hers is the door with the symbols from the old language carved on it. Don't use the door. It's been protected against intruders. Use the window before it. Her bedroom is upstairs. Do we have a deal?"

"You'll answer all my questions about the Wild

Hunt and the current Gwyl if I hide my iron necklace near her bed." She gestured towards the building.

"Only the questions you ask today. I'm not having you think you can come back whenever you want. Pestering me for years."

"Today's questions and questions from another four days."

Derwyn shook his head, still remaining close enough to glare down at her. "One other day. And only questions about the Wild Hunt and the current Gwyl. You have other questions, you ask them of someone else."

She wanted to argue, but his expression was set and his glare didn't waver.

Chapter Sixteen

"Okay." Quinn took the hand Derwyn held out to her and shook it. The smell of jasmine filled the air and she eyed him. How had such an angry Fae ended up with so sweet a smelling magic?

"Get moving. I want her gone as soon as possible."

She stepped back from him, trying to figure out the best way to get behind the buildings that were closely packed together.

"Go on." He pointed in the opposite direction to the wood Fae's place. "Out the back and through her window. You're wasting time."

She headed in the direction he'd indicated, glancing over her shoulder a couple of times to see he watched her. It didn't take long to find the narrow alley leading between two buildings. Out the back of the buildings was a laneway filled with rubbish and shadows, the buildings behind looming over her. None of this seemed like a good idea.

Straightening her shoulders, she hurried along the laneway looking for the door with the carved symbols. Finding it, she stared at the red paint that had been used to highlight each symbol. A shiver went through her. That didn't look good. Shouting from out the front of the building caught her attention and she strained to hear. Was that two voices? The banging from inside the building had stopped so the wood Fae might be distracted enough for her to enter the house.

Returning to the open window she'd passed, she climbed over the sill, wincing at the creak of the timber floorboard she stood on. Derwyn accused the woman of deliberately annoying him and Quinn couldn't resist smiling when the woman told him he was delusional. He probably was, but that wasn't her problem. All she had to worry about was getting the answers she needed. Tiptoeing across the room, which was filled with junk, she paused at the doorway to peer into a dark hallway. A pity she didn't know the layout of this place. She hadn't thought to ask Derwyn exact details.

Turning to the left she soon found she'd chosen the wrong direction and hurried back the way she'd come. The argument grew louder as she came near the end of the hall and she froze in a doorway. A woman stood with her back to her, arguing with Derwyn.

"Stop coming around here spouting nonsense." The woman slammed the door shut.

Quinn barely managed to remain quiet as she scurried to the end of the hallway and up a set of stairs, wincing when several of them creaked. So much for Derwyn distracting his neighbour. Peeking into a couple of rooms along the upstairs hallway, she found the bedroom halfway along. There was a large timber bed in the middle of the room, tangled sheets lying haphazardly across the mattress. Along one wall was a large mirror, the edges damaged and the reflection tarnished. On the opposite wall was an old timber wardrobe that no longer closed properly because it leaned to one side.

She searched under the bed first, looking for a suitable hiding place. The only thing she found was dust. Would the wardrobe be close enough for the iron to work? And did Fae recover from iron sickness? A creaking sound drew her to the doorway and she peered out. Catching a glimpse of the woman, she ducked back into the room, her heart racing and an uneasiness churning in the pit of her stomach.

She needed to get out of here. Silently crossing the room she looked out the window. It was too great a drop. The sound of footsteps came closer and Quinn's gaze darted around the room. She took a step towards the wardrobe before scurrying over to the bed and hiding underneath.

The woman entered her bedroom, muttering under her breath about Derwyn. A door creaked.

Quinn turned her head in the direction of the sound and saw the woman stood in front of the wardrobe. Relief momentarily washed over her at the thought of how close she'd come to hiding there. She looked to the other side, trying to find an escape. Dust stirred and tickled her nose. Holding it until the urge to sneeze passed, she stared at the bottom of the mattress. Her gaze was drawn to a small hole that appeared to have straw poking out of it. She cautiously put her fingers in the hole, her attention partially on the woman who continued to rummage in the wardrobe. What was she doing? How long did she plan to remain in here? It better not be too long.

Several strands of straw rained down on her and she grabbed at her nose again to prevent a second sneeze from escaping. There looked to be plenty of room for her to slide the necklace inside the mattress and the straw would prevent the woman from feeling it. She raised her head and slipped the necklace off, freezing when she made a noise. Holding her breath, she watched the woman. Nothing changed. She continued to rummage in the wardrobe and mutter about Derwyn.

Letting her breath out slowly, Quinn pushed the necklace into the hole. At every slight sound she winced, glancing towards the woman. It seemed to take forever to hide the necklace in the mattress and make sure it wouldn't easily fall out. Hopefully Gideon wouldn't be annoyed she'd given it away. Maybe she could buy some iron necklaces when she returned home tomorrow night. One each.

She continued to lie under the bed, wishing the woman would hurry up and leave the room. What if she stayed here all day? When the woman closed the wardrobe she tensed, waiting for her to go, her gaze fixed on the woman's feet. Instead of heading towards the door, like she'd expected, the feet came towards the bed.

Muttering under her breath, the woman sat on the edge of the bed, continuing to complain about Derwyn. After a few minutes she lay down, several strands of straw drifting from the hole onto Quinn.

Once again Quinn found herself holding her nose and desperately trying not to sneeze. When the feeling passed, she eased to the side of the bed with the mirror. She raised her head as much as she could, but it didn't help. She couldn't use the mirror to see what the woman was doing. Lowering her head, she closed her eyes, tiredness washing over her. She couldn't be caught here after dark. Gwyl would come and she'd be easily cornered if she remained in the building.

She debated making a run for it, having nearly reached the decision to leave when the woman started to snore. She stared at the bottom of the mattress. How heavy a sleeper was the woman? It didn't matter. She couldn't stay here. Easing out from under the bed, she slowly sat up, peering above the mattress at the woman who lay there. She looked far younger than Quinn had expected, auburn hair spread across the bed and an arm flung out towards her. There was a hitch in the snoring and Quinn came up in a crouch, creeping towards the door.

She'd nearly reached the doorway when a floorboard groaned. The woman stopped snoring. Quinn didn't risk looking behind, but scurried out the door and, straightening, hurried to the stairs.

"Is anyone there?"

The words sounded far too loud in the otherwise quiet house. Trying not to make any noise, she took the stairs two at a time, headed for the front door. Fearing it was spelled against intruders, she reached for the door and opened it, slipping outside. Nothing happened. Closing it behind her she ran to Derwyn's house and knocked on his door, worried the woman would follow. Glancing continually towards her place, she knocked again. It was far later in the day than she liked. The sun was nearly overhead and she still needed sleep before her shift started. And to have her questions answered.

Derwyn flung the door open. "Always impatient."

"Can I come in? She heard me."

Derwyn looked up the street before stepping back and letting her in, closing the door behind her. "She better not have figured out you hid the necklace." His gaze fell on her neck. "You did hide it, didn't you?"

"Yes." She told him about the location she'd chosen.

He chuckled. "That should do the trick. Won't take long and she'll be moving out of there."

"It won't kill her, will it?"

"Only if she's stupid enough to stay."

That hadn't been what she'd wanted to hear. "I

don't want to kill anyone. Will she be fine once she moves?"

"She'll recover. Eventually. If she stays away from iron."

Guilt hit her and she was tempted to run back to the woman and tell her about the iron necklace. What if she ended up killing her like Gideon had killed the Dryad?

Derwyn's eyes narrowed. "You better not be thinking about going back on our deal. You made a promise. Things won't go well for you if you try to break it. Magic isn't gentle when you go against it."

She shook her head. "Of course not. I need my questions answered." She held his gaze, his dark eyes still narrowed. She wasn't that stupid. Did he really think she'd admit something like that to him?

"What do you want to know?"

She glanced around the room they were in, her gaze drawn to the two armchairs in front of an empty fireplace, small tables cluttered with junk and crammed bookcases lining the walls. "Can we sit down?"

"No. Ask your questions."

"Who did the new Gwyl used to be?"

"I never asked their names. Not any of them. They'd come to me wanting revenge. When they couldn't get justice, they sought revenge. I never asked questions as long as they could pay the price. If they couldn't, they'd often join the Hunt in the hope they could take revenge into their own hands or earn the money to buy their revenge. Some joined for other reasons."

"How do you become Gwyl?"

"When the previous Gwyl breaks his curse another needs to take his place. Only Fae can be Gwyl. Usually dark or light Fae, but occasionally wood Fae. You give up yourself when you lead the Wild Hunt. You become the Hunt. Once night arrives you can only think about tracking those you need to punish. Days bring some sanity, but the nights are full of howls and hunting. Chasing and tracking. And catching prey." His eyes gleamed as if in anticipation.

She wanted to run at the look in his eyes. Running her thumb over the back of her ring, feeling the engraving, she held her ground. "Is it only males who can lead the Hunt?"

"No, but it usually is."

"How is the leader chosen? What made him the next Gwyl after you?"

"Revenge. It burned in him the brightest."

A shiver went through her at the tone of his voice. Obviously it had once burned in Derwyn the brightest. "Do you remember what revenge he wanted?"

"A man killed. He wanted him tracked and taken down. Destroyed."

"Who was it?"

"I can give you a name, but it won't help much. Not without a scent. He had that too. In a velvet drawstring pouch he carried with him. It was midnight blue. That's the important part. Something personal to track them. Unless of course the leader has met you. Then they need nothing to be able to hunt. They carry the scent with them always." He breathed in, his eyes gleaming as if he could smell his prey and was ready to hunt.

Fear raced through her and she was tempted to run. Holding her ground, she wondered what the Dryad had used to help Gwyl track Gideon. "If you steal back the scent used to track someone, does that stop them from tracking that person?"

"Sometimes. But if Gwyl has ever come close enough to breath it in himself, it's too late. He has the scent. Nothing else is needed to find his prey."

She was tempted to ask if he'd got his revenge, but the look in his eyes made her keep the question to herself. "Did Gwyl destroy the man he wanted revenge against?"

Chapter Seventeen

Derwyn laughed. A mocking, cruel sound. "They always think that. They believe they can go against the nature of the Hunt. It doesn't work like that. The only time they can hunt someone of their own choice is if that person interferes in a current hunt or helps the hunted to escape. They're forced to follow the rules like everyone else. Gwyl is the Hunt. The rest of the pack are pale imitations. When night falls he must hunt his prey. The urge is too great to fight. Until the curse is broken, he'll remain the Hunt and each night he'll track down those others need revenge against, while burning with the need of his own. With or without the pack he'll be compelled to continue the hunt." His final words had a hollow sound to them.

Did he remember what that had felt like? That was another question she didn't dare ask. "How do you break the curse?"

"Gwyl must have his revenge. Only the one whose revenge burns brightest can lead the Wild Hunt. It's what drives Gwyl."

"What was his name? The one Gwyl wanted tracked?"

"Tamek. He's part dark Fae." Derwyn paused. "Tamek of Ganat Castle. I could see it in his eyes how badly he wanted the man dead. He would have given anything to have seen it done. But he had nothing to give."

"What did you ask for?"

"Tamek has a castle. They're always a problem to hunt. I asked a perfectly reasonable amount. Ten thousand gold coins."

She tried to imagine what ten thousand gold coins would look like. It was a fail. She could only picture the four she'd seen in Gideon's hand. "Surely you could have quoted him a lower figure."

"Everyone needs to follow the rules that govern magic. The least I could have asked for would have been seven thousand gold coins."

Her heart plummeted. Plans to pay Gwyl to go after the man he wanted revenge against, faded. The two gold coins and handful of silver in her pocket were nowhere near enough. Uneasiness made her stomach turn. Just because Gwyl was the one seeking revenge, that didn't make him the person in the right. "How do I find out why Gwyl wants Tamek dead?"

"You could ask him, but I doubt he'd tell you. These things are almost impossible to speak of. Even though the burning desire for revenge is always present, you lose the rest of your past, including the reason you felt that way. Sometimes bits and pieces come through in disjointed memories, but most of the time life is all about the hunt."

Everything seemed completely impossible. There had to be a way to fix it. She couldn't remain here for seven years. Even if she had Buddy with her, there'd still be far too many she'd be leaving behind. She couldn't bear never being able to see her family again. "Isn't there another way to break the curse or stop the Wild Hunt?"

He laughed, a mocking sound that filled the room. "The hunt can never be turned aside, stopped or tricked. They can only be outsmarted. And few have managed to last the seven years necessary to win against the Wild Hunt. Some try to remain in sanctuary. It can be nearly impossible to spend so long a time there. Others have tried shifting between the realms. It takes a day or two for the Hunt to register the change. Water throws them off the scent, but few, other than the water folk, can spend so long a time in it. And the foolish ones, upon learning the Hunt is after them, throw themselves on its mercy."

When he fell silent, she asked the question she dreaded hearing the answer to. "What happens to them?"

The gleam in his eyes became a glitter. "The Wild Hunt has no mercy."

That's what she'd feared. "Isn't there anything you can tell me that will help against them?"

"The deal was that you have to ask questions if you want the answers."

"What happens if Gwyl dies?"

"A new Gwyl will be born. He'll gather the items the last Gwyl had to track the prey and the hunt will continue. That's rare. A curse is more likely to be broken than Gwyl to die. The pack will protect him with their lives."

Gwyl's death would set her free, but not Gideon. Not that she'd be able to bring herself to end his life. There had to be another way. She tried to think of other questions to ask, but it was impossible. Everything was impossible. How was she going to survive seven years in the realms of the Fae? Her heart lurched and her stomach did a slow turn. She wouldn't. "I have to go." She turned away before the tears that were forming could fall.

"You can only return once more to question me."

She nodded, flinging the door open and hurrying from the shack. The world wavered around her and she tried to blink back the tears. She couldn't stop them. Nor could she stop the same words repeating themselves over and over in her head. I don't want to die. There was so much she hadn't done. She had so many plans for her future. Her throat tightened, aching from trying to hold back the flood of tears. I don't want to die.

No one told her she wouldn't. If she hadn't been alone, would someone have told her there was hope? How had Gideon survived a month on his own? She wasn't coping with a day. And it wasn't even a full day.

As soon as she was far enough from the shack, she broke into a run, eventually slowing to a jog. She was relieved to make it back to the stables without running into anyone. After using the bathroom, she kicked off her sneakers and dropped onto the bed. Sleep claimed her nearly instantly. It didn't help. She tossed and turned and nightmares continually woke her. Each time she woke it was because Gwyl had caught her and she couldn't escape from his grip, his green eyes pinning her in place. She was almost relieved when Finch knocked on her door to wake her for her shift.

Dragging herself from bed, she used the bathroom and then offered to bring food back for Finch, heading to the kitchen to collect it. Both Marley and Gideon were there. She didn't want to talk to either of them. It only took a slight shake of her head to dash the hope in Gideon's eyes. She half listened to Marley's chatter while she waited for the food, her gaze following Gideon as he turned and left the room. What she'd learned probably couldn't help him. She wasn't certain if she could use it to help herself. Gideon worried that he might be a murderer. What would it make her if she sent Gwyl after Tamek? Or found a way to end Gwyl's life. She shied away from those thoughts.

Taking the two plates the cook gave her, Quinn told Marley she'd see her later and returned to the stables. After eating the food and returning the plates to the kitchen, she once again made her way to the stables, relieved to find Gwyl's mare wasn't in the stall. She didn't think she could have faced him after all she'd learned.

Like the previous night, Finch strolled off and left her to take care of the stables. It seemed busier than usual and she was glad because it didn't leave her time to think about what she needed to do tomorrow.

Finch sauntered into the stables well after midnight and with a nod in her direction, headed to bed. Yawning, she wished she could do the same. By the time morning arrived, she wanted to drop into bed, not listen to Marley who'd arrived with sunrise to tell her everything that had happened in the restaurant during the night.

Gwyl entered the stables, leading his mare. His gaze went directly to Quinn.

She didn't take her gaze from him. "Marley, go inside." She kept her voice low in the hope that Gwyl wouldn't hear her.

Marley glanced at Gwyl. "You're worrying about nothing. We're safe here." With a heavy sigh, she headed for the doorway. "I'll bring breakfast back."

"And for Finch too." Her gaze remained on Gwyl, who stayed where he'd stopped, not far inside the stables. As soon as Marley stepped outside, she moved forward, collecting the silver disk from the stall door and holding it out to Gwyl.

He held her gaze a moment longer before he handed over the reins and took the disk.

She couldn't stop glancing over her shoulder as she led the horse to the stall. He continued to watch her. This morning she didn't bother to brush the horse, only removed the tack and hung it up. She was too tired for anything else. The entire time Gwyl remained inside and she couldn't stop thinking about everything Derwyn had said. Slowly crossing the room to stand in front of him, she drew in a steadying breath. It didn't help, but she spoke anyway. "I was told about Tamek." He seemed to change before her eyes. His jaw tightened and his eyes narrowed, a glitter making them appear even greener.

"Stay out of my business." The words were sharp.

"Then how about you stay out of my business?"

"Your life is my business."

The words made her want to run. She held her ground. It's sanctuary. The words didn't help. She still wanted to run.

"What would you want to go after him?" She tried to decipher the expressions that crossed his face, but all she could think was that he struggled against something.

"Six thousand gold coins. If I could, I would do it for free." His voice was harsh.

This time she did take a step back, even though she tried not to. "Would you accept something else in exchange?" Not that she knew whether or not Tamek deserved Gwyl hunting him down, or even if she'd be able to send Gwyl after him.

"Something of equal value." He crossed the distance between them in one large step. "Pay the price and I'll set aside all other hunts to pursue him. That is a promise." The scent of rich earth rose up around them.

"What did he do?" She wanted to escape the heat radiating from his body. It seemed unnatural. Unnatural and dangerous.

Confusion crossed his face to be replaced by a hard look. "He needs to die."

"You don't know, do you?"

"I know he deserves to die." The words hung in the air a moment before he spoke again. "See if Mairwin waits in the courtyard for me."

It took a moment for his words to make sense. She hadn't been expecting such an abrupt change of subject. She started to refuse, but decided it'd make a good excuse to move away from him. Stepping around him, she headed for the doorway and saw Mairwin pacing in the courtyard. "If you're looking for Gwyl, you're too late again."

"I saw him come down here."

"Have you considered looking inside?" She gestured towards the main building.

Mairwin stared at her suspiciously for a moment before she strode to the far door. The sharp sound of the door closing rang out in the courtyard.

Mairwin seemed the sort to eventually want to shoot the messenger. That didn't bode well for her future. She spun when she felt the heat of Gwyl behind her, taking a step away from him before she spoke. "She's inside Masquerade's main building now."

"If you could pay the price, would you send me after Tamek?"

She stared at him, trying to figure out how to answer. "I don't know. It would depend on what he's done." Even then she wasn't sure if she could, knowing what the results were likely to be. "If what he did was so bad, why did you go to the Hunt instead of to whatever law you have in this realm?"

"The Hunt is the law."

"What about your police, soldiers, something?"

"There is the law of magic. For all else, that is what the Hunt is for."

"Then why must you be paid?"

"That is the law of magic. All must be fair and equal between exchanges." His lips twisted into a smile that made fear race through Quinn. "Or at least perceived to be equal." His smile vanished as quickly as it had come. "Would you pay the price?"

Chapter Eighteen

Quinn was still no closer to a decision. "I don't know. What's your name? The one you were born with."

"Gwyl." He held her gaze a moment longer before he withdrew coins from his belt pouch and dropped them in her hand.

She watched as he strode towards the alley, not looking at the coins until he was out of sight. Her jaw dropped when she saw there were ten gold coins. Her hand closed over them and she shut her eyes, trying to figure out what to do. Did he plan to keep overpaying her until she had the six thousand needed to send him after Tamek?

"Why are you standing there?"

She opened her eyes to see her sister carried three plates of food. There was no answer she could give her. "I'll wake Finch." Slipping the coins in her pocket, she strode to his room and knocked on the door, letting him know his breakfast was here.

After they'd eaten Marley returned to the main building, taking the plates, and Quinn retreated to her room planning to sleep. She only managed to step into her room before Gideon arrived with endless questions about her trip to see the last Gwyl. They sat beside each other on the bed as Quinn told him everything that had happened, including her morning run in with Gwyl. She withdrew the coins from her pocket, holding them out.

"If you had the money, would you pay him?"

"I don't know." It seemed wrong. Like hiring a killer.

"Things are different here. We can't look at it the way we would look at the same situation back home."

"Would you pay him?"

Gideon shrugged. "I don't know. If there's no real law, what else can you do?"

She didn't have a clue. "I suppose there's no banks here either."

"No."

"What am I going to do with these?" She continued to stare at the coins in her hand.

Gideon shrugged.

She added the two gold coins she'd earned from

Mairwin, keeping only the silver ones in her pocket, and held them out to him. "Can you look after them for me?"

Gideon took the coins from her. "If you end up with six thousand I hope you don't expect me to look after them too."

"I have no idea what I'm going to do."

"Do you think if there was a new Gwyl, and you took what the Dryad gave them for tracking me, that the Hunt would leave me alone?"

Quinn shrugged. "I have no idea." She was beginning to wonder if she knew anything.

"It'd be worth a try, wouldn't it?"

Even if she'd felt it was useless, there was no way she would have been able to say no to the hopeful expression in his usually sad eyes. "I think we should find out what Tamek did before we make any decisions."

"Okay. Are you still going tonight?"

She nodded, words deserting her at the thought of what she needed to do. She couldn't wander the streets after dark. She needed to be hidden before the sun set.

Gideon rose to his feet. "I'll let you get some sleep then."

She followed him to the door. "I don't know if

Finch is waking me since I'm not working tonight, so do you think you could come over an hour before sunset and check I'm awake?"

"Yeah."

She didn't bother watching him walk away. Closing the door she slipped off her sneakers, took the handful of steps to her bed and fell onto it. Sleep came instantly, but once again was constantly disturbed by nightmares. In the end, she didn't need anyone to wake her. She stumbled from bed well before sunset, unable to sleep any longer.

She wanted to remain in bed and even the thought of temporarily returning home didn't make her feel any better. She wouldn't be able to let anyone know she was there. Otherwise it would be impossible to return for Marley. There was no way she'd be able to convince anyone of the truth. If she hadn't seen the realms of the Fae with her own eyes, she would have thought anyone who told her about them was crazy.

She ran her fingers through her hair, wishing she had a brush and a change of clothes. Somehow she was going to have to sneak into her home and take, not only her dog, but some of her belongings to make life a little easier in the realms of the Fae. She wasn't sure exactly how she was going to manage it.

Taking a deep breath didn't help. The sense of

impending doom, that had been growing ever since waking, remained. Opening the door, she strode through the silent stables, not seeing Finch anywhere. She reached the courtyard as Gideon stepped out of the main building. Like Gideon, she froze and stared across the courtyard at him. She couldn't do this. She couldn't leave sanctuary.

Gideon crossed the courtyard and stopped in front of her, reaching for her hand. "Can you see if you can find out if my father is okay?" He frowned. "What's wrong?"

She shook her head, unable to voice her fears.

"Did something happen?"

Marley came outside and stopped beside them. "I thought you said he's not your boyfriend." She grinned.

Gideon continued to hold Quinn's hands. "That's narrow minded of you. Do you also believe males and females can't be friends?"

Marley glared at him. "I was only joking around."

Hardly able to believe that someone hadn't fallen for Marley's charms, she drew her hands from Gideon. "If you give me some details, I'll see what I can find out about your father for you."

With a last daggered look for Marley, Gideon turned to Quinn with a nod. He withdrew a piece of paper in a resealable plastic bag and held it out to her. "I was hoping you'd say that. Is there anything else you need?"

No Hunt. Knowing it was pointless to speak the words she shook her head, taking the bag from him. "I need to have something to eat and then I can leave." She couldn't resist looking skywards and noting how little of the day was left.

"Weren't you going to say goodbye to me?" Marley demanded.

"Of course I was. I thought you might like to sit with me while I ate."

Marley shot a look towards Gideon. "Is he joining us?"

After how little sleep she'd had, she wasn't in the mood for Marley's theatrics. "Gideon is welcome to eat with us if he wants."

Gideon rested his hand on her shoulder for a moment. "I'll see you later." He strode towards the alley.

Marley tugged on her arm. "Come on. I'm hungry."

She trailed behind Marley, wishing there was some other way to go home.

Marley stopped abruptly when she reached the

door, turning to face Quinn. "Will you see Scout while you're at home?"

"I doubt it. I probably won't see anyone." If she was lucky.

"Why not?"

"What would I tell them?"

Marley stared at her, open mouthed. "What are we going to tell them?"

"Nothing. You'll tell them you can't remember a thing. They'd think you were crazy if you started talking about this place."

"But you could tell them-"

"Marley. No." She shook her head. "They wouldn't believe either of us. Tell them you can't remember." She couldn't bring herself to tell Marley she wouldn't be going back with her. "Come on. I need to eat so I can leave before the sun sets."

Marley glared at her a moment longer before opening the door. "I still think they'd believe us. Especially if both of us told them the truth."

Marley continued to grumble and complain through most of the meal and Quinn was almost relieved to tell her she was leaving. Marley threw her arms around Quinn, holding on tight. "Take me with you. Don't leave me behind."

Quinn pulled away from her sister. "You know I

can't." She tried to smile, but it was a fail. "I won't be gone long." She was extremely tempted to tell Marley it was her own fault she'd ended up here. Taking a step away from her sister, she kept silent.

"What if something happens and you can't get back?" Tears pooled in Marley's eyes. "What if I'm stuck here forever?"

"I will come back for you." She turned away, heading for the door, trying to ignore the sob she heard behind her. In the courtyard, she paused long enough to put the note from Marley and the directions from Darci into the resealable plastic bag before returning them to her pocket. She stood there a moment, trying to convince herself to head to the river. It took far more effort than she'd thought possible to take the first step towards the alley. Reaching it, she saw Gideon waited for her.

He pushed away from the wall he leaned against, coming towards her. "Are you sure you're okay?"

She nodded, gesturing in the direction she needed to go. "I have to hide before sunset."

Gideon took a reed from his backpack and held it out to her. "I thought you might need one of these."

She took the reed from him. "Thanks." She'd planned to ask him for one, but had completely forgotten about it.

"Take care."

"You too."

"I'll watch out for your sister for you."

"You don't sound happy about that."

He shrugged. "I don't like her very much. Sorry, I know she's your sister." He shrugged again. "I don't like how she expects everyone to do things for her. Particularly you. Instead of trying to sort them out for herself. "

"What do you mean?"

"They all gossip about each other in there." He nodded towards the main building. "They were talking about how your sister spent all her time crying until you turned up."

"She was scared."

"You didn't do that."

He hadn't seen her on the way back from visiting Derwyn. "She's younger than me."

"Not by that much."

She glanced away. "I have to go."

"Don't go putting yourself in danger for her. She wouldn't do the same for you."

"You don't know that."

"No, but I'd be surprised if she did."

She wanted to defend her sister, but if experience was anything to go by, it could go either way with

Marley. "She's my sister." Her tone was firm. "I need to go." She gestured towards the river.

Gideon gestured in the same direction. "Do you want me to walk with you for a bit?"

She was tempted. "No. Thank you."

Gideon shifted from one foot to the other. "This feels like a really bad idea."

His words surprised a fleeting smile from her. "You're probably right."

"I feel like I should be doing more. It's my fault you're being hunted."

Maybe that's why he was so bothered about her sister expecting to be saved. "If it's anyone's fault at all, it's that of the Fae. Them and all their stupid rules. If we knew they existed we wouldn't get caught up in their world."

"Could you imagine the lengths some people would go to, so they could possess Fae magic, if humans knew about them?"

She dreaded to think. "Okay, fine. It's better most humans don't know about them." She looked past him. "I have to go." She still had to find somewhere to hide.

He nodded, remaining silent.

She stared at him a moment more before she walked away, headed for the river.

Chapter Nineteen

Following the river, Quinn went further into the Fringes. Finding a place where the water was murky and the buildings weren't as close or as tall, she sat on the banks and watched the light fade from the sky. There was no way she was getting into the water any sooner than she had to. She shivered at the thought of remaining in the water until the moon was overhead. How many hours was that likely to take?

When the last of the light faded from the sky she slipped into the cold water. Raising the reed to her lips, she slid below the surface and tried to get comfortable while she waited for the moon to be overhead. As the night wore on she grew colder, shivering as she remained below the surface. In the distance she heard the wolves howl and she wished Gideon was with her. Even Marley's company would have been better than huddling here on her own.

The sound of the wolves grew closer and her fear increased. The next time she looked towards the surface of the water to check for the moon, she saw the Hunt through the murky depths. Her gaze scanned the creatures at the water's edge, but she didn't see the familiar antlers rising from any of them. Where was Gwyl? When the Hunt turned away from the river and moved off, she guessed he was probably at the head of the pack. She didn't relax until she heard the howling further away.

By the time she could see the moon overhead, she was shivering and wouldn't have been surprised if she ended up sick from being cold for so long. With how hard she was shivering, it was nearly impossible to clamber out of the river. A hand reached down and grabbed her upper arm, pulling her from the water. Her gaze rose, taking in the bare chest silvered by moonlight and stopping at the face that was half in shadows, antlers rising upwards. The glitter in his eyes froze her in place and it took her a moment to register that she should run.

Jerking her arm from his grip she tried to escape. She'd taken no more than a couple of steps when he crashed into her. The breath was knocked from her lungs as she collided with the ground, twisting as she tried to escape. Gwyl landed on top of her and the reed was knocked from her hand to clatter across the cobblestones.

His hands wrapped around her neck. "I owe you one release and head start. Do you want to take it?"

The unnatural heat of his hands and the look in his eyes made panic race through her. She concentrated on the iron ring she wore, trying to think clearly. "What is the name you were born with? The name Tamek would know you by?" An unreadable expression crossed his face and she began to hope that somehow she could reach the person he'd once been.

His expression cleared, the gleam returning to his eyes, bright in the moonlight. "He will eventually know me by the name Gwyl. No other name exists. Do you want to call in your favour? Or would you give up?"

"I can't give up." How could she fail Marley who needed her help to return home? Or desert Gideon, with his sad eyes that reminded her of Buddy, who'd helped her survive her initial days in the realms of the Fae and wanted news of his father. She tried to push Gwyl away, but he was far stronger than her.

"Then call in your favour." His hands tightened around her throat. "I can't wait all night."

Fear raced through her as his grip tightened a little more and breathing became more difficult. She barely managed to stop herself from screaming and struggling ineffectually. Recalling the pouch he'd taken the coins from that morning, she slid her fingers in, searching for a weapon. Panic threatened to take hold from the look in his eyes. "And if I don't call in the favour?" Her fingers came into contact with something soft and velvety. She drew it out.

"Then you must die."

She held up the item. A dark blue drawstring bag. Hopefully it was Tamek's scent. "Want it?" She tossed it towards the river. When he released her with a roar, she scrambled to her feet. The drawstring bag floated in the reflection of the moon on the water. Before Gwyl had a chance to move, she dived into the river, a hand closing over the drawstring bag as she slid through the reflection of the moon.

The murkiness of the water seemed to become clearer as she swam downwards, the outstretched fingers of her left hand touching sand. Pressing her feet against the ground, she pushed upwards, bursting through the water to see she was in the ocean. A moment of panic hit her. How far was she from land? Treading water, she turned around, relief causing her to draw in a shuddering breath when she spotted the lights of houses on the shore. She'd expected to be in the dam.

Tucking the drawstring bag into a pocket, she swam to shore, the waves buffeting her. As soon as it was shallow enough, she rose and walked the rest of the way, wanting to drop onto the beach when she left the water behind. There wasn't time. She eyed the moon that was low in the sky, barely a slither.

Looking around, she soon figured out she had no idea where she was. Why hadn't she ended up in the dam? Weariness washed over her. She needed help. The only money she had was from the realms of the Fae. She had no idea if it could be used in this world. Dripping wet and shivering, she headed for the houses that looked onto the beach. Before she walked between two houses, aiming for the road she could see, she looked over her shoulder. The sea was empty. Gwyl hadn't followed. Her fingers brushed against her pocket that contained his drawstring bag. She'd half expected him to chase after her. Maybe he couldn't yet.

It took her about ten minutes to figure out where she was. About a twenty-minute drive further up the coast from where she lived. She didn't have time to walk and certainly didn't have money for a taxi. There was no help for it. She'd have to ring someone. Daisy was her first thought, but her parents would want to know where she was going and why. Scout was the only one who could pick her up without people wondering what he was up to. All he needed to do was give his usual shrug and say 'exploring'. Everyone expected it of him.

It took her a bit to figure out a plan of action and several more minutes before she could decide which of the three houses, that had their lights on, to approach. The one she chose had an immaculate front yard, a double garage that was closed and a car parked out the front with a P plate on it. If she was lucky the teenager who owned the car parked out the front would answer.

Knocking on the door, she found she wasn't lucky. A man in his fifties, wearing pyjamas, opened the door. He looked half asleep.

His gaze travelled from her head to her toes then back again, the sleepy look disappearing. "Are you all right? Should I call an ambulance? The police?"

"No." She shook her head, worried he'd ignore her and call them anyway. "Can I use your phone? I need to call someone to pick me up."

"What happened? Are you sure you're not hurt?"

"I was in an inflatable dinghy." She shrugged. "I'm not sure how it got punctured."

He stepped out of the doorway, waving her in. "Come inside. I'll get the phone for you."

"It's okay, I'll wait here." There was no way she was about to go in the house if she didn't need to.

"Of course." He took a step back from her. "I'll only be a minute."

"Dad?" A boy, several inches taller than his father, came to the door. "What's going on?" He frowned. "You look familiar."

She didn't recognise him, but her heart skipped a beat anyway. "I doubt it. I've never seen you before."

His father pushed him away from the doorway. "Stop trying to chat the girl up. She's been in an accident. Get the phone for her."

"I wasn't. She does look familiar." The boy strolled from the room.

"Sorry about that." The man looked embarrassed. "Can I get you anything? A drink. Something to eat?"

Quinn was glad the boy returned to the room, saving her from needing to answer. A girl, a couple of years younger than him, followed. He held out the phone to her.

"Thank you." She took the phone, staring at the date on the screen. The fifteenth of October. She'd been gone eighteen days. It hardly seemed possible so many had passed.

"She is familiar," the girl said.

Quinn looked at her, shaking her head. "I haven't met either of you before."

"I know who she is." The girl's eyes widened. "She's the one who went missing with her sister a few weeks ago."

Dread hit and she nearly ran. "I think sometimes my Dad wishes I would disappear." She forced herself to laugh. "Especially with how accident prone I am. The inflatable dinghy is a perfect example. He'll probably lecture me for a week. And tell me I should quit trying to do anything with even the slightest bit of risk. It never goes well."

"You are the missing girl. You were all over the TV. They even dredged the dam you were lost in," the girl insisted.

"I think I should know who I am," Quinn said.

The father stepped between Quinn and his daughter, standing sideways so he could talk to both of them. "Go finish getting ready. We need to be on the road in an hour." He looked at Quinn. "Did you still want to make a call?"

She nodded, stepping out of the doorway and turning her back on the family, hearing the girl complaining that her father wasn't ready either. She was surprised to see her hands shook when she dialled Scout's number.

He answered on the second ring. "If it's not life or death I will murder you for waking me." His words were mumbled and he sounded like he was asleep.

"It is."

"Quinn?" Sleepiness vanished from his voice.

She glanced over her shoulder and saw the family had moved away from the doorway to give her some privacy. She kept her voice low. "I need you to pick me up without telling anyone."

"Is that really you? Is Marley with you? What happened?"

"Please, Scout. I'll tell you everything when you get here."

"Where are you?"

"Hang on." She turned to the father. "What's your address?" When he gave her the address, she relayed it to Scout. "Don't tell anyone, okay? Or I might not be able to get Marley back."

"Okay."

"Bring a jumper and a towel." When she hung up, she dialled a random number and hung up, hoping that would prevent them from easily figuring out what number she'd called. She held out the phone and the father stepped forward to take it. "I'll wait out the front. My lift won't be too long."

"Are you sure you don't want to come inside? Or maybe you'd like a towel?"

Seeing a woman around the age of the man enter the room, she shook her head, stepping back from the doorway. "No, thanks. I'll be fine." She took another step back before she turned and hurried to the roadside edge.

Several times she looked at the house and each time she saw the silhouette of someone at a window. She had no idea what she'd do if the girl convinced them she was right and they called the police. What were they doing going somewhere on a school day? Figuring out the direction Scout would be coming from, she headed down the street and stopped at a house several doors away.

By the time he pulled up, she'd half expected the sound of the approaching vehicle to be the police. She took the towel he held out to her and put it on the seat before she sat in the front and buckled up. "Go."

Chapter Twenty

Scout pulled out onto the road. "Where are we going?"

Quinn awkwardly pulled on the jumper that was lying between the seats, tugging it into place below the seat belt. "I don't know. Not home. Not yet anyway."

"Where were you?"

She smiled, staring at Scout in the glow from the dash. He'd been the right one to ring. He wasn't the sort to freak out until he had all the facts. "You'll never believe me."

"Try me." He glanced towards her, returning her smile.

She was surprised by the amount of relief in it. "Can we go somewhere and sit while I tell you?"

"I know just the place."

Of course he did. He always knew the right place

to go. He was Scout. "Thank you." She tilted her head back, closing her eyes as she slowly warmed. Her eyes opened and she faced Scout when he rested his hand on hers. The warmth of his hand sank into her thigh.

"We were worried about you. And Marley. Everyone thinks you're both dead. Except your parents. They go out to the dam every day looking for you. Even though it's been eighteen days."

She stared at his hand on her thigh, before looking at him. He seemed different, less than he used to be. It took her a moment to realise it wasn't him that was different. It was her. She wouldn't recommend a trip to the realms of the Fae to cure a broken heart, but it obviously worked. Slipping her hand from under his, she patted his a couple of times. "I didn't know it had been that long." She gestured towards the steering wheel. "Think you can keep both hands on it? I wouldn't want you to have an accident."

He glanced towards her before returning his hand to the steering wheel. "You've changed."

She had no idea what had made him say that, but she couldn't argue what she'd already figured out for herself. "Yeah." If she'd changed this much after only a few days in the realms of the Fae she dreaded to think how different she'd be after seven years. Looking out the window, she tried to figure out where they were. The world outside seemed both familiar and unfamiliar. When had forests, lakes and ramshackle cities filled with strange creatures become normal? A shiver went through her and this one wasn't from the cold. She had to find a way to leave the realms of the Fae before she risked more than her life. Another few weeks and she might not be able to recognise herself.

When Scout pulled up and opened the door, she almost bolted from the confines of the vehicle. Looking around, she didn't recognise the park he'd brought her to. Hearing the boot lid shut, she turned to see him walk towards her with the blanket he kept in the car for when he was too tired to return from his scouting expeditions.

"I could have brought you some dry clothes if you'd said you were wet."

Wrapping the blanket around her, she grinned. "I don't think we wear the same size clothes."

"Why can't I tell anyone?"

Spotting a bench seat under a light, she gestured towards it. "Can we sit down first?" At his nod, she walked silently beside him.

He spoke the moment they were seated. "Where's Marley?"

She really didn't want to have to explain

everything, but guessed she needed to tell him some things. Watching his expression, she told him about arriving in the realms of the Fae, meeting Gideon and becoming marked by the Hunt. She kept everything to the basics, but she could see he didn't believe her. Explaining she needed to take Buddy back so Marley could return home had him shaking his head. She dug in her pocket and took out some of the silver coins she'd earned at the stables. "It's true, Scout."

He stared at the coins for a moment before shaking his head. "How can it be? You're talking about fairies. Children's stories." His eyes were filled with concern.

"Fae and they're no children's story." She couldn't help thinking about the Hunt, led by Gwyl with his antlers rising from his head, the glitter in his eyes when he was on the trail of his prey. "I don't know how to convince you."

"You could take me there."

"No way." She shook her head. "You don't want to risk getting stuck there."

"But–"

"No."

"If it really exists, think of the places to explore."

The dreamy look in his eyes had panic racing through her. "I need someone to look out for Marley. I won't be able to come back with her." Gideon's comments came to mind. Unable to think about them, she pushed them aside. Some people needed more help than others. Her sister was obviously one of them.

"What about your parents? You should see them. They're walking around like zombies."

"I can't stay here. The Hunt would find me." She rubbed her neck, trying to forget the sensation of Gwyl's hands wrapped around it. "I thought you'd help me. Didn't you say I was like a sister to you?" It made her feel guilty to use that tactic, but she was desperate.

"Did someone kidnap you?"

She shook her head. "Can't you trust me? Please, Scout. Help me get everything together and take me to where I need to go so I can return to the realms of the Fae. And wait for Marley to call you so you can pick her up."

He stared at her for nearly a minute before he nodded. "Okay. What do you need done?"

"You believe me?"

He shook his head. "I'll give you the chance to prove it exists. Either that or I'll take care of whoever you're heading back to and help you get Marley away from him."

"We weren't kidnapped." She paused. "Well, Marley kind of was, but she agreed to that."

"How can you agree to be kidnapped?"

"Never mind. I don't have long before the Hunt can find me here."

"Where do you need to go?"

She took out the resealable plastic bag and withdrew the directions Darci had given her, handing it over to him.

"Out from Bundaberg? Seriously?"

She half shrugged. What could she say? Nothing he'd believe. "Yeah. You still helping?"

He rose to his feet, handing back the directions. "What do we need to do first?"

Relief washed over her and she stood up. "There are things I need from home, including Buddy. I also need to buy two iron necklaces."

He nodded towards her ring. "Is that what it's made of?"

"Yeah. They don't cope with iron. It gives them iron sickness." She still wasn't completely certain what it was or how it affected them. As long as it worked she guessed she didn't really need to know all the details. "You ready?"

"Time to get on the road. There are places to explore."

She walked beside him, the familiar words making her feel a little less worried. Before she got in the car, she tossed the blanket onto the back seat. Staring out the window, she saw the day had lightened. A day or two before the Hunt could find her, according to Derwyn. That didn't seem like much time. There was so much she needed to do. She thought of Gideon's father. "Can I borrow your phone? I need to check something out on the internet."

He took it from his pocket, handing it over without a word.

It didn't take her long to find some information. She watched the most recent news clip, surprised to find Gideon's parents were together. At the start they talked about how difficult it was surviving the loss of a child. Towards the end of the clip they stood with arms around each other, looking a little uncomfortable with all the attention.

"I hear you have some good news after all the heartbreak you've suffered," the reporter said.

Gideon's mother nodded, her hand going to her stomach. "We're privileged to be having another child. He could never take our first son's place, but it's a comfort to know we'll have Jacob in our lives next year." She turned to Gideon's father with a smile. "This is the second wake up call I've had in my life.

I didn't understand the message the first time. This time I have and I've discovered too late what's really important. I won't make that mistake again."

Quinn closed the browser the moment the clip ended. She had no idea how Gideon would feel about the news. She only hoped Truman didn't cut down any more Dryad trees. It seemed like an extremely hazardous line of work to be in when you had to worry about the Fae too.

"Who was that?" Scout took his phone she held out to him and dropped it onto his lap.

"Gideon's parents."

"The one who helped you?"

"Yeah."

"Do you think you should trust him? Why would he help you?"

She couldn't resist smiling. The comments were similar to what she'd first thought. "Yeah, I do." She understood now. The Fae were different to humans and it was necessary to be different around them. It was nice to be human sometimes.

"Is there something between you two?" He glanced towards her.

"No." She fell silent. Why did everyone have to keep asking her that?

Scout didn't talk until they reached their street.

"Duck down until I see who's about. Unless you've changed your mind about letting everyone know you're here."

"I can't." She leaned forward, keeping her head below the window. "I wish I could, but I don't think anyone would understand."

Scout pulled up. "Wait here."

She was tempted to peek out the window when he got out of the car. When the minutes stretched out, she nearly did. "What took you so long?" she demanded when he opened her door.

"They've gone already."

"Who?"

"Your parents. And the key was still in the usual place out the back." He held the front door key up.

"It's safe to get out?"

Scout glanced around. "Hang on." He rummaged amongst the handful of gear on the back seat and a moment later held up a cap.

"Thanks." Putting it on her head, she pulled it down low.

"Hurry up. Unless you want to be spotted."

She got out of the car and followed Scout to her front door. As soon as she stepped inside, she was hit by the familiar sights and smells. And sounds. The click of Buddy's nails against the floor had her smiling and throwing her arms around him when she bent to greet him. "I'm happy to see you too." She giggled when he licked her cheek.

"Can we not take so long in here? I'm feeling like a burglar or something." Scout's gaze darted around the lounge room.

Letting Buddy go, she straightened. "Okay. You get my dad's fishing knife from the garage, the one with a sheath, and the small waterproof torch. I'll get what I need from my room." She didn't wait for him to agree before striding through the house.

Chapter Twenty-One

It didn't take Quinn long to grab her backpack that had a faded sunflower print on it. She shoved in a couple of changes of clothes, her handful of valuable jewellery she'd rarely worn and hoped her parents wouldn't miss, toiletries, the bit of cash she'd left in her underwear drawer and headed to the kitchen for some resealable plastic bags and a water bottle. Passing the linen cupboard she took an old towel she hoped wouldn't be missed. Buddy followed close on her heels. In the kitchen she grabbed the resealable plastic bags, filled a water bottle and threw in an unopened packet of biscuits and an orange.

Scout entered the kitchen with the knife and torch. "What next?"

A shower would have been nice, to wash off the salt, but there wasn't time. She needed to be somewhere safe before dark. She couldn't risk it. "Iron necklaces." Taking the knife and torch she put them in her backpack. "Actually, give me a minute." She headed to the back door and opened it, leaving it ajar and locking it again. The door always had to be checked to make sure it shut properly or it swung open. Hopefully her parents would think they forgot to check and Buddy had wandered off. She turned to find that not only had Buddy followed her, but also Scout. "We can go now."

Scout left her and Buddy in the car while he returned the key. When he got in the driver's seat, he handed her his phone again. "See if you can find somewhere that sells iron necklaces. Although we might have to wait around a bit for them to open."

Keeping down low, until they were well away from their street, she found a shop on the way to Bundaberg. He remained silent when she told him and after checking out the window, she sat up. "I don't know if I'll be able to give you much fuel money. Not and buy the necklaces too."

"That's okay. I haven't done much driving lately."

She stared at him, not sure what to say. 'I'm sorry' would make it sound like it was her fault, and it hadn't been. She had no idea whose fault it was. Her sister's for not believing the Fae existed? That was ridiculous. No, it would have to be Kaeder's fault. But even that didn't seem right. He'd been completely honest with Marley.

Scout glanced towards her. "What's up?"

"Thank you for picking me up."

"Of course I did." He sounded offended.

She smiled wryly. "It probably would have been more accurate if I'd said thanks for not telling anyone you were picking me up."

He glanced towards her again. "I nearly did. I was going to call Ted, but then I thought he'd tell Daisy and their parents would have got involved and they would have rung your parents." He shrugged. "It seemed easiest to get you and bring you home." He paused for a moment. "I didn't realise you hadn't planned to stay."

"I can't." She felt like she should apologise again so kept silent. This wasn't her fault. She looked out the window, her eyes eventually growing heavy. Next time she opened them, the sun was well up and they were at a service station. Blinking sleepily, she looked around for Scout. After a minute, he came out of the building and she guessed he'd been paying for fuel.

Scout opened the car door and looked at her before he got in. "I didn't mean to wake you yet. Not for another ten minutes or so."

"Where are we?"

"Last stop before we get to the bridge."

"What about-"

"You slept through my shopping expedition." He gestured towards the back seat before he started the engine. "I bought you two necklaces and a ring."

She reached for the bag and Buddy, who was lying on the back seat, opened one eye before returning to sleep. Facing forward, she took the jewellery from the bag and put it on. "Thanks. I've got some money you can have."

"You keep it."

"It's no use to me. Not in the realms of the Fae." She took the notes out and slid them under the dash mat, keeping only the three two-dollar coins for Marley to use when she returned home. If she ended up in the same place she'd need to make a phone call. It'd probably be best if she didn't have to go knocking on some stranger's door. The next person might call the police.

Scout remained silent for a minute. "Can I look at those directions again?"

She took the piece of paper from the resealable plastic bag, holding it out to him.

He didn't take it, only glanced at it several times before nodding. "Thanks."

Silence fell again and she returned the paper to

the bag and stared out the window, wondering how much time would have passed in the realms of the Fae. It took them about twenty minutes to reach the bridge and they parked in a gravelled area beside a sedan. Unable to answer the questions she could see in Scout's expression, she got out of the car and opened the back door for Buddy. He raced towards the bushland surrounding the gravelled clearing.

"Here, boy." She was relieved he immediately returned. She slipped her fingers through his collar. "I should have brought your lead." She smiled at his expression. "Don't look at me like that. I know you hate it, but it's better than getting lost."

Scout came to stand beside her. "I've got a piece of rope in the boot."

"That'd probably be a good idea." While she waited, she checked out the area, her gaze drawn to the bridge that had dark metal railings along the sides. It seemed so ordinary. Well, a little fancy with the dark metal railings, but not something you'd expect to take you to another realm. An ordinary bridge crossing an ordinary river. How many other places that she'd visited over the years would have been able to take her to the realms of the Fae? She took the rope Scout had taken from the boot. "Thanks."

"I want to come with you."

She made a loop in the rope and threaded it through Buddy's collar, putting the end of the rope through the loop and pulling it tight. "Who will pick Marley up?"

"How do you know this will work?"

She met his gaze. "I don't."

"Then it might not."

"I think it will. Darci had no reason to lie." She turned away and took her backpack from the floor in the front of the car, swinging it into place on her back. "I need to return before night falls here." The leaves scattered across the gravelled area made her steps sound loud as she headed for the riverbank.

Scout walked beside her. "Marley doesn't need me. She can ring Ted and Daisy to pick her up. Or even your parents." He paused. "I don't need your permission to go."

She stopped on the riverbank and stared at him, trying to think of a way to explain how dangerous it was. A smile slowly formed. Telling him that would only have the opposite effect.

"What?"

"You were born in the wrong century."

"I've been saying that for years. Finally someone gets it." He returned her smile.

"I'm not going to tell you that you can never go

there. But don't go unprepared. Research all you can, wait till Marley returns and ask her everything she knows and take the things you need. I'd tell you more if I had the time." A sound drew her attention and she turned towards it, staring at the boy and girl on a black horse on the opposite side of the bank. They looked to be around her age.

"What are you doing here?" The girl was seated behind the boy, leaning so she could see around his broad shoulders.

Quinn watched them cross the river, remaining on the horse. They both had sun streaked sandy brown hair. His was just past his shoulders while hers was nearly halfway down her back, strands of it hanging around her face. The girl's eyes were green while the boy had vivid blue eyes and his face had a chiselled look to it. When the horse reached the bank she stood on, the two of them dismounted. Quinn's gaze was drawn to the swords both wore. She took a step back, tugging Buddy with her. He didn't make a very good guard dog because all he wanted to do was greet the newcomers enthusiastically. "You're Fae?"

The girl shared a look with the boy before facing Quinn again. "No, I'm a Knight Commander. What does a human know about the Fae?"

"Why did you ask them that?" Scout asked.

"Their swords." Quinn nodded towards the two strangers.

"What swords?"

The boy chuckled. "He can't see them. They're glamoured. If you weren't wearing iron you wouldn't see them either."

Scout looked at each of them. "What's going on?"

Quinn took off her new ring and held it out to Scout. She smiled when he hesitated to take it. "You don't need to wear it, just hold it."

It took another few seconds before he did, his jaw dropping when he looked towards the strangers. "They're wearing swords."

The girl laughed, turning to the boy. "Tell me I never once had that expression when I first met you."

The boy grinned. "The first time you met me, or when you re-met me?"

Quinn didn't have time for this. It had to be at least lunchtime judging by how hungry she felt. "I have to get somewhere safe before dark."

"Why?" the girl asked.

Quinn hesitated, not sure if she really wanted to tell these people her problems. "What's a Knight Commander?"

"We protect humans from the Fae."

"Like a soldier or some kind of law?"

"Neither," the girl said.

"Then how do you protect humans?" Quinn took the iron ring, sending Scout a look of annoyance when he took it straight back.

"Sorry." Scout was grinning and didn't look in the least bit sorry. "It's amazing. As soon as I let go of the ring I can't see their swords. You were right. I need some gear before I go exploring."

Quinn gave him another look before she returned her attention to the Knight Commander. "How do you protect humans?"

The girl glanced towards the bridge. "Why are you here first?"

The girl's cautious tone reminded her of what Gideon had said. 'Could you imagine the lengths some people would go to so they could possess Fae magic if humans knew about them?' Her own gaze was drawn to the bridge. "I need to return to the realms of the Fae."

"Why?" the girl asked.

"I've been marked by the Wild Hunt. I need to return to Masquerade Nightclub." Quinn gestured towards the reflection of the bridge in the water. "Are you going to stop me?"

"What did you do to make someone send the Hunt after you?" the boy asked.

"Saved someone who is being hunted by them. I didn't know it'd mean they'd be after me too." She didn't bother telling them she probably would have done it even knowing the consequences. Especially after all Gideon had done for her. "Are you going to let me through?"

Chapter Twenty-Two

"You do know time doesn't run the same between here and there, don't you?" the girl asked.

Quinn nodded.

"That means it could be night when you go through to the realms of the Fae."

Quinn's stomached plummeted at the girl's words. "Is there a way to find out?"

"Only by going through. And it'd be no point one of us going through and checking because who knows how much time would pass between when we returned and you go back there." The boy turned to the horse with a smile when it snorted. He patted his neck before facing Quinn again. "Can you ride?"

Quinn nodded, watching as the girl rested her hand on the boy's arm and he turned to her. They shared another look before her hand returned to her side.

The boy looked at Quinn again. "My horse can take you to Masquerade, but if you dismount or fall off he will leave you and return to me. You need to make sure you hold on tight as he'll move fast. Faster than any human horse."

"What about my dog? He has to go back with me so my sister can return here."

"It sounds like you've left a lot of details out of your explanation," the girl said.

"Not really. My younger sister accidentally made a bargain with a Demi Fae and has to remain at Masquerade until my dog no longer lives in this world."

"She made a deal with Kaeder?" the boy asked.

Quinn nodded.

"How old is she?" the girl asked.

Quinn was starting to feel annoyed by all the questions. She doubted telling them it wasn't any of their business would get her the help she needed. "Fifteen."

"Poor kid," the girl muttered.

"What do you plan to do when you return to the realms of the Fae? Other than rescue your sister from Kaeder." The boy absently patted his horse.

She almost told them she planned to wait out the seven years. "I've been trying to find out about Gwyl.

About what Tamek of Ganat Castle did to him to send him seeking revenge and cause him to become cursed and the leader of the Wild Hunt." The look the two of them shared made her heart leap with anticipation. "What? Do you know something?"

"What have you found out?" the boy asked.

"All I've learned is that he's a wood Fae." She thought of the drawstring pouch in her pocket. They didn't need to know about it.

The boy shared another look with the girl before he faced Quinn. "Tamek was the first son of a wood Fae named Glade, who remarried after losing his first wife, a dark Fae. Glade's second wife, also a wood Fae, owned Ganat Castle and they had three sons. When Glade died, the second wife asked Tamek to leave and live in the manor house his mother had left him. She didn't like the way he tormented his brothers and treated her people. About two years ago, when the youngest brother was away with friends, Tamek came visiting. He was all smiles until his warriors were in place. He killed Glade's second wife while his warriors killed the two older brothers and the wife and child of the oldest one. He took the castle for his own, killing the people who tried to go against him. No one knew what had happened to the youngest brother. Until today."

"Didn't anyone do something?" Scout asked. "I mean, your police or something."

Quinn nodded at his words. It was the question she'd wanted to ask. Surely something like that should have been dealt with by someone. No wonder Gwyl had wanted revenge. The thought of her entire family being slaughtered made her think similar thoughts.

"The realms of the Fae are dangerous." The girl stared at Scout. "Many humans don't survive it."

Scout took a step back. "Are there maps of the place?"

The girl shrugged. "There might be a few. But there are many places no one has ever been. Especially not a human."

Quinn could have shaken the girl. She'd said the very words that would make Scout want to explore the realms of the Fae more than ever. She could see it in his eyes, the gleam of excitement that said one day soon he'd be visiting. Unable to do anything about Scout, she turned to the boy again. "What was his name? The youngest brother."

"Baenen. Baenen of Ganat Castle."

She had a name. She didn't know if it would help, but she now knew his name. And the reason why he wanted revenge. "How old was he when it happened?"

"About seventeen or eighteen."

She wished she hadn't asked. He'd been about her age when he'd lost his entire family. "Thank you. For everything."

The boy nodded. "Are you ready to return?"

It took her a moment to nod. She wanted to say no, but that wasn't a good idea. Not with the Hunt after her.

The boy led the horse closer. "Do you need help?" He waved towards the saddle.

She shook her head, stepping forward so she could swing up into the saddle, still holding the rope attached to Buddy's collar.

The boy lifted Buddy like he weighed nothing and placed him in front of her. "Remember to remain on my horse until you reach Masquerade."

She nodded. When the boy stepped out of the way, Scout took his place, holding out the ring. She slipped it onto her finger, not sure what to say to him.

Scout grinned. "I'll see you in the realms of the Fae one day."

A reluctant chuckle escaped. "You be careful. And look out for my sister when she first returns."

He rested his hand on her calf. "I will. If you leave

Masquerade before I get over there, leave a message for me."

She nodded, not sure how to take his comment. It took her a few seconds to think of a reply to make sure he hadn't stopped thinking of her as a sister. "It'll be good to catch up. You never know when a brother will come in handy." She forced herself to grin. "Just don't go scaring off any potential boyfriends like you do for Daisy."

Scout chuckled, letting his arm fall back to his side as he stepped away. "I can't promise anything."

When the horse started forward, moving slowly so he didn't disturb the water, she raised her hand in farewell. The other she rested on Buddy while she held the reins. With how long it took the horse to walk through the river, she was able to rethink her decision to return far too many times. She wanted to urge him to hurry, but knew he couldn't disturb the reflection or the portal wouldn't work. At least according to the instructions Darci had written, along with the directions.

One moment she headed through sun dappled water and the next the horse walked out from under the bridge and through the reflection of a full moon. Her heart plummeted at the sight of the moon, the same size as she'd left it. Not that she'd wanted a lot of time to have passed, but it would have been nice to have arrived during daylight.

In the distance she heard a wolf howl and hoped it wasn't one that belonged to the Hunt. A sound behind her made her turn in the saddle and she saw a Troll trying to sneak up on her, holding a large hammer.

Bending low over the horse in an effort to not only keep herself on, but also Buddy, she urged him forward. It felt like he leapt from the river, racing through the trees. She clung to his back, her arms also wrapped around Buddy who whimpered at the change of pace.

"I know, boy. But it's safer." She murmured the words against his fur. She didn't dare look behind her and see if the Troll chased them for fear she might fall off. She hadn't expected the horse to go so fast. After awhile, her body began to ache with how tense her muscles were and how tight she clung to the horse. Finch's ability to talk to animals would have come in handy. For all she knew, Masquerade could be several hours away. She really hoped not. She doubted she could hold on that long. If she could have understood the horse, she would have asked him how fast he could travel the same distance it would take her half a day to walk.

It wasn't until she could see the Fringes in the distance, that she heard the howls of the Hunt ahead of her. This time she knew it wasn't an ordinary pack of wolves because of the fear that raced through her. She wanted to urge the horse to go faster, but didn't know if that was possible. She also wanted to tell him to run away from the Hunt, but that wouldn't help her reach safety. Remaining low over the horse, she stared at the city in the distance. It seemed a long way off.

The beat of hooves behind her had her wanting to turn to see who followed. Ahead the Hunt cried out, the howls making a shiver race through her body. Behind her was an answering howl. She recognised his voice and her heart beat even faster. Like it might burst from her chest.

"Go faster. Please go faster." She whispered the words to the horse, even as she told herself not to demand more of him. The sound of hooves came closer and the horse she rode kept to the same pace. She had one reprieve, but how would she survive seven years of being hunted if she used it so soon? It would be impossible.

Something hard collided with her and she let go of Buddy as heat washed over her. She was driven from the horse so her side slammed against the ground. She gasped for breath as his hands wrapped around her neck.

Gwyl hissed, drawing back as if burned.

She finally managed to draw in a breath and twist away, leaping to her feet to run towards the Fringes, her backpack feeling cumbersome. Ahead of her she saw the black horse slow to a walk and Buddy jump from his back, the rope trailing behind him. When the horse turned and headed in the direction they'd come from, she wanted to call him back. She heard the sound of running footsteps behind her and she tried to run faster. It didn't help. Shrugging out of her backpack, she let it fall to the ground. That didn't help either.

Gwyl tackled her, pinning her to the ground, his eyes glittering. This time he kept his hands away from the chains at her neck, pressing her shoulders into the ground. "Do you call in your favour?"

Before she had a chance to speak, Buddy launched himself at Gwyl, his teeth bared. "No, Buddy. No." She didn't want him hurt.

Gwyl released one of her shoulders to raise his hand.

She tried to escape, fearing he'd hit her dog.

He placed his hand on Buddy's forehead, narrowly

avoiding the snapping teeth. "I have no fight with you. This is between your master and me alone."

Buddy stopped trying to bite him, but his teeth remained bared and a growl rose from deep within him.

"What are you doing to my dog?"

Gwyl ignored her. "Step back. Cover your teeth. I would rather not call my wolf."

She couldn't see how that would end well for Buddy. She stilled. "If you can make him understand you, tell him to go to Marley. Tell him she needs his protection, not me." The thought of sending Buddy away so she'd be left alone with Gwyl, scared her. The thought of him being attacked by a wolf terrified her more. She pointed in the direction of the Fringes. "She's that way. Tell him she's that way." Her voice broke on the last words.

Chapter Twenty-Three

"You heard her." Gwyl took his hand from Buddy's forehead when he stopped growling.

Quinn nearly burst into tears when Buddy licked her cheek before turning and running towards the Fringes. She stared after him for a moment, the moon nearly out of view so it was harder to see him. Her gaze was drawn to Gwyl.

He looked down at her. "Do you call in your favour?"

"Baenen."

His grip on her loosened and confusion crossed his face.

She slammed her hands into his chest, surprised when he was knocked back. Scrambling to her feet, she started to run away. He grabbed hold of her ankle and she crashed to the ground. Rolling, she checked where he was and saw him rise to his feet and throw his head back. Fearing he was about to call his pack, she threw herself at him, knocking him to the ground, crashing onto him. His arms came around her, trapping her against him.

"Do you call in your favour?"

She wanted to yell the word 'no' at him. Wanted to tell him he didn't have to do this. "I know who you are. You're Baenen."

"I am Gwyl."

"Baenen!" She tore herself from his grip, staggering to her feet. Seeing his horse, she ran to the mare and tried to swing up into the saddle. The horse danced away. She clung to the saddle, her foot in the stirrup as she tried to keep from being thrown. At least now there was a horse between them. She finally managed to get her leg over the horse and clung on as the mare reared. Again and again. The horse tried to throw her and she clung tightly.

When the horse had all feet on the ground, Gwyl dragged her off. "Last chance. Do you call in your favour?"

She blinked back tears, about to say yes when she noticed a change. Day was coming. "You're Baenen and you want to kill Tamek. I have his scent." She drew the bag from her pocket, holding it up so he could see it. When he went to snatch it from her, she threw it as far as she could. The moment his grip on her loosened, she twisted out of it and ran towards the Fringes. The light increased, the day a pale greyness as it awaited the sun.

Even though she told herself not to, Quinn couldn't help checking over her shoulder. She came to a stumbling stop, watching as Gwyl stood there, facing where the sun was about to rise, the drawstring bag clenched in one hand. His antlers rose above him and his horse came to stand at his shoulder. She took one step towards him before wondering what she was doing. She should be running, not staring at him.

The sky filled with colour as the sun rose. Gwyl turned to face her, remaining where he was. The glitter had gone from his eyes, but the look of confusion remained.

She took another step towards him. He wasn't some creature with sad eyes in need of a home. He was a hunter. One that would chase her as soon as night fell if she wasn't somewhere safe. "Baenen."

He stared at her a moment longer before he turned away and walked towards her backpack. His horse followed at his shoulder. After he picked up the backpack, he swung into the saddle and headed towards her.

Running wasn't possible. There was no way she

could outrun a horse. Yet now the sun had risen, the fear that had clung to her had left. She stared up at him when he stopped the horse near her, holding out a hand.

"What?"

He didn't answer, only kept his hand out.

"What are you offering?"

"Night has ended. I'll hunt again when the sun sets."

"What are you offering? Baenen." She caught a glimpse of someone else in his eyes when she spoke his birth name. Someone young and gentle. A lost soul staring back at her before the hard look of Gwyl returned.

"That name means nothing to me."

She knew better. "Why won't you answer me?"

He held up the drawstring bag. "Thank you for returning this." He slid it into his belt pouch, her backpack slung over his arm. The other hand he kept out.

A glance towards the Fringes, that were still a fair way in the distance, had her making up her mind. She took hold of his hand, the heat of it far too familiar. Once she was seated, the horse broke into a trot and she grabbed hold of his waist, her grip tightening when the horse went faster, trying not to let the iron rings touch him.

They entered the Fringes from a different direction than she'd first arrived, winding through narrow streets until Masquerade could be seen ahead of them. Quinn felt strange sitting behind the one who'd hunted her. It was like he was two different people. Or maybe three. The lost soul she'd seen deep in his eyes, the one who waited for nightfall so he could hunt and the hunter. The hunter terrified her.

Gwyl drew his horse to a stop and looked over his shoulder at her. "Call me when you're ready for the Hunt. We'll finish this soon. You and me. You don't have the skill to last seven years. And it seems like you're not willing to take your only other option."

Guessing that was his way of telling her to get off, she swung down off the horse, taking the backpack he held out to her. She held his gaze a moment before she spoke. "I have nothing valuable enough, but if I could I'd send the Hunt after Tamek." It was the only way she knew to break the curse. And he was right. She couldn't last seven years. It also didn't seem right that Tamek should live considering the amount of lives he'd taken.

"There are places a human can go that a Fae would

not be able to pass unnoticed." He wheeled his horse around and galloped down the street.

She stared after him. That had made no sense at all. What had he been trying to tell her? Pushing it from her mind, she slung her backpack on and headed towards the alley that led to Masquerade's stables. She was halfway along the building when Gideon came around the corner.

He stopped, a mixture of emotions crossing his face before he ran towards her, wrapping her in his arms. "I was going to look for you."

She returned his hug before letting go. "Why?"

"Buddy arrived. Marley is adamant you're dead and hasn't stopped crying since he scratched at the back door, whining." He looked her up and down. "What happened? Are you okay?"

She had no idea how to answer the second question. "The Hunt nearly caught me. It was only Gwyl. If the entire pack had been there I doubt I could have escaped."

He reached for her shoulder, his grip tight. "But you're okay, aren't you?"

"Yeah." She had a few bruises, but she'd live. "I need to let Marley know I survived."

He walked beside her, a wry smile forming. "I think everyone in the kitchen would appreciate that."

She chuckled. "Marley doesn't do quiet when it comes to crying." She stepped in the back door to chaos.

Kaeder stood over Marley who sat on the floor, hugging Buddy. "This changes nothing. If you kill the dog then you can go free."

Quinn pushed past the handful of people who were watching. "It changes everything. Tonight she returns home. All obligations to you are ended. The terms of the deal have been met. And you will not touch my dog." When Buddy whimpered, she glanced down to see Marley continued to hold him even though he struggled to reach her side. "Let him go, Marley."

Kaeder glared at the dog that went to Quinn's side and sat. "He's not staying here."

"He can stay in the stables with me."

Kaeder pointed a finger at Quinn. "You can't keep him here."

She opened her mouth to argue, but closed it instead. She barely managed to prevent a smile from escaping. "Fine. I won't keep him here." She took a step towards Kaeder. "But tonight, my sister returns home. Her obligations to you are done."

Kaeder's lips twisted into a smile. "She found her own way here, she can find her own way back." He glared at everyone standing around. "What are you all doing? Get back to work." He turned abruptly, leaving the kitchen.

Not wanting to discuss anything in front of the rest of the kitchen staff, Quinn pulled Marley to her feet, keeping hold of her arm, and headed for the back door. Buddy followed and she beckoned Gideon to come too. She nearly groaned when she saw Mairwin pacing the courtyard. So much for a place to talk in private. "If you're looking for Gwyl, I saw him riding away from Masquerade not that long ago."

Mairwin's eyes narrowed. "I'm beginning to think you're covering for him."

Quinn nearly laughed. It was the only time she hadn't been. She shrugged. "Believe me or not, I don't care. You can waste your time waiting for him if you want." It looked like she'd have to talk in the stables and hope that Finch wasn't around.

"Do you see him every day?"

She gestured towards the stables. "I see him when he leaves or collects his horse."

"Is his horse in there now?"

"Shouldn't be, but I'll check for you." She kept hold of Marley, taking her to the stables with her, Gideon and Buddy following. A glance around showed Gwyl's horse wasn't here. She looked at Buddy first.

"Stay." When he sat, looking up at her with his sad eyes, she turned her attention to Gideon and Marley. "Can you wait here for me?"

They both nodded, tears still staining Marley's face.

Quinn looked at them for a moment longer before she turned and headed outside. "His horse isn't here."

Mairwin held out a folded piece of paper and a gold coin. "See he gets this as soon as possible."

With a nod, Quinn took the coin and paper and pocketed them.

"Do not go reading it or you'll regret it. The letter is for Gwyl only." Mairwin's tone was as haughty as the look she gave Quinn.

"Right. As soon as I see him." After facing Gwyl that morning, Mairwin didn't worry her in the least. "Was that all?"

Mairwin walked away without replying.

Quinn stared after her, slowly shaking her head. No wonder Gwyl kept avoiding Mairwin. Pushing thoughts of the annoying Fae from her mind, she went inside the stables. She smiled when she saw Finch was talking to Buddy, who was enthusiastically greeting him with numerous licks on his face. Unlike most people Buddy had tried to do that to, Finch didn't seem to be bothered by his attentions. In fact, he actually seemed pleased by them.

"What did she want?" Gideon gestured towards the doorway.

"For me to get a message to Gwyl." She paused. "Can you keep Buddy here?"

Gideon laughed. "You'll probably want to keep him out of sight. Kaeder won't be impressed."

She grinned. "I know."

Gideon's laughter faded. "You're starting to think like a Fae."

Chapter Twenty-Four

Quinn stared at Gideon for a moment, thinking over his words. "No. I'm thinking like a human who has learned how to outsmart some Fae."

Before Gideon could reply, Marley interrupted. "How am I going to get home?"

"Exactly how I'd always planned. Through a moon portal. As long as you go tonight, it should be full enough for you to get through." She took the three two-dollar coins from her pocket and held them out. "If you end up where I did, it'll be about a twenty minute drive from home. I'll write down Scout's number for you. He's agreed to pick you up."

"You saw him? How is he?" Marley frowned. "Hang on, why can't you ring him when we go home?"

It was the moment she'd been dreading.

Gideon took a step backwards. "You don't need me anymore, do you?"

She didn't blame him wanting to run. "No."

"What's going on?" Marley demanded when they were alone.

Quinn glanced towards Finch who was at the far end of the stables introducing Buddy to one of the horses that always seemed to be there. A glance towards the doorway also showed no help. "I can't go back with you."

"Why not?"

"Because I'm marked by the Hunt."

"What!"

Quinn looked over to see Finch glance in their direction before returning his attention to the horse he was talking to. "Keep it down."

"How did that happen? When did it happen? When will you be able to come home?"

She really didn't want to answer the first two questions. "In seven years."

"What!"

"Will you stop screeching?"

"I'll be twenty-two before I see you again."

"No, you'll be older. Time doesn't run the same here as it does in the human world, remember?"

"What am I going to tell Mum and Dad?"

"We've already sorted this out. Tell them nothing. Say you can't remember a thing."

"Ever? I thought one day we might…" Marley's voice trailed off.

"The only person you'll be able to talk to about it is Scout. Everyone else will think you're crazy."

"Maybe I should wait and we can go back together."

Quinn felt like shaking her sister. "Eighteen days have already passed since we left home."

"But–"

"You're going tonight. As soon as the moon is overhead you're walking down to the river and diving through the reflection of the moon."

"On my own?"

Quinn nodded.

"No! You can't expect me to wander about the Fringes after dark."

Finch sauntered towards them. "Will you stop scaring the horses?"

Marley pointed at Quinn, glaring at her. "She expects me to walk to the river on my own tonight."

"If you stop making all this noise, I'll walk with you," Finch said. "And if you leave the stables now." He turned to Quinn. "Can I borrow Buddy?"

"I don't–"

Quinn interrupted before Marley could decline the offer. "What do you mean by borrow Buddy?"

"I had no sleep last night as I had to do your shift too. I want to sleep when it's quiet and have him wake me if anyone comes in."

"You can do that?" Quinn looked from Finch to Buddy and back again.

Finch nodded. "He agreed. Is it a deal?"

"I don't know him." Marley continued to glare at Quinn.

"Buddy can go with Finch when he walks you to the river." Quinn turned to Finch. "Can you ask Buddy to do that for me during my shift?"

Finch nodded. "It's not hard at all." He gestured towards Marley. "Is she going now?"

She interrupted Marley's protests, propelling her to the doorway. "Yeah." As soon as they were in the courtyard, she let go of Marley. "Don't be difficult. Do you really want to stay here working for Kaeder?"

"We don't have to stay here."

"Yeah, we do. I can't leave without risking being killed by the Hunt."

Marley's mouth dropped open and she tried several times to speak. "You were marked before you went back home?"

She nodded.

"Are you crazy?"

Quinn winced. "Stop screeching."

"You must be. Is that why you keep telling me to stay away from Gwyl? How long have you been marked?"

"Not long after I arrived." When she saw her sister open her mouth, she spoke again. "And don't you dare screech about it."

Marley closed her mouth with a glare.

She shifted the straps of her backpack, wanting to put it in her room. "I'll see you before I start work. I'll give you Scout's number then."

"This is wrong. I didn't know I'd have to go back on my own."

She sighed heavily. "Can you drop it already, Marley?"

"It's still wrong."

She shrugged one shoulder then readjusted the strap of her backpack. "I'm going to have a sleep. It was a long night."

"Goodnight." Marley grumbled the words, muttering under her breath as she headed to the main building. "It's wrong." She slammed the door behind her.

The sigh that escaped this time was one of relief. Soon she could stop worrying about getting her sister home and focus on dealing with the Hunt. She started to turn towards the stables, freezing when she saw Gwyl stood near the alley, his horse behind him. How long had he been there? And what did he want? She thought of the note from Mairwin.

Taking it from her pocket, she strode towards him, holding it out when she stopped. "Mairwin asked me to give this to you. She was disappointed to miss you again."

He didn't even look at the note. His gaze remained on her face. "I'm not interested in anything she has to say. I've heard all I need to from her."

"What do I do with her note? What do I tell her when she asks?"

A look of amusement fleetingly crossed his face. "I don't think you have a problem with skating around the truth from what I've noticed." He took a step closer. "It's a nice change from the usual lies humans tell."

Guessing that was probably a compliment, she struggled to think of something to say. Only awkward comments came to mind. "You'll have to see her again sometime. She's extremely persistent and is beginning to think I'm covering for you." She slid the note back into her pocket rather than continue to hold it out.

"Are you?"

She didn't think so, but couldn't be a hundred percent certain. "You were the one who first asked me to deal with her."

He stared at her, expressionlessly, eventually nodding. "Then it seems I owe you for your service." He withdrew some gold coins from his belt pouch and held them out to her.

She watched the ten coins fall onto her outstretched hand. "That's a bit excessive."

"We all place different values on things."

"If you continue to pay me ten gold coins a day, it'll still take six hundred days before I have enough to send the Hunt after Tamek." She doubted she could survive nearly two years marked by the Hunt. Not judging by her current efforts.

His gaze searched her face a moment before he reached out and grasped hold of her jaw. "Are you serious about this?" He paused. "You do understand what it means to send the Hunt after someone, don't you?"

Even though she knew, she couldn't resist asking. She wanted to see his reaction. "What did he do to you?" When his expression didn't change, she tried again. "Why do you want Tamek dead?" She thought she saw a flicker in the depths of his eyes at the name. "Baenen." His grip tightened on her jaw.

"He doesn't deserve to live." His voice was as hard as his expression.

"Why?" She watched him struggle with the answer until his face became expressionless again.

"He's evil." He released her jaw, taking a step back.

She could see it, he didn't know. All he knew was the man needed to die, not the reason for it. "How can you stand it?" The words were soft. "How can you stand having lost yourself like that?"

His expression remained closed. "Put my horse in her stall. Leave the disk in the door." A gleam entered his eyes. "I doubt anyone would dare steal her."

She took the reins from him, wishing she had the courage to push further. It would be crazy to continue to push when he had that look in his eye. Just like it would be crazy for anyone to steal his horse. "You never said what you wanted me to do with Mairwin's note."

He held out another ten gold coins. "I don't care about the note. All you need to worry about is unsaddling my horse." As soon as she'd taken the coins, he headed inside Masquerade's main building.

She stared after him. Twenty coins a day would still mean it'd take nearly a year. Not knowing what else to do, she put the coins in her pocket and took the horse to the stall she was usually stabled in. Finch was nowhere in sight and Buddy raised his head to look at her. "It's okay, I've got this one."

He lowered his head onto his paws and closed his eyes, going back to sleep.

As soon as Quinn had put the horse in the stall and removed the tack, she was tempted to have a shower and change into some fresh clothes, but she was too tired. Stepping into her room, she saw it was as she'd left it. Leaving her backpack on top of the chest and putting her coins into the backpack, she slipped off her sneakers and dropped onto the bed.

Chapter Twenty-Five

Quinn slept surprisingly well, woken after dark by Buddy scratching at the door. Staggering from bed, feeling every bruise, she slipped her feet into her sneakers before she opened the door and saw a Fae waited for someone to take his horse. Yawning, she wondered where Finch was as she took a disk from one of the stall doors she passed and exchanged it with the Fae for the reins. He tossed her a silver coin before he strode outside. She fumbled the catch and ended up having to pick it up off the floor.

After she put the horse away, she stared at the stall where Gwyl's horse had been. He'd obviously collected it already. She doubted someone would have stolen it on him. About to knock on Finch's door, she smiled when he sauntered in with three plates, placing one on the floor for Buddy.

She took the plate he handed her. "Thanks."

"It was the least I could do for leaving your dog on duty today. Think he could do the same again tomorrow?"

The meal now made sense. He wanted a favour. "Yeah."

"I don't know why I didn't think to get a dog before this. You're not looking for a home for him, are you?"

She shook her head, looking at Buddy who seemed more interested in his food than their conversation.

"If you ever are…" Finch left the rest of his sentence unspoken.

"Okay." Finishing her food, she rose to her feet. "Thanks for letting me sleep in." She was surprised she hadn't been up earlier considering she'd had a few hours' sleep in the car yesterday. She frowned. At least she guessed it had been yesterday. Time was too confusing.

"What's the matter?"

"Time. How do you keep track of the differences between the realms of the Fae and the human world?"

Finch grinned. "You don't. And why would you need to? It's not like there's anything worth going back to."

"Maybe not for you."

"Not for you either after some time passes."

She shied away from that thought. "Did you see Marley when you were getting food?"

"Are you sure she's your sister? Not much alike, are you?"

"What happened?"

"If her eyes were any sharper I'd have been shredded into tiny pieces."

"You'll still walk with her to the river, won't you?"

Finch nodded. "I'll make sure she gets home. You remember me if you need someone to take in Buddy."

"Okay."

Rising, he took her empty plate. "I'll be back when the moon's overhead."

She watched him go. He paused to take Buddy's empty plate and give his head a rub. When Buddy came to lean against her, she asked, "What do you think, boy?" It would have been handy to be able to understand animals when Buddy made a few noises that bordered on whining. "Sorry. You might have to tell Finch so he can pass on the message." Once she would have pretended to understand him. Now she knew better.

Two Fae entered the stables and she was kept busy taking care of their horses, more Fae following on their heels. When Finch and Marley arrived, the evening was quiet and she had Scout's number written on a torn off piece of paper and inside a resealable plastic bag.

Marley took the bag from her and slipped it inside a pocket of the trousers she wore. "I can't believe you're making me go home on my own."

"I can't believe you'd want your sister to risk her life to go home with you," Finch said before Quinn had a chance to speak.

Not wanting an argument to start, she interrupted Marley. "Have you got everything?"

"I didn't bring anything with me."

"Be careful."

Marley threw her arms around her. "Come home with me. I bet Mum and Dad could figure something out."

Her arms tightened around her sister for a moment before she let go and stepped back, shaking her head. "By the time we'd convinced them, it'd be too late. I'm safer here."

"But we'll never see you again," Marley wailed.

"Are we going or standing around here all night?" Finch asked.

"You're going." Quinn spoke before Marley could. "I'll see you to the alley, but I can't go any further than that."

They walked together silently, Buddy between Finch and Quinn. When they reached the alley, Marley threw herself at Quinn again, tears forming. "Will you be able to visit?"

She hugged her sister once more before letting her go. "Probably not." It would only cause problems. And who would she call to pick her up if Scout turned up here? "You better go before the moon is no longer overhead."

Marley started down the alley, throwing several looks over her shoulder until she stumbled and Finch grabbed her arm to keep her from falling. She pulled away from him. With one last look and a wave, she kept her gaze directly ahead of her.

Quinn remained at the edge of the alley watching Marley, Finch and Buddy until they were swallowed by the shadows, wishing she could have gone with them. She stayed there for several minutes, unable to bring herself to move. About to turn away, she heard a scream pierce the night. Recognising it as her sister's she ran towards the sound. Halfway down the street, she froze. Marley backed away from the horseman in the middle of the street, Finch tugging her towards the direction of the river.

Gwyl turned his head to stare at her, as if he sensed her standing there.

"Quinn! Run." Marley tried to come towards her, but Buddy got in her way and Finch kept tugging her towards her destination.

"Marley, go. If I have to save you, I will be caught." Seeing Gwyl ride towards her she turned and ran for the alley that led to Masquerade. The pound of hooves grew closer and her breath burned in her lungs as she forced herself to move faster. He crashed into her as she reached the start of the alley, making her feel every bruise from their last encounter. She fought to escape, safety so close.

Gwyl pinned her so she could barely move. "Ask for your favour."

Surprised by the pleading quality of his words, she tried to see his expression in the darkness. It was a fail. "Haven't we been through this before?" Even as she spoke the words, they felt like a lie. Everything about it felt different. Even his grip on her wasn't as tight.

"Ask." His voice was a demand, the pleading gone.

"Baenen."

"Do you want to die?"

As harsh as his voice was, the words didn't sound like that of the leader of the Wild Hunt. She slipped her fingers into his belt pouch, feeling around for the drawstring bag. It wasn't there. "No."

"Then ask for your favour."

She wrapped her arms around him so she could slide one of her rings off, pushing it into the band of his trousers. When he roared, she pushed against him with the hand that still had a ring on it. He recoiled from her and she staggered to her feet, running towards the end of the alley. Behind her she heard the sound of metal bouncing across the cobblestone alley followed by running footsteps. She threw herself forward, landing half out of the alley as he crashed into her legs.

Gwyl howled, holding onto her legs and trying to pull her to him. In the distance came answering howls.

She kicked out at him. "Let me go."

"Are you asking for your favour?"

She didn't dare answer him. When her foot connected with his jaw, she winced at the sound he made, scrambling further away from him. She was nearly completely out of the alley, but he still had hold of one of her legs. Drawing a necklace over her head, she struck out at him with it. The moment he released his grip on her leg, she scurried backwards. Remaining on the ground, she stared at him.

He stayed on the ground too, watching her, a glitter in his eyes. "You keep taking risks and your life will be over."

She didn't know if it was a warning or a promise and wasn't about to ask him. When he rose to his feet, she remained half sprawled on the ground, her arms propping her up. When he turned and walked away her arms gave out and she lay flat on the ground. She was still lying there when Finch and Buddy returned. She pushed Buddy away when he licked her face.

"Your sister left through the moon portal." Finch held out his hand.

She eyed it, not sure if she wanted to get up yet.

"You look like you need a drink."

"I don't know about a drink, but I could certainly use a shower."

"I can take care of things while you take one." Finch continued to hold out his hand.

She put the necklace back on before she took his hand and let him pull her up. "I'll probably be covered in bruises by morning."

"I have a balm that will help." Finch let go of her hand, walking beside her to the stables. "It's good for all minor injuries."

"Okay. I think I will have that shower. You right to take care of things for now?" When Finch nodded, she walked faster. "Thanks." Heading to her room she took a change of clothes from her backpack before entering the stable bathroom.

As soon as she was under the warm spray, she started shaking. Leaning her head against the shower wall, she tried to pull herself together. She was alive, her sister had returned home and she had Buddy with her. And if Gwyl kept paying her as much as he was, she'd have the money to help him break his curse within a year or two. She shied away from thinking about exactly what would have to happen to break the curse. Tamek had killed an entire family. Including a young child.

Turning off the water and stepping out of the shower, she realised she hadn't brought the towel. She ran her hands quickly over her body to get some of the water droplets off, but her skin was still damp when she tried to dress. It didn't make pulling jeans on very easy. Before she left the bathroom she took the leaf and coins from the pocket of her dirty jeans and slid them into the pockets of the ones she wore.

Stepping out of the bathroom, she thanked Finch and when he strode outside, she asked Buddy to let her know if anyone arrived and retreated to her room. She took out her waterproof torch and turning it on was surprised to find a small glass jar sitting on the chest. The hand drawn label read 'balm'. Her legs trembled and she staggered to the bed before she collapsed onto the floor. It took several attempts to open the jar so she could apply some of the sweet smelling balm. She didn't worry about most of her legs as she wasn't about to go to the effort of taking her jeans off and on again.

Why had Marley screamed? She'd have to ask Finch when he returned. After everything she'd gone through, hearing her sister's scream had made her think it might all have been for nothing. Slipping off her sneakers, she drew her legs up and wrapped her arms around them. She wanted to go home. Wanted to have left with Marley and be picked up by Scout and be on her way back to the house she'd grown up in. Her sister had been right. It was wrong she couldn't leave. Turning the torch off, since she had no other batteries, she sat in the dark.

Chapter Twenty-Six

Quinn had no idea how long she sat there before Buddy came to scratch and whine at her door. Slipping her feet back into her sneakers, she left the room to find a Fae wanting her horse. Finch didn't return until the early hours of the morning and he looked half asleep.

"Why did Marley scream?"

"Gwyl came out of nowhere and scared her. She wasn't wearing any iron so she felt the fear he brings when the sun sets."

"Thank you for not letting her try and help me." Both of them marked by the Hunt was the last thing she'd needed.

Finch grinned, his eyes half closed. "Does that mean you'll let me go to sleep now?"

She laughed reluctantly. "Yeah." After Finch shut

his door, she turned to Buddy. "Sorry. I forgot to ask him to translate. In the morning."

Buddy gave a soft yip and returned to sleep.

Thinking that was a good idea, she returned to her room, kicking off her sneakers before she lay down. It seemed like she'd barely got settled before Buddy was at her door again. The rest of the night was fairly similar until the early morning rush of Fae heading home.

Finch was still asleep when the steady flow of Fae ended and the sun rose. Gwyl arrived with his horse. She couldn't stop staring at him. Did he ever regret his hunts? Not willing to ask him, she took the coins and the reins he held out and put his horse in her stall, removing the tack. Once she'd brushed her over, she closed the stall door and left the disk in place. Gwyl was still where she'd left him. She had no idea what to say to him. The last hunt was too fresh in her mind.

"Would you like to join me for the morning meal?"

It took several attempts before she could answer him. "You tried to kill me earlier this morning."

He nodded once. "That's the nature of the Hunt."

"Why would you ask me to join you for a meal?"

He remained silent for long drawn out seconds. "I thought you might be one person who would actually be willing to." He started to turn away.

She reached out and grabbed hold of his arm before he could finish turning away. "Wait." She could have sworn she'd caught a glimpse of that lost soul within his eyes again. Even though the heat of his arm reminded her of who he was, she couldn't prevent herself from saying, "Okay. As long as it's a meal for humans." When he smiled, her breath caught in her throat. It faded as quickly as it had arrived and she was left wishing she'd known him before he was consumed by the Hunt. She let go of his arm, taking a step back from him.

"Is something wrong?"

Where should she start? Keeping the long list to herself, she shook her head. "I have to let Finch know it's his shift." When Gwyl nodded, she went to the far end of the stables and knocked on the door.

"Yes?" came the half distinct reply.

"It's your shift."

"Tell Buddy to wake me."

She turned to Buddy who'd followed her. "You get that?" When he barked softly, she guessed he did. "Okay. I'll see you later." She looked towards Gwyl, wondering what on earth she was doing. It was completely and utterly crazy. But she couldn't forget the glimpse of the lost soul she'd seen in the depths of his eyes. It took her a moment before she could bring herself to cross the distance between them.

When she reached his side, Gwyl turned and headed for the doorway. Walking beside him, she sent several glances his way as they headed for the main building. He entered the far door and she looked around the hallway, thick carpet on the floor. They passed several doors and a stairwell before taking another hallway that led into the one that continued to the front door.

Darci came forward to greet them when they entered the restaurant. Her initial expression of shock was masked by a smile. "Let me show you to a table. I'll be back with drinks. That'll give you time to think about what to order." She gave them menus.

Quinn sat across from Gwyl at a table for two. She had no idea what to say to him. She wasn't about to ask him how his night had been. She already knew more than she wanted to about that. "What is your horse's name?"

"Sweet Pea."

"Your horse." She couldn't help the disbelief that filled her tone.

Gwyl nodded once.

"Why did you call her that?"

A look of confusion crossed his face before it cleared and became expressionless. "That's her name."

There hadn't been anything sweet about the horse when she'd been trying to throw her that morning. "Are you sure that's her name?"

"It's the name she's always had." He pointed to the menu she was fiddling with. "Darci is on her way back. You might want to decide what you wish to eat."

She glanced through the numerous pages, the style of writing reminding her of the sign at the front of the building. Half the meals had strange names and she had no idea what they were or if they were safe to eat. She closed the menu and put it to the side like he'd done with his. "I've decided." She'd order what she'd had last time. That was probably the safest option.

Darci placed drinks on the table. "Are you both ready to order?"

"I will have my usual," Gwyl said.

Quinn nodded towards the drink that had been placed in front of her. "Is that fine for a human?" When Darci nodded, she continued. "I'll have the same as I had last time."

Darci collected the menus. "Your meals will be brought out to you soon."

Quinn watched Darci stride away, wondering why she'd served them. She'd expected someone else, like Oscar. When Darci opened the staff door and stepped through to the kitchen, Quinn saw half a dozen humans stumble back from where they'd been trying to peer through the slightly open door. She faced Gwyl. "Have you ever dined with anyone here before?"

"No."

Well that explained all the attention they were getting. She glanced around the restaurant. They were the only ones dining. Struggling to think of something to talk about, she couldn't help thinking about her sister. Marley was able to chat to anyone in any situation, but she bet even she would have been having problems right now. Hopefully she'd made it home safely. There were so many things she'd miss about her world. Other things she wouldn't.

"What are you thinking of?"

"The human world. Have you ever been there?"

"I can only leave this realm to hunt my prey."

She shuddered at the thought of him hunting her. "Does that mean you've never been there?" She frowned. No, he'd hunted Gideon in the human world. It had been what had driven him here.

"I've been there a few times hunting prey and I've

also been there on the longest nights of the year. The winter solstice in the north and the south. A pity no one has lured Tamek there on those nights. The Hunt can go after any prey we wish, in the human world, during the nights of the winter solstice. Many a human has whispered names, crimes and locations into the breeze as the sun sets on the winter solstice in the hope we'll hear their pleas."

She was tempted to ask if it bothered him. Was there any hunt he regretted? Her courage failed her. Seeing Darci stride towards the table with their meals, she was relieved. Joining Gwyl for breakfast hadn't been the smartest of ideas.

They remained silent as they ate and every now and then Quinn noticed someone peeked around the edge of the door. After she'd eaten, she laid her cutlery together in the middle of the plate.

Not having anything else to talk about, she drew Mairwin's note from her pocket and opened it. She read it aloud. "Tell my brother our parents will pay the price to have so high a noble hunted. If he comes home they'll give him the money he wants. But it's to be on his head. They'll give him the money, it's up to him what he chooses to do with it. But he must come home to collect it." She looked up from the note. "Are you going to pass on the message?"

He shook his head. "It makes no difference now. If they want him released, they'll have to bring the money to him. He can't leave the Hunt until he's fulfilled his terms."

"What are the terms when you join the hunt?"

"They aren't the same for everyone. All seek something different."

She couldn't resist asking, her voice low. "What did you seek?"

He stared at her, a gleam in his green eyes. "Why ask what you already know? I see it in your eyes."

She was surprised to hear he could see something in her eyes like she could see things in his. "You don't, do you?"

"Then it must not matter."

She wanted to argue his words, but knew it was pointless when his face was expressionless. Rising to her feet, she tried not to feel pity for the boy who'd lost his family. "Thank you for the meal."

Again he stared at her for a moment before he answered. "I'll see you before the sun sets." He rose to his feet. "You won't want to see me after."

She watched him drop coins onto the table before he strode away. His words rang in her mind. She was still standing by the table when Darci joined her.

"What do you think you're doing? You wouldn't

let your sister serve him, but you'll dine with him? Have you forgotten Gwyl leads the Wild Hunt? There's no harm in waiting on him when he comes to the restaurant or taking care of his horse when he leaves her at the stables, but you don't befriend him. One little accident and you could end up being marked by him."

She nearly told Darci it was too late. Remembering Gideon's warning, she kept quiet. "I know who he is."

"Then use your brain. Don't get close to him. Take care of his horse, stay in the stables. Don't speak to him any more than necessary."

"Is that an order?"

"Of course not. It's good sense." Darci scooped the coins up off the table. "If you bring the Hunt to the door, Kaeder won't be impressed. You'll be out quicker than you can blink. And I don't want to lose someone who's good with the horses." Darci strode back to the kitchen, not bothering to wait for a reply.

Chapter Twenty-Seven

Quinn knew Darci made sense. Knew she should keep Gwyl at a distance. But Baenen was another matter. What would it be like to be trapped by a curse? She never wanted to find out.

Not wanting to walk past the curious eyes of the rest of the staff in the kitchen, she left the same way she'd entered. She was nearly across the courtyard when Gideon came out the staff back door, headed straight for her. "I hope you're not about to lecture me too."

Gideon shook his head, looking slightly confused. "I was going to ask about your sister. Did she get home okay?"

"Finch said she went through the moon portal."

"Do you trust him?"

"Buddy does."

The corners of Gideon's mouth tilted up. "Only

here does that make complete sense." The humour left his expression and even though he looked like he wanted to speak, he remained silent.

"What's wrong?"

"Did something happen to my Dad? When you didn't say anything I began to worry something had happened to him."

Guilt hit her. "I'm so sorry. He's fine. More than fine. It's just with everything that's happened…" she finished her sentence with a movement of her hand. "I can't believe I forgot." She lifted one of the necklaces over her head. "I even brought this back for you since I gave away your last one."

He held up his hand, shaking his head. "You keep it. I can't wear it in the bar. Especially not when I dance with so many Fae each night. I've even had to stop wearing my dagger."

She slipped it back over her head, telling him about his parents, how they believed him dead and the brother that would be born next year. When he remained silent, she crossed the space between them, resting her hand on his shoulder. "Are you okay?"

"They're moving on. I was worried he'd have no one." He met her gaze. "I don't need to go home."

"Don't you want to?"

"Do you remember the human I told you about?

The one who helped me when I first came here." Colour spread across his cheeks.

She nodded.

"He's been visiting of an evening."

She was confused. "You like him?"

"Yeah."

"I thought you said you weren't gay." She frowned. "Actually, you didn't really answer the question."

"I'm not gay." He grinned. "I'm bi."

Her grin matched his. "And you reckon I'm sounding like the Fae. What's his name? How old is he? Didn't you say he's been here for a decade?"

"He was only fifteen when he arrived here a decade ago. He gained some Fae magic, for his own, after he was here about two years. He told me that would probably put us about the same age. When I told him he'd be much older than that with the time difference between our worlds he laughed. Said it didn't count. I don't know what to think. I'll be eighteen in four months. Or maybe longer. I don't know. Time's confusing here. Do I go by human time or the amount of time that's passed since I've arrived?"

"I know exactly what you mean. I wouldn't have a clue either."

"What do you think I should do? Tell him to stay

away? Return home when I can? Or let my parents finish mourning me and stay here with Grant."

"What do you want to do?"

"Stay here."

"Then stay."

"What about my parents?"

"They have their own lives to live."

"So you think I should let them continue to think I might be dead? Do you think they ever wonder what happened to me?"

When he put it like that, it didn't sound right. "What will they think if you turn up in their lives fifteen years or more after you disappeared, looking pretty much the same?"

"Dad would probably have a heart attack." He slowly shook his head. "I want to stay, but I feel guilty. Right now I'm almost glad I'm marked by the Hunt so I don't have to choose."

"Does that mean you don't want me to do anything if I get the chance to take your scent from Gwyl? If I end up freeing him from his curse."

Gideon hesitated. "Take it. If it'll help." He placed his hand on hers that still rested on his shoulder. "Thank you. For finding everything out for me."

"Sorry for not telling you sooner."

His hand tightened on hers before he let go,

stepping away before he smiled. "I understand. You've been worried about your sister." His smile faded. "I'm going to have a brother. That's going to take a lot of getting used to." With a bemused smile, he headed inside the main building.

She stood in the courtyard, not sure what to do. Normally she'd be exhausted and more than ready for bed, but after the frequent naps all night, she didn't feel tired.

"Did you see him?"

Hearing Mairwin's voice behind her, she wished she'd headed to bed after all. Facing her, she nodded.

"Did he say anything?"

"The money will have to be brought to your brother. He has to fulfil his terms before he can leave the Hunt."

"That's impossible. Did he say what the terms are? Maybe I can help him meet them."

Judging from what she'd read in the note she had a feeling that what had driven Mairwin's brother to seek out the Hunt was similar to Baenen's reason and it would take a similar task for him to fulfil his terms. "I believe bringing the money to him will help him fulfil his terms."

"Did Gwyl say that?"

"Gwyl said very little." At least on that matter.

"But he was very clear that the money needed to be brought to your brother."

Mairwin turned away, striding down the alley.

Quinn glared at Mairwin's retreating back. Maybe she should have a sleep before some other haughty Fae turned up to try and ruin her day. Deciding that was the best plan, she grabbed a change of clothes and her towel and took her dirty clothes from yesterday to the bathroom. Once her and her clothes were clean she hung her clothes over some of the doors of the empty stalls near her room. While she was doing that Finch came out of his room.

"For five silver coins a week you can have your laundry taken care of. Talk to Darci about it if you're interested."

"Thanks, I'll think about it." She couldn't afford to waste any of her money. Six thousand gold coins were a lot to save up.

"I can hang a rope in the empty stall next to your room. Your clothes will dry better hung on a rope."

"I suppose." She watched as he headed to the front of the stables where bits and pieces were kept, returning a minute later with a length of rope.

He entered the stall to hang up the rope. "Have you thought about if you're planning to keep Buddy?"

She should have known. She started to say she'd

never give him up, but watching Buddy follow Finch around made her feel guilty. Was she being selfish wanting to keep him? She didn't know, but she couldn't bring herself to let him go. Not right now. "I've barely had a chance to think about anything."

Finch finished tying off the rope. "There you go." He stepped out of the stall. "Will you let me know when you decide?"

She gathered up her washing from the stall doors. "Of course."

"I'm going to get something to eat, do you want anything?"

"No." She was now tired enough to want to sleep. "I'm heading to bed soon."

"I'll wake you when it's your shift." Finch strode from the stables, leaving Buddy behind.

She started to ask Buddy who he preferred, then decided she really didn't want to know. Not yet. Finished hanging out her washing, she went to her room. Kicking off her sneakers, she stripped down to her underwear and used the balm on the rest of the places she'd missed. She'd been surprised at how well it had worked. After putting the jar on the chest and dressing again, she crawled into bed and lay there for far too long before she fell asleep.

When Finch woke her, she found Gwyl had

already collected Sweet Pea. She wasn't certain if she was disappointed or relieved. But she was worried there was the possibility she might be disappointed. Taking the plate of food Finch had brought her, she sat down beside Buddy and shared bits from her plate with him. Once she'd finished eating, she offered to take the plates back to the kitchen. She was halfway across the courtyard when Gideon came out the back door. Her steps slowed to a stop.

"I should have asked what you meant earlier when you wanted to know if I was going to lecture you. I only learned a few minutes ago that you had breakfast with Gwyl this morning."

"Does that mean I get the lecture now?"

He shook his head. "He will kill you. If you're trying to make friends with him in the hope he won't, he has no choice. If someone paid him the right amount to kill his best friend, from before he became Gwyl, and he was compelled to accept the offer, he'd have to do it."

"It wasn't like that."

"Then why did you eat with him?"

She shrugged. She had no answers for herself let alone him.

"Be careful. Getting close to him would be like making friends with a murderer."

"It's different. Like you said, he has no choice. He is the Hunt once the sun sets."

"If you want to be pedantic about it then you can't argue the word killer."

She wanted to defend Baenen, but it was illogical to argue the truth. "I want to break the curse."

"I thought you were waiting to find out more about Tamek first."

Guilt struck her again. "Sorry. I really should tell you everything that happened while I was gone."

"I've got about half an hour before I have to start work."

She held up the plates. "Let me return these to the kitchen and I'll meet you in the stables." Thinking of Finch, she changed her mind. "In my room."

"Okay." He crossed the courtyard and went inside the stables.

Chapter Twenty-Eight

Quinn entered the kitchen, feeling uncomfortable with the sudden silence at her entrance. It felt like every eye in the room was on her. Leaving the dirty dishes by the sink, she hurried outside and headed to her room. She was tempted to take one of the lanterns from the stables with her so she didn't have to waste the batteries in her torch. She'd ask about a lantern for her room later.

Gideon sat at one end of the chest, leaning against the wall. One leg was bent across the chest and the other remained on the floor. He was little more than a shadow in the nearly dark room. "You don't have to tell me if you don't want to."

Before she closed the door, she took out her torch and turned it on. "It wasn't that. There's been so much going on. We've barely had time to talk in the last couple of days." She continued speaking, telling him almost everything that had happened. Including the possibility of Scout following her to the realms of the Fae. A couple of times she had to take a break and put horses in stalls.

Gideon slowly shook his head. "No wonder you didn't tell me everything." He smiled. "And I thought my life had been busy lately."

"Mine's been a little too busy."

Gideon rose from the chest. "I better start work." He stopped in the doorway and looked back at her. "If you have some time around midnight, I'd like you to meet Grant."

"If things aren't busy I'll come over and meet him for a few minutes."

"Thanks." He grinned before he walked away.

Gideon had barely left when Buddy was scratching on her door to let her know someone had arrived with a horse. She was kept busy for a while, and when things were slow around midnight, she went to the bar so she could meet Grant.

They were dancing. The crowd watched them as they glided gracefully across the floor. She could see why Gideon was attracted to him. It was the way he looked at Gideon. It was similar to the way she'd often caught Marley looking at Scout, only with a hundred times more feeling behind it. He would be crazy to walk away from someone who looked at him like that.

The song ended and Gideon spotted her, bringing Grant over. He was beaming while Grant looked cautious. "Quinn, I want you to meet Grant."

Grant held out his hand. He was nearly as tall as Gideon, but could have almost been mistaken for a Fae with his slim body and elegant looks. "It is a pleasure to meet you. Gideon often speaks of you."

She shook his hand. "The two of you are perfect together on the dance floor. I could have watched you for ages."

Grant's cautious look was replaced with a smile. "I learned to dance in the realms of the Fae. It's something they're fond of."

Gideon gestured towards a table. "Did you want to sit down for a while?"

"Sorry, I can't. I have no idea where Finch is and can't leave the stables unattended for long." Her gaze returned to Grant. "I wanted to come and meet you."

Grant slid his arm around Gideon's waist, the cautious look having returned. "So you could decide if you approved?"

"No, because Gideon asked it of me." She couldn't resist grinning. "But I do approve." When Grant looked towards Gideon, she said, "And that's exactly why."

"What do you mean?" Grant looked and sounded confused.

"You have a very expressive face. Particularly when you look at Gideon."

Grant sighed heavily. "I've been trying to break that habit ever since I arrived here. It's not a good one to have among the Fae."

"I suppose not." She paused. "I'd better go before someone complains about no one being at the stables." She couldn't afford to lose her job and be kicked out of Masquerade. An image of Gwyl's green eyes came to mind, a glitter in them. She pushed it aside.

Grant nodded. "It was nice to meet you. Hopefully the next time will be longer."

"I'd like that."

"I'll see you later," Gideon said.

She was still smiling when she returned to the stables. Now if only she could sort her own life out. Maybe she could be content to remain at Masquerade like Gideon was, waiting for the seven years to be over. It took her only a few seconds to know she wouldn't manage. As much as she liked horses, she couldn't do this for the next seven years. Or even one or two years if she gained enough coins from tips. Particularly with Gwyl's excessive tips. She had to do something before then. She didn't have it in her to patiently wait and hope nothing went wrong.

By the time morning had arrived, she'd come up with numerous outlandish ideas to earn the six thousand gold coins, but nothing practical. She was still discarding crazy ideas after the morning rush was over when Gwyl arrived. He watched her as she put Sweet Pea in her stall and removed her tack. It annoyed her. Surely he could trust her to take care of his horse by now.

Closing the stall door, she left the disk in place, striding towards him. "Don't you trust me with her?"

Instead of answering, he held out a small, leather bound book. It looked like a diary or journal.

"What is that?" She eyed it warily. "And what are those stains on it?"

"Blood."

"What?" She felt like her sister with the way she screeched the word. "Whose blood?"

"Arnall of Ganat Castle."

"Who is that?" She had a bad feeling she already knew.

"One of his servants brought it to me a year ago. Said Arnall told him with his dying breath to take it to someone who'd avenge him against Tamek. The servant apologised for taking so long to bring it to me, refusing to listen when I told him I couldn't help him and he should take it to another. Since I'm unable to do anything with the book I'm giving it to you."

"Does the name mean nothing to you?" She watched him carefully. "Baenen?"

"I've already told you, my name is Gwyl."

"Was your name Gwyl when the servant gave you the book?"

"Yes."

She took it from him, being careful to avoid the rust coloured marks. "What am I meant to do with it?"

"Use it to bring about the fall of Tamek." He turned and strode from the stables.

She started after him, not quite sure what had happened. She flicked through some of the pages. After a bit she realised it wasn't a diary or a journal. It was details about the castle. Some of it would no longer be relevant, such as guard duties and patrols, but she doubted hidden passageways and secret entrances would have changed. Including a secret entrance to a treasure room. Surely he hadn't given her the means to steal six thousand gold coins or something of equal value. Turning to the next page, her jaw dropped. There was a list of family jewels, including drawings of them and estimated worth. Each was kept in its own hidden panel in the walls of the treasure room.

Running outside, she found the courtyard empty. Her shoulders slumped and she started to return inside. Freezing, her gaze was drawn to the far entrance to Masquerade's main building. She took a single step forward. She didn't know what to do. In the end, she straightened her shoulders and marched inside, heading to the dining room. Standing in the doorway, she almost missed spotting him. He was off to one side, the area filled with shadows. When her gaze stopped on him, she found he was staring at her. It took her nearly a minute to convince herself to cross the room and sit in the other chair at the small table.

"Did you wish to join me for the morning meal again?" He gestured towards his half eaten meal.

She shook her head, placing the book on the table in front of her. "Have you read this book?"

"Yes."

"What do you expect me to do with it?"

"I've already told you."

Annoyance arrowed through her. "But how do you expect me to use it to do that?"

"You'll have to make that decision for yourself. I gave it to you because the servant wanted the book given to someone wanting revenge against Tamek. Since you do, I handed it on to you."

She opened her mouth to correct him, closing it instead of speaking. She doubted it'd make a difference. "How would I get there?"

"If you were ready at sunrise I could take you. But you must be quick if you want me to return you here before sunset."

It seemed like a really bad idea. So many things could go wrong. "If I was caught out after sunset an hour head start wouldn't help with me on foot and you on horseback."

"If you asked for your favour I'd tell Sweet Pea to allow you to ride her."

It still felt like a bad idea. "Why would you help me like this?"

Confusion and what appeared to be a struggle crossed his face before the expressionless look replaced them. "Sometimes we must follow rules even when we don't wish to."

She almost laughed. A humourless laugh at her own expense. Typical. The one guy who might actually like her spent half his time wanting to kill her. As her sister would say, it was wrong.

Completely and utterly wrong. She nearly said yes, but forced herself to be cautious. There had to be a safer way to get the money. "I need to think about it."

"Have an answer before sunset."

She nodded, rising to her feet, carefully picking up the book. She stared at him a moment longer, trying to see Baenen in the depths of his eyes. There was nothing. Turning, she walked away, heading for her room.

Chapter Twenty-Nine

Quinn found Gideon waiting for her by her door. Finch was nowhere in sight and Buddy slept on the floor between their two rooms.

"Kaeder found out."

"About what?" She almost crossed her fingers, hoping she was wrong about what she expected to hear him say.

"He said I've either got to leave or pay him a gold coin a day to be able to remain here. If I want sanctuary, I've got a pay for it. I don't earn enough silver coins in tips once he takes his cut."

It had been as she'd feared. "How many silver coins do you need a day?"

"Twenty."

She didn't earn enough each day either. She was lucky to get ten to fifteen silver coins if she didn't count the ones Gwyl gave her. She couldn't bring herself to offer them. The gold coins didn't feel like they belonged to her. Drawing out the handful of silver coins in her pockets, she held them out to him. "I have some more in my room you can have."

"I can't take all your money. What if-" He broke off, glancing around and taking a step closer. "What if he finds out you're marked by the Hunt too."

Her gaze was drawn to the book she held. "I'm going to try and break the curse tomorrow." She met his gaze. "Take the coins. I don't need them."

He took the handful of silver coins and put them in his pocket. "How did you get the money?"

"I haven't yet. I'm hoping to have it tomorrow." Again her gaze was drawn back to the book. She had a feeling that if she failed to get the money, it'd probably be because she'd been caught. Being marked by the Hunt would be the least of her problems.

"Is there anything I can do to help?"

She started to shake her head. "Can you look after Buddy? I can't take him with me where I'm going."

Gideon called Buddy to him and crouched in front of the dog, rubbing his head. "I hear you have my eyes." He glanced towards Quinn, a grin fleetingly appearing.

"That was Marley's comment."

He rose to his feet, Buddy continuing to sit in front of him. "I'll take care of Buddy for you."

Finch's head appeared above the stall door across from them. "What's going on? Why does he need to take care of Buddy? Are you giving him to Gideon?" He vaulted over the stall door to walk closer.

"No. I was only expecting him to make sure Buddy had food and water."

"I can do that. It's not a hardship. Don't you trust me to look after him?"

Several comments formed in her mind, but none seemed right. "I didn't know where you were."

"I'm never far. Did you try looking?"

"I was going to ask you as well. Later, when you woke me for my shift."

"You were?"

She nodded, even though she hadn't even thought of asking Finch. "Of course I was."

"That's all right then. But I can manage without help."

She looked towards Gideon, not sure what to say.

"I'm sure Finch is right. He won't need my help." Gideon gestured towards her door. "Do you think I can have a couple of those coins?"

"Yeah." She opened the door. Before she could step into her room, Finch spoke.

"When are you going? How long will you be gone?"

"At sunrise. And hopefully only a day. But I don't know for certain." When Finch nodded and turned away, she stepped into her room, Gideon on her heels.

He closed the door and stepped in front of her when she would have picked up her backpack. "I don't need the coins." He kept his voice low. "I need to talk to you in private."

"What's wrong?"

"What are you planning on doing?"

Something completely and utterly crazy. But she wasn't crazy enough to say those words aloud. "I have a treasure map." She held up the book.

"Where did you get it?"

"Gwyl." She could almost hear the comments he was keeping to himself. Particularly with his expression she could barely see from the limited light entering the room through the curtain that moved in the breeze. "I know what I'm doing." If Kaeder found out she was marked by the Hunt, she'd be in the same predicament as Gideon.

He reached for her, grasping her shoulder momentarily. "I hope so. I've only got two friends in this realm and I'd hate to lose one of them."

In an effort to lighten the conversation, she grinned. "Does Grant know he's only a friend?"

Gideon chuckled softly. "He's something more as well. But the point is, don't go getting yourself killed."

"That's the last thing I want. Which is why I'm going treasure hunting with Gwyl tomorrow morning." She regretted the words the moment she spoke them.

"Are you insane? You're actually going with him?"

"He's a different person when the sun is up." Even to her, the excuse sounded lame.

"And what happens if you're still with him when the sun goes down?"

"It's not like I have any other way to get there."

"Do you want me to see if Grant can borrow a horse for you?"

She shook her head. "It's more than that. Without Gwyl I have no idea how to get there."

"You're not doing this for me, are you? Because Kaeder will throw me out when I run out of money."

"No. I'm doing it for me. What happens when he finds out I'm marked too?"

"Take care."

"I plan to."

Gideon stood there silently a moment longer before he nodded and turned away, leaving the room.

After dropping the book on the chest, she stared at the closed door. Deciding to use the bathroom before she headed to bed, she opened the door to see Buddy lay on the floor between the two rooms, sleeping. He opened one eye and seeing it was her, closed it again. Finch didn't seem to be around. After she'd finished in the bathroom, she crouched in front of Buddy and patted his head. Guilt twisted through her. She'd put off the words long enough.

"Buddy?" She waited until his eyes opened again. "It's your choice, boy. Who do you want to stay with? Finch or me? Go and sit in front of the door to one of our rooms. Whichever door you sit in front of, that's who you're choosing to stay with."

Buddy sat up, looking from one door to the other. He stood, licking her face several times before he walked over and sat in front of Finch's closed door.

She wanted to tell him no. Beg him to stay with her. "I wish you could tell me why."

Buddy barked once, loud and clear.

Finch's door swung open and he stood there, yawning. "What's wrong? Why did you call me?" He looked at Buddy when he spoke.

Buddy made several sounds that were a cross between a yip and a whine.

Finch grinned, turning to Quinn. "He's staying with me?" When Buddy barked softly, Finch looked down at him. "Okay. I will." He faced Quinn again. "He said to tell you I can understand him. He likes that."

"I don't blame him. I'm glad he's found someone who does."

Finch's grin vanished. "You won't change your mind? You aren't going to take him away?"

"No. He can stay with you for as long as he likes." She couldn't help smiling when Finch knelt on the floor to throw his arms around Buddy. She decided to leave them to it.

Kicking off her sneakers, she tumbled into bed, trying not to think about Buddy's decision. Even though she could understand why, it hurt. Closing her eyes, she drifted off to sleep. Surprisingly undisturbed by nightmares.

She was woken by the door being hesitantly knocked on. Stumbling over her sneakers, she slid her feet into them before answering the door. Finch stood there, looking between her and the exit. When he stepped back, she looked in the direction he had continually glanced and saw Gwyl standing in the doorway. "Thanks."

"He said you'd saddle his horse. He's never said that before. Do you think he's unhappy with the way I do it?"

She dragged her gaze away from Gwyl. "No. He wants to talk to me."

"I'll–" He sent another glance towards Gwyl. "Well–" Again he struggled to finish a sentence. "If you–" He gestured towards his room. "I'll leave you to…" this time his sentence trailed off instead of ending abruptly. He made another gesture towards his room before retreating to it, closing the door. Buddy remained sitting between the two rooms.

Quinn was almost tempted to ask him if he was going to desert her too. She returned her attention to Gwyl, who continued to wait in the doorway. The light from outside was rapidly fading. Not wanting to have to talk to him once the sun set, she hurried towards him.

"My horse."

She looked between him and Sweet Pea, having expected he'd want her answer first. "Okay." It didn't take her long to saddle the blood bay and lead her to Gwyl.

He took the reins from her. "You have made your decision?"

"Yes." When he appeared to still be waiting, she clarified her answer. "I'll go with you to Ganat Castle at sunrise tomorrow."

He swung up into his saddle. "Come alone and bring only the book. I'll meet you in the courtyard."

She watched him ride away. She felt the sun set, fear filling her with how close he was. What had she done? Reminding herself she'd chosen the only option possible didn't make the fear go. That went when Gwyl left the area, the cries of the hunt sounding in the far distance. She needed food, a shower and a lantern. Before the sun rose she wanted to know that book off by heart.

All throughout the night, she read the book between stabling and saddling horses. As dawn grew near, she began to wish she'd used some of those moments to sleep. Tomorrow was probably going to be far longer than she wished.

Gideon came to see her a little before sunrise, wishing her luck. She'd already woken Finch and stood in the courtyard, returning Gideon's hug, the book clutched in one hand.

Gideon drew away from her. "Be careful."

"I will."

"I wish I could help you."

"It's okay."

"I still feel like it's my fault."

She smiled. "We could spend all day trying to figure out who's to blame and still not be able to choose anyone." When fear rushed in on her, she looked towards the alley. She was surprise to see Gwyl standing there when the sun hadn't risen yet, Sweet Pea at his shoulder.

"Do you want me to wait with you until the sun rises?"

She shook her head, not bothering to look towards Gideon. "I'll see you this afternoon."

"I hope so." He stayed beside her a moment longer before he went inside the main building.

Chapter Thirty

Quinn remained where she stood, not daring to take a single step towards him until the sun rose. She remembered far too clearly last time she'd faced him here. His eyes glittered as much now as they had then. As the fear continued to surround her, she tightened her fist. The iron she wore felt solid and comforting, but it wasn't enough to completely cut through the fear.

It disappeared the moment the sun rose and she watched the change in Gwyl. The predatory look faded and the glitter left his eyes. Even the way he held himself changed. He no longer looked like he was barely restraining himself from leaping on his prey. She slowly walked towards him, ready to run if the hunter remained.

He held up a leather pouch when she stopped in front of him. "This is yours."

She frowned. "I've never owned a leather pouch."

A smile escaped, gone as quick as it had come. "The contents."

She took the pouch and tipped it into her hand, surprised to see the other iron ring. The one she'd lost in her fight against him. Slipping it on her finger, she handed back the pouch.

He put it in his belt pouch. "Do you have something to carry the book in? Something not as cumbersome as your bag of flowers."

This time it was her that momentarily smiled. "No."

"We'll deal with that first." He swung up into the saddle and held out his hand.

She hesitated, but was obviously as insane as Gideon thought she was. Taking his hand, she was soon seated behind him, holding him in a way that didn't let her rings touch him. They headed further into the Fringes and she clung to Gwyl even though Sweet Pea wasn't going fast. The area they travelled through was full of half fallen down buildings and piles of rubbish. She wouldn't have been surprised if the people in this neighbourhood would have been willing to take on the leader of the Hunt. They stopped in front of a building that seemed a little more intact than the others on the street, both dismounting.

"Wait out here for me. If anyone approaches, call me. Do you still have the leaf I gave you?"

"Yes." Her gaze kept darting to the shadowy areas along the street. "You won't be long, will you?"

He didn't bother answering, striding inside.

She stared after him for several minutes until she remembered to keep an eye on her surroundings. She saw a flicker of movement in some of the tumbledown buildings around her and she was sure a creature had peered around the corner of the building across the street. A noise behind her had her spinning to face the building Gwyl had entered. Seeing him didn't bring the relief she'd expected. There was a definite gleam in his eyes and she wondered what had put it there.

Reaching her, he held out a leather satchel. "More than enough space for the book and whatever you might find at the castle." After she took the satchel from him, he swung into the saddle.

She stared up at him. His words brought to mind exactly what she needed to do. "I'm not sure if I'm going to be able to steal from Tamek." How many times, when she was younger, had she been told that stealing was wrong?

"Tamek doesn't own anything you will take. The ones everything belongs to no longer live. Their blood stains the cover of the book." He held out his hand.

Trying to ignore the images his words brought to mind, she slipped the book into the satchel and dropped the strap over her head, putting one arm through it so it sat against her hip. Taking his hand, she let him seat her behind him.

Gwyl turned the horse in the direction they'd come from and they soon left the Fringes behind. As the day grew warmer, Quinn wished she could put more space between her and Gwyl's unnatural heat. She kept glancing in the direction of the sun, trying to figure out how much time had passed by how it crept up the sky. She had no idea, but guessed it had to be over an hour by the time Gwyl stopped in a forest by a stone wall that towered over them.

"Where are we?" She slipped off the horse.

Gwyl joined her on the ground. "The external wall of Ganat Castle. According to the book, one of the entrances is nearby."

She studied the wall. It all looked exactly the same to her. Opening up the satchel, she took out the book and flicked through it. Finding the appropriate page she read it over again. Even with using landmarks and knowing where the hidden catch was, it still took several minutes to find the location of the secret entrance. She returned the book to the satchel and opened the door, staring at the blackness a set of steps lead into. "I should have brought my torch."

"Human devices are unreliable." He held up his hand and after a few seconds, a dozen fireflies landed on his palm. He moved his hand to her shoulder. "Go with her and light the way unless you are asked to hide. If she should need you to light the way again, she'll ask you to shine."

Watching the fireflies land on her shoulder made her feel uncomfortable. She would have preferred her torch. But she guessed they had to be better than something like cockroaches.

"This is as far as I can go. I'll wait for you here."

She wanted to beg him to come with her. The darkness didn't look safe. Anything could be hiding in it. "Why can't you come any further?"

"Do you really wish to stand here talking when the day continues getting closer to sunset?"

She almost said yes. Forcing herself to enter the secret entrance, she tried not to let her imagination run wild. It was impossible. Each step towards the darkness had her coming up with more fearsome creatures hiding in there. It didn't help that the fireflies didn't light very far ahead of her. Several times she looked over her shoulder towards the exit and the daylight that was getting further away. Not long after leaving the flight of steps behind, she reached a crossroads. Recalling the diagrams in the book, she went right.

The further in she travelled, the more she wanted to turn and run back to the daylight she could no longer see. Ahead in the darkness she heard the occasional noise and dreaded to think what might be down here with her. She finally reached the hidden door that led to the rooms beneath the castle where the treasure room was located. Taking a deep breath, she tried to steady the racing of her heart. It didn't help.

Before opening the hidden door, she took out the book and refreshed her memory on where to go. When she found herself with her ear pressed against the door before she opened it, she realised she was looking for flimsy excuses to postpone the inevitable.

Steadying shaking hands, she found the catch to make the door swing open and stepped inside. She didn't manage to get far before she was stopped by a barred gate across her way. Trying it, she found it locked. Panic rushed in on her and she needed to take several deep breaths before she was calm enough to go through the book and find an alternate route. She'd have to go nearly all the way back to the start. Again panic rushed through her and it took a minute to calm herself.

Returning the book to the satchel, she headed to the point where she needed to take a different direction. She had no idea how much time she'd wasted, but as long as she got out a couple of hours before dark everything would be fine. Gwyl would be able to return her to Masquerade's stables before it was time for him to hunt. And tonight he could go after Tamek.

She finally came to one of the other hidden doors leading to the rooms under the castle. When she entered it, she was relieved to find there was nothing preventing her from continuing. In this section occasional lanterns hung from the ceiling. They looked nothing like the ones at Masquerade. Those ones were ordinary oil lamps while these ones appeared to glow. She had no idea how they were lit, but suspected it was from magic.

Reaching the treasure room, she pressed her ear against it. Like last time she'd done that, she couldn't hear a thing. The only way she'd be able to find out what was inside was by entering. Taking out the book again, she went to the appropriate section.

She'd try and find the hidden areas to the right when she entered. Following the directions, she opened the door to the treasure room.

It wasn't what she'd expected. She supposed she'd been thinking something along the lines of Ali Baba. There were no chests overflowing with gold here. In the centre of the room were statues. Some were embellished with gold and jewels. The smaller statues were solid gold. Around the outside were large timber chests, all closed and locked with padlocks hanging on the front. Everything was surprisingly neat and tidy with lanterns hanging from the ceiling similar to the ones in the corridor.

Closing the door behind her, she headed right, trying to figure out the correct spot on the wall. It took far longer than she'd expected. Opening up the hidden compartment, she was relieved to find a diamond necklace. Another five items to gather. According to the book, that would bring the total to around the ten thousand mark, but she wanted to make sure the prices hadn't changed much in the past couple of years. No one had updated it since the previous owner had died. She tried not to think about the bloodstains on the cover. It was a fail. If she was caught would her blood end up staining the cover too? She shied away from that thought.

Wishing she had a watch, she continued to gather the rest of the jewellery she'd decided to take. The longer she was in the room, the more nervous she became. There was really only one exit. The other exit had a barred gate partway along the corridor leading from it and she didn't have the key to unlock it.

Putting the last of the jewellery into the satchel, she headed for the door, freezing when she heard sounds outside. When someone spoke, her legs nearly gave way. Forcing them to work, she scurried across the room to the other exit. It took all her effort to concentrate on getting the door open instead of continually looking towards the main door. The moment the hidden door opened she slipped inside, closing it behind her. Worried there might be some small gaps light could shine through she whispered, "Hide."

The fireflies went out immediately and the corridor was plunged into darkness. Pressing her hand against the door, she barely managed not to tell them to shine. She'd never been scared of the dark before today. Or maybe it was the small area that felt like it was closing in on her. Pressing her ear against the door, she listened. There seemed to be two people talking. She had no idea what they were saying through the stone and could only hear indistinct voices.

Time seemed to drag and she didn't know what to do if they remained in there once the sun set. Would Gwyl come after her in the castle? Would he remember all the hidden passages? He didn't seem to recall any other things from when he was Baenen. Scared to move away from the door, but equally scared to remain by it waiting for Gwyl to come hunting, she kept one hand on the wall and stretched the other one out in front of her as she shuffled along the passageway. Maybe she'd get lucky and the locked door partway along could be opened.

Her fingers connected with a metal bar and she ran them across the bars looking for the latch. Unable to immediately find it, she clung to the bars, fighting against the panic that rose. Gaining control, she slid her hands across the barred door near the wall. The latch was lower than she'd expected. She tried it. Her heart plummeted. The only way out of this passage was the hidden door behind her.

She rested her head against the bars, still clinging to them. It took her several minutes before she could face the direction she'd come from. It was another couple of minutes before she was able to shuffle her way back along the passage, hand outstretched and one against the wall. Reaching the hidden door, she pressed her ear against the stone. For a moment she thought they'd left. Until one of them spoke. She closed her eyes, not knowing what to do. How much time had passed? She slid down the door to sit on the cold floor. What was she going to do?

Chapter Thirty-One

Time stretched out and Quinn drifted off to sleep a couple of times as she waited for whoever was in the treasure room to leave. What were they doing? She would have loved to have been able to open the door slightly and peer through at them. A new noise could be heard and she realised it was the sound of coins being poured into something. She strained to hear anything else, but everything was silent on the other side.

She continued to listen carefully, but nothing else could be heard. Had they left? She counted to a hundred. Was that enough time? She counted to five hundred. Surely she'd waited long enough.

Rising to her feet, she ran her hand over the door, searching for the mechanism to open it. Finding it, she activated it and the door started to swing open. She grabbed hold of the door, her hand tightening on it as her gaze scanned the room. Seeing it empty, she sagged against the doorway.

Forcing herself to enter the treasure room, she closed the hidden door behind her. One of the chests was slightly ajar, the padlock on the floor in front of it. She couldn't resist opening the lid. Now that was what she'd expected of a treasure room. It was half full of small gold coins. She started to close the chest, stopping with the lid half open. Grabbing a handful, she dropped them into her satchel. She didn't want to risk not having enough. No way was she returning to the treasure room ever again. She stared at the coins for nearly a minute before she shut the lid. It was odd thinking that in a way Tamek would be paying for the Hunt to take him down.

Frowning, she glanced around the room. No, not Tamek. This treasure room had been here long before him. Those he'd killed would pay the Hunt. Feeling a little better about having raided the treasure room, she strode to the main door and opened it enough to peer out. The corridor was empty. Stepping out of the room, she closed the door behind her.

She'd done it. She'd finally escaped from the treasure room. A smile started to form as she took a step forward. Freezing, she stared at the man who came into the corridor ahead of her, also stopping when he saw her. She moved first, spinning to run in the opposite direction.

"Stop!"

She clutched the satchel to her side, racing through corridors as she tried to think of the many drawings she'd poured over throughout the night. Nothing came to mind. All she could think of was the pound of feet behind her and the warnings to stop. Running through a doorway, she found the only option was a flight of steps. Taking them two at a time, she struggled to work out where she was.

It came to her in a flash, gasping as she continued to run, trying to ignore the burning sensation in her legs and lungs. She was heading to the ground floor of the castle. An area likely to be filled with people. She was dead. Forget about worrying if she'd be caught by the Hunt. A castle full of Fae were about to do Gwyl's job for him.

Bursting into a large room, she raced past several startled people. Running through the doorway at the other side of the room, she collided with someone. Wincing at the pain in her shoulder she stumbled, but kept going. There was no way she was about to obey any of the people shouting after her to stop.

Something whistled past and her mouth dropped

open as an arrow punched a hole in a glass window across the room from her, cracks radiating out from the hole. Glancing over her shoulder, she nearly tripped when she saw the amount of people following, many wielding weapons. She was so dead. Changing direction, she headed for the broken window, grabbing a timber chair as she passed a small dining setting.

Reaching the window, she swung the chair at it several times. As soon as enough of the glass was gone from the window, she tossed the chair at those following, hitting a man who'd nearly reached her, wishing they'd stop yelling. Placing her hands on the sill, she ignored the sharp pain, vaulting outside, the fireflies leaving her. Not stopping, she glanced at her hand. Blood spread across her palm. Her stomach turned and she closed her fist, breathing in sharply at the increase in pain. There was no time to do anything about it. From the sounds behind her, she was still being chased. Looking skywards, she saw the day was drawing to a close.

Taking the autumn leaf from her pocket, she clutched it tightly. Gwyl had mentioned it, but with how close it was to sunset would he take it as an invitation to hunt her? Ahead of her a man came out of a smaller building. It didn't take him long to decide to run towards her. A glance over her shoulder showed those following were gaining on her.

Raising the leaf to her lips, she spoke his name, the satchel bumping against her hip. A breeze dragged the leaf from her fingers and she watched as it swirled away. The man running towards her came closer and she veered off to the side. She had no idea where she was going. All the diagrams she'd studied were forgotten in the sounds of pursuit.

Ahead she spotted a castle gate. Through it she caught glimpses of the forest surrounding the castle. There was no way she could make it. But she wasn't about to slow down. A body crashed into her and she sprawled across the grass, gasping for breath.

Hands roughly dragged her to her feet, remaining on her arms to prevent her from escaping. People surrounded her, including soldiers with weapons. There was no escape, but she wasn't about to go quietly.

She stepped back hard on the foot of the man who held her. He barely loosened his grip. She tried to elbow him. It didn't help. He lifted her off the ground so she hung limply in his grip. A man pushed through the crowd, coming to a stop in front of her. He had dark brown eyes and features a little similar to Gwyl's.

"Who are you and what are you doing here?"

She pressed her lips together. Telling him wouldn't help.

"You won't like the methods I'll use if you don't answer me."

She doubted she'd like the methods he'd use if he found out why she was here. "Are you Tamek?"

"Why?"

"I have a message for Tamek."

"What is the message?"

"Are you Tamek?"

The man nodded once. "Now tell me the message."

"Set me down first."

Tamek laughed, a sharp mocking sound. "You will tell me without anyone letting you go." His gaze went past her to the man holding her. "Take her to the dungeons."

Before anyone could move, Gwyl galloped through the castle gates, leaning low over Sweet Pea. People scattered out of his way and Tamek spun to face the noise. The man holding her let go, diving to the side when Gwyl came straight for him.

Tamek dived in the other direction. "Baenen!"

Gwyl scooped Quinn up and deposited her behind him on Sweet Pea.

She clung to him, the heat of his body warming

hers. The light was fading and she had no idea what to do once the sun set.

"Shoot him!" Tamek bellowed.

Arrows whistled past as they raced out the castle gates. Sweet Pea didn't slow and the two of them remained low as they galloped across the road that led into the forest. Once the castle was out of sight, the horse slowed and Gwyl sat up, guiding her into the trees.

When the horse stopped, Quinn slid off, watching as Gwyl joined her on the ground. "Thank you." Meeting his gaze, she noticed the gleam in his eyes. Sunset wasn't far away.

He looked down at his side where her blood was smeared across his skin. Reaching out, he checked her hand. Without speaking, he took a piece of cloth from his belt pouch and wrapped it around her hand.

"Thanks." Her hand still ached, but the flow of blood had slowed.

"It isn't possible to return you to Masquerade in the few minutes left until sunset." He glanced towards the satchel. "Did you get something of sufficient value? I promised to set aside all other hunts to track down Tamek if you did."

Some of her worries faded. She might actually survive the night after all. "Take what you want." She slid the strap of the satchel over her head and held it out to him.

Gwyl rummaged around in the satchel and took out several pieces of jewellery, dropping them into his belt pouch. He handed the satchel back. "You need to tell me who you want hunted. Who do you send the Hunt after?"

A shiver went through her as the sun set and the gleam in his eyes turned to a glitter. His body tensed and fearing he might attack her, she spoke. "Tamek of Ganat Castle." The words tumbled over each other in her hurry. She said them again. This time slower. "Tamek of Ganat Castle." Her heart pounded as she stared into his glittering eyes.

"It will be done." He gathered Sweet Pea's reins.

"Wait. How will I get back to Masquerade?" She placed her uninjured hand on his arm and he shrugged it off. "Baenen." She wanted to beg him not to desert her in the forest. There were wolves and who knew what else.

The glitter in his eyes momentarily faded and he drew Sweet Pea's head down to whisper in her ear. "Stable her when you're done with her." The glitter returned to his eyes before he turned and ran through the forest towards Ganat Castle, leaving Sweet Pea behind.

The last glimpse Quinn caught of him was with his head thrown back as his howl echoed through the forest. A moment later she heard answering cries. She rubbed at the goosebumps that rose on her arms. Not sure if Sweet Pea would let her on, she gathered the reins and cautiously reached for the saddle. When the horse remained still, she swung into it. Remembering Mairwin's carriage horses, she said, "Take me to Masquerade Nightclub, please." Sweet Pea turned towards the road and Quinn hoped she'd understood.

When she eventually saw the Fringes in the distance, she nearly sagged against the horse in relief. "Thank you, girl." She patted the horse's neck.

As soon as they reached the courtyard, she slid off the horse and led her the rest of the way into the stables. She'd nearly finished putting Sweet Pea in her stall when Finch strode inside.

"Gideon has been out here every ten minutes asking if you're back yet."

She closed the stall door behind her. "I'll go in and let him know. Is he in the bar?"

"I wouldn't worry about it, he'll be out here again in another two minutes."

She started to stride towards the door, not wanting to leave Gideon wondering.

"Quinn."

She looked over her shoulder at Finch.

"I'm glad you made it back from wherever you went."

"Thanks." She had no idea if he knew all the details of what she'd been up to, but had no plans to tell him. She ignored the prompt in his words. The less people who knew the Hunt wanted her, the better.

He gestured towards her hand. "Try the balm on it."

With a nod, she continued to the doorway. Stepping into the courtyard she saw Gideon come out of the far door.

Chapter Thirty-Two

The moment Gideon saw Quinn, he ran towards her, engulfing her in a hug. "I thought they'd caught you. When I heard them howling, I thought they'd caught you. I didn't know what to do."

She returned his hug. "Things didn't go as smoothly as I'd hoped." She let him go.

"What happened?"

She gave him the highlights. Glancing past him to the main building, she asked, "Shouldn't you be inside? Dancing?"

He shrugged. "It's a slow night."

"Maybe that's because you've been out here every ten minutes. Finch told me."

Gideon chuckled. "He was exaggerating. I'm sure it was only every twelve." He sobered. "What happens next?"

"I don't know."

"How will you know if the Hunt is no longer after you? Or if you can stop them from hunting me?"

"I don't know." When he started to speak again, she interrupted. "I really don't know anything, Gideon. But I will let you know as soon as I figure it all out."

"Okay." He glanced over his shoulder. "I should probably get back and see if I can earn a few more coins. In case."

She nodded, watching as he strode to the door, looking back once before he entered the building. Her hand still aching, she decided to try Finch's balm. He waited for her inside.

"You look beat. Get some sleep."

"But–"

"Buddy and I can take care of things here."

She started to argue again then decided she'd be an idiot if she did. "Thanks." Walking past Sweet Pea, her steps slowed. How would she know what had happened? And how long until she knew? Should she tell Finch to wake her if Gwyl returned for his horse? She paused near her door. Surely he wouldn't be back before sunrise.

After using the bathroom she entered her room. She didn't close the door until she'd lit the lamp she'd got yesterday, when she'd been reading the book. Sitting on the bed, she unwrapped her hand and applied balm to the cuts, wincing at the pain. If the balm didn't work, she had no idea what to do. Did they have doctors around here?

Yawning, she kicked off her shoes and dropped the satchel onto the floor, lying back. Closing her eyes for a minute, she fell asleep with the lantern on. It felt like only a moment before a sound had her opening them, but guessed it was far longer with how rested she felt.

Gwyl stood above her, blood streaking his chest. Far more than she'd left on him. His antlers were gone and there was a wolf at his side, one of the ones that were as big as a small pony. She continued to lie on her bed, not sure there was enough space in her little room for her to rise to her feet. In the distance she heard the howl of wolves and the one at Gwyl's side glanced in that direction.

"You–" She didn't know how to ask him what had happened. 'You killed him' sounded wrong.

"I can't go inside looking like this. I need to ask Kaeder for sanctuary."

Her gaze met his and she realised what else was different. "Baenen?"

He smiled, the one she'd only glimpsed twice. "Yes. Thank you." He held out his hand, drawing her to her feet when she took it. "You asked me once if I regretted joining the Hunt." He remained silent for a moment. "I can't regret something I sought out of grief, but if I'd been forced to take your life, then I would have had regrets."

"There's no kill you made that you regretted?"

"No one seeks out the Hunt unless they're desperate. None are innocent if the Hunt has been sent after them."

"Gideon is."

"The boy who killed a Dryad?"

"The human who helped his father chop down a tree that he didn't know belonged to a Dryad. The Fae don't exist in our world."

He reached out and ran his thumb across her cheekbone. "We don't?"

She ignored the amusement in his tone. "Obviously you do, but we don't know that. He thought he was removing a tree that was ruining someone's fence and was far too big for the yard it was planted in."

Baenen dug into his belt pouch, drawing out a green cloth bag. "Give him this. It's of no use to me anyway. If I don't have it on me when Gwyl collects them in a week, then I can't give it to him."

"This is what you've been using to track down

Gideon?" At his nod, she looked in the bag and found short strands of sandy brown hair. Closing the bag, she looked at him. "The Hunt won't be able to go after him now?"

Baenen shook his head. "They'll think the hunt has been completed since the scent isn't with the others I carry."

Her gaze momentarily dropped to his belt pouch. "You carry all the scents in there?"

He shook his head. "Only the active hunts. Some take longer than others to complete. Ones that take too long eventually gain less attention as other hunts are focused on. Especially when we know they're in a sanctuary."

"I'll go and get Kaeder for you." She needed to give Gideon the strands of his hair.

The wolf left the room and Baenen started to follow her. He stopped when the cry of the Hunt seemed to echo all around them.

"What's going on?"

"Don't leave Masquerade. Whatever you do, don't leave."

"Why?"

"They will hunt us for the next seven days."

"What!" She nearly winced at the sound of her screech, sounding far too much like Marley. "Why?"

"It's the way of things. The new Gwyl has seven days to hunt the old Gwyl and the one who broke the curse."

"Why didn't you tell me?"

"Seven days is far less than seven years."

"Yes, but–" She'd thought it was over. That she was safe.

"Go and ask Kaeder to speak to me." He stepped out of her room.

Slipping her feet into her sneakers, she followed, freezing when Kaeder burst into the stables.

"They're surrounding the place." His finger pointed at Baenen. "They want him. I offered them the other boy, but they weren't interested. Said they wanted the old Gwyl. And the one who broke the curse." He pointed his finger at Quinn. "Is that you?"

Baenen stepped forward, the wolf at his side. "I can pay you."

"It wouldn't be enough. No one can get in or out with that pack surrounding the place. You have to go. Now."

A howl started up outside, lasting for ages, making goosebumps rise on Quinn's arms. "They'll kill us."

"That isn't my problem." Kaeder glared at her. "You've been nothing but trouble. I should have negotiated a deal with the Fae wanting a diplomat. He asked for you."

She remembered him. It had been the first day she'd worked in the stables. "You can't go making deals on my behalf. You don't own me."

"You would have done it. For your sister." Kaeder's lips twisted into a smile.

Quinn forced herself to hold her ground, refusing to step back from his unsettling expression. "You would have regretted it." She wasn't about to let Kaeder think he could get away with making deals over her in the future.

"It doesn't matter. The opportunity is gone and I want you out."

Gideon entered the stables. "Don't throw her out."

Kaeder spun to face Gideon. "Do you want me to throw you out too?"

Quinn hurried forward, pressing the bag into Gideon's hands. "Don't get yourself into trouble over me. Not when you're finally out of it."

He opened the bag. "Is this…"

She smiled. "Yeah."

"I–"

"No more talk. Out. Both of you out. And anyone else who wants to argue about it."

When Gideon opened his mouth to speak, Quinn

interrupted. "You're safe now. Don't interfere with the Hunt. You know what happens when you do that." She smiled wryly. "I'll see you in the morning." If she was lucky.

"Is anyone listening to me?" Kaeder demanded.

"I would ask that you allow my wolf to remain the night," Baenen said.

"It's not a kennel."

"I'll take care of her." Finch stood in the doorway of his room, Buddy hiding in the shadows behind him. "It'll be no hardship."

Quinn hoped Kaeder couldn't see Buddy from where he stood.

"Five gold coins."

Baenen withdrew them from his belt pouch and gave them to Kaeder before saddling his horse. As soon as he was mounted, he rode over to Quinn and held out his hand.

She glanced at Kaeder before she took Baenen's hand. Kaeder wasn't about to relent. She hoped Baenen knew what he was doing. The regular howls from the Hunt sounded like there'd be no place they could sneak out from. Not unless Sweet Pea could fly.

Baenen rode the horse to the courtyard, stopping well back from the start of the alley and the pack that stood there waiting for him. In the middle was a young man with antlers rising from his head and no shirt. "Hold on."

She clung to Baenen, realising that the unnatural heat no longer radiated from him. "What are we going to do?"

"Run."

She wasn't certain if he'd been answering her or giving an order to Sweet Pea, or possibly both. The horse leapt forward, racing across the courtyard and jumping those waiting for them. Sweet Pea didn't slow. She galloped through the streets, the Hunt following, howls filling the night.

Quinn continued to cling to Baenen listening to the pursuing Hunt. There was no way they could escape. Nor would they be able to outrun them. The Hunt was slowly gaining on them. She wondered who'd taken his place. Which member of the Hunt had wanted revenge the most? If they survived the night, she'd ask.

They left the Fringes behind, taking the road through the forest, the Hunt continuing to follow. Quinn couldn't stop checking over her shoulder. They were as fearsome as ever. Weapons gleamed in flaming torchlight. Large wolves ran with the horse riders, sharp teeth clearly visible. They weren't about to let them live if they caught them.

They burst into a clearing and Quinn noticed the sky was growing lighter. She began to pray the sun would rise even though she'd never before prayed in her life. Did the Fae have their own gods? She didn't know. But if they did and she'd known who they were, she would have prayed to them too. Another glance over her shoulder had her closing her eyes, unwilling to check again. If the sun took much longer to rise, it would be too late.

Chapter Thirty-Three

Quinn noticed the change immediately. The fear she hadn't registered, she'd become so accustomed to feeling it each night, disappeared. The sounds of the Hunt ended and when she looked, she saw they were turning away, riding back the way they'd come. She was surprised when Sweet Pea continued at the same pace, not slowing now the Hunt was no longer chasing them.

Sweet Pea didn't begin to slow until Ganat Castle came into sight. "What are you doing?" Surely he didn't think going there was a good idea.

"Going home."

"You killed someone there."

Baenen glanced at her over his shoulder. "The pack did. And it was more than one. Any who tried to protect him lost their lives. The smart ones ran. Those that were left are loyal to my family and await my return."

She had no idea what to say so remained quiet. When Sweet Pea stopped at the front of the castle, she half expected soldiers to run out brandishing weapons. Instead, a boy about half her age came to take Sweet Pea once they'd dismounted. She watched the boy until he was out of sight, not realising Baenen had walked away until he spoke from near the castle door.

"Is something wrong?"

She started to shake her head, but shrugged instead. "The rest of the things I took from your treasure room are still at Masquerade."

He came forward, holding out his hand. "We'll get them later."

She stared at him. He looked young. As young as her. And lost. Or was that sorrow deep in his eyes? There were far more differences in him than she'd first thought. Even with the blood streaking his body he didn't look like the menacing hunter he'd once been. "What happened to the antlers?"

"I left them where they fell. Near Tamek's body."

She quickly spoke before he had the chance to give her any details she might not want to hear. "How will we manage to avoid the Hunt for seven nights? Or is it only six now?"

He lowered his hand that she hadn't taken. "Six. Do you want me to apologise?"

"No."

"What do you want?"

"What do you mean?"

"You've broken my curse."

She frowned, still not understanding what he was trying to say. "I know."

Baenen stared at her a moment more before he smiled. "You don't understand what that means, do you?"

She shook her head.

"I owe you a great debt."

She shook her head again. "It set Gideon and me free too. Well, in six days I'll be free."

"In seven years you would have been free if you could have remained at Masquerade. Or some other sanctuary. In seven years I would still have been cursed to seek revenge for others when I most needed it for myself."

"Oh."

His smile remained in place and he held out his hand again. "At least let me offer you the hospitality of my home. I know it's far from full payment for everything I owe you, but at least it's a start."

She placed her hand in his. "Who is the new Gwyl?"

"Mairwin's brother."

"That can't be good." She remembered what Gideon had said after they'd helped Mairwin with her carriage. 'You don't annoy the Fae. Ever. They always retaliate.' Mairwin was certainly the type to want her revenge.

"I doubt it will be good." Baenen led her inside, sending a servant ahead to prepare a room. They followed at a more leisurely pace and he showed her to a room where clothes were laid out for her and a door stood open, leading to a bathroom. "I'll return to escort you to the dining room." Stepping into the hallway, he closed the door behind him.

She stared after him, dazed. Going from stablehand to valued guest in a castle was not something she'd expected. Especially not after spending the previous day breaking into the castle and stealing some of the family jewels. Not knowing how long it would be before Baenen returned, she gathered the dress and retreated to the bathroom.

Once she was clean and dressed, her hair still damp, she stared at her hand, only a pink scar where the worst cut had been. Finch's balm was amazing. Lowering her hand, she stared at the bathroom door. She couldn't hide in here the rest of the day. Opening the door she saw Baenen waited for her. He stood beside the bed, coming forward to run his hand over her hair. The smell of rich earth filled the room and a gentle breeze tugged at her hair. She felt it dry. "How did you do that?"

"Wood Fae find it easy to work with nature. I drew the moisture from your hair."

"Can anyone do that?"

"Is that what you want? Your own magic? You would have to remove your iron first. Do you plan to stay in this realm forever?"

She could go home. Once the next six nights were ended, she could return home. The thought jarred her. Marley would be thrilled. Her parents would be ecstatic. Buddy would be safe with Finch. She didn't know how she felt about it anymore. She should be happy, but she wasn't. "I don't know. I thought returning home was what I wanted." An image of Scout came to mind. Excited to learn the realms of the Fae had plenty of unmapped territory. Was she like Scout? She hadn't thought so. Not after her own failed attempt at exploring.

"You don't have to decide immediately." Baenen

held out his hand. "Would you like to join me for our second meal together?"

She couldn't help smiling at the memory of their first meal. "Does it count? You were a different person then."

"It wasn't Gwyl who asked you to dine." He continued to hold out his hand.

Staring at him, she took a step forward. "Who was it?"

"Do you really need to ask?"

Taking his hand, she could see the answer in his eyes. The moment their hands touched she saw a change in his face. "What's wrong?"

"Nothing of importance." He continued to hold her hand, stepping into the hallway.

Wanting an answer, she drew her hand from his. She was about to demand what was wrong again when he stopped and faced her. She knew. "Why didn't you say something?" She took off her rings.

"They're a good weapon and the Hunt is after us."

He'd suffered enough. Turning back to the room, she tossed them onto the bed before facing him again. "I have my necklaces." She tried to figure out what his expression meant. "What's wrong now?"

"You know very little about this world."

She shrugged. "Hardly anything at all." But she

was learning all the time. She remembered all the questions she'd asked Derwyn. She wouldn't need to return for her second day of questioning.

"Standing near iron is almost as painful as touching it."

"What do you want me to do?"

"Leave them on. Or at least one. You'll be safer that way, for now."

She hesitated. She didn't want to remove the necklaces or hurt him. In the end she drew them over her head and tossed them on the bed with the rings. If she needed them, she could put them on later. "You said something about food?"

He nodded, taking her hand again and leading her to the dining room. Servants dished out the food as soon as they were seated.

Quinn looked from the food to Baenen twice before she could bring herself to speak. "Is this safe for me? For a human?"

"Of course it is." He sounded offended.

"You already pointed out I know very little about your world."

He reached across the table and took her hand. "I'd never willingly do anything to harm you."

"Willingly? What about unwillingly?"

"I already have, while I was cursed."

"Oh." She couldn't think of a single intelligent comment to make.

Smiling, he let go of her hand. "Eat. We need sleep before the sun sets."

She didn't want to think about what sunset would bring. "How will we hide from them?"

"We'll travel to your world. When we hear them calling out, then we'll return here. My magic isn't strong enough to be able to travel endlessly between the realms to make it difficult for them to keep track of us."

"Where in my world?" She had a mouthful of food while she waited for him to answer.

"Wherever you wish. It needs to be somewhere you've been before and that you can picture clearly."

"Don't portals lead to particular places?"

"Most do, but we won't be using portals. They're usually too risky. Natural ones often have someone guarding them."

She remembered the Trolls at the bridge portal. And the Knight Commander. "How will we get there?"

"With magic." He opened his hand to show an autumn leaf. Closing it, he moved his hand closer to her before opening it again. This time a dainty white flower lay in his palm.

Once again she found herself speechless. Taking the flower, she examined it. As far as she could tell, it seemed real. Raising it to her nose, she breathed in the delicate scent. "So the next six days should be a breeze?"

"I'll do whatever is necessary to keep you safe."

He hadn't really answered her question. Deciding she didn't want to push for an answer, she placed the flower beside her plate. "It's pretty."

"It was my mother's favourite flower."

"What were they like, your family?" For a moment she thought he might not answer.

His words were hesitant at first, but by the time they'd finished eating he'd told her about his family and some of the trouble he'd followed his brothers into as a child. Eventually he rose from the table, holding out his hand. "I'll show you to your room. We should sleep. It'll be a long night."

Chapter Thirty-Four

Picking up the flower, Quinn took Baenen's hand and walked silently beside him to the room she'd used earlier. Stopping at the door, she looked up at him. "Will we be able to collect my clothes before we go to my world this afternoon? I much prefer jeans."

"Yours will be cleaned and returned to you before you wake. We will need to go to Masquerade so I can check on Maya."

"Who?"

"My wolf."

"How did she leave the Hunt?"

"She was never part of the Hunt, only ran at my side. I had her long before I was Gwyl." He continued to hold her hand.

"And Sweet Pea? Did you have her before too?"

He smiled. "She was born by flowering Sweet Peas and was so curious about them." He chuckled softly.

"I was about five and as fascinated by her as she was by the flowers."

She stared at him, caught by the tone of his voice and the expression on his face. "You care for her."

"She's part of my family. Her and Maya are all I have left of it. We wood Fae often tend to treat our animals like family." He chuckled again. "I remember my mother making me send Sweet Pea outside when she found her in my room. We've grown up together, like siblings." He took a step back from her, still holding her hand. "I should let you sleep."

Staring at her hand in his, she wanted to ask him so many questions. Obviously he liked her, but was that only because she'd broken his curse?

His hand tightened on hers. "Is something wrong?"

She met his gaze. How could she explain? Her gaze lowered to his lips. Let him figure it out. Leaning forward, her lips momentarily met his. "Goodnight." She took a step back, drawing her hand from his. "Or morning." Noticing his bemused expression she grinned before disappearing into the room, shutting the door. She leaned against the door, closing her eyes, her grin still in place as she clutched the flower. She was still there when he whispered the word 'goodnight' and she heard his footsteps travel down the hallway. Pushing away from the door, she headed to the bed, leaving the flower on the bedside table. The bed looked far more comfortable than the one she'd been using at Masquerade. Turning back the linen it didn't take her long to find out she was right. It was extremely comfortable. It was so comfortable she fell almost instantly asleep to be woken by a knock on her door.

"Who is it?" Her voice sounded unused and she wondered what time it was.

"I have your clean clothes, mistress."

"Uhm, bring them in?" She wasn't used to being waited on by servants. Normally she would have had her mum complaining she hadn't put away her folded and laundered clothes.

The servant, a human, opened the door. "I'll set them out in the bathroom for you. Lord Baenen requests that you join him in the dining room. I'll wait for you in the hallway and show you the way once you're ready for the day."

She nodded, not knowing what else to do. As soon as the servant stepped into the corridor, closing the door, she got out of bed and headed to the bathroom. It didn't take her long to get ready for the day. Dressed in her own clothes she felt more like herself.

Before she left the room she gathered her iron jewellery and slid it into a pocket, putting the flower in a separate pocket. She couldn't decide if she should take the jewellery with her tonight or not.

The servant left her in the dining room where Baenen waited for her. He took her hand, leading her to the table. When she was seated he was full of polite questions about how she'd slept and if there was anything she needed. She started to feel awkward.

Was he uncomfortable with her because she'd kissed him? There was probably only one way to find out. She didn't work up the courage to ask until they'd finished eating and he'd risen to his feet, holding out his hand as he waited to escort her outside to Sweet Pea.

She took his hand. "What's wrong? You seem extremely polite this afternoon."

"Nothing new is wrong."

"Are you sure?" She paused. "You don't have to worry about me kissing you again if you tell me you're not interested."

He stared at her a moment, surprise in his eyes. It was replaced by amusement. "What if the problem happens to be that I wish to kiss you again?"

She laughed, letting go of his hand to throw her arms around him. "This better not be because you feel you owe me or anything."

"The way I feel has nothing to do with my obligation to you." His lips met hers.

She clung to him, wishing they could remain here the rest of the afternoon. But it wasn't safe. Baenen had proven that when he'd broken the curse. She reluctantly drew away from him. "I suppose we should probably go."

"Sadly, yes." He led the way outside where he helped her sit behind him on Sweet Pea.

Wrapping her arms around him, she rested her head against him, disappointed that these days he wore a shirt. She could understand why he never had with the heat that had radiated off him when he was Gwyl.

The ride seemed far too short. When they dismounted, Quinn nearly groaned when she saw Mairwin paced Masquerade's courtyard. "Looks like she might have found out." She kept her voice low, not wanting Mairwin to hear.

The moment she spotted them, Mairwin strode forward. She jabbed a finger at Baenen's chest. "This is your fault."

Baenen pushed her hand away. "I wasn't the one who made him join the hunt. That was his choice."

"You didn't have to make him Gwyl after you."

"I had no control over that. The member of the

pack that wants revenge the most is always the new Gwyl."

Mairwin shook her head. "No. He isn't like that. You don't know him like I do."

"You don't know him like I do." Baenen's words were soft.

"He isn't a killer." Tears glittered in Mairwin's eyes. "If you don't return my brother to me, you will regret it."

"I'm sorry, Mairwin. I can't help you. This was your brother's choice. You and your family had more than enough chances to save him from this, but you didn't like your options. This is the result."

Quinn started to tell Mairwin that it was possible to break the curse. She had done it. Mairwin spoke before she could.

"No. Make someone else Gwyl. Take those antlers from him and give them to someone else."

"It doesn't work like that. They grew when he became Gwyl."

"I'll send the Hunt after you. Both of you. You've destroyed my family." Mairwin strode towards her horse.

Quinn hurried after her. "No. Wait. I know how to break the curse." The last thing she needed was the Hunt after her for seven years again.

Ignoring Quinn, Mairwin swung up into the saddle and turned the mare towards the alley.

"Mairwin, I can help you get your brother back." She crossed the distance between them, reaching for the woman.

Mairwin urged her horse forward, galloping down the alley.

Quinn stared after her, wanting to call her back. Her hands tightened into fists. There had to be some way to convince Mairwin. She couldn't survive with the Hunt after her for seven years.

Baenen stood at her shoulder, wrapping an arm around her waist. "You need to gather all your things. Don't leave a single strand of hair behind. If she has nothing to use for a scent she can't send them after us."

She doubted Mairwin was the sort of person to give up that easily, but she'd do as Baenen suggested. Inside the stables, both Finch and Gideon waited for them. She left Baenen to talk to Finch and asked Gideon to join her in her room. There was no time to waste if they wanted to be away from here before sunset.

"What are you going to do about Mairwin?" Gideon asked.

She wasn't surprised he'd heard with how loud

she'd been. "Try to make it impossible for her to find something to give to the Hunt." She packed up her gear. Most of it was still in her backpack. She had no idea how to figure out if she'd left any strands of hair behind.

"I don't think that'll stop her." He handed her a piece of paper. "I wanted to tell you I'm leaving with Grant today." He gestured to the paper she'd taken. "That's the directions to his place. If you ever wanted to visit me."

"Of course I'll visit."

"Where will you be staying?"

"Uhm…" She had no idea what to tell him.

"Ganat Castle."

She turned to see Baenen stood in the doorway, Maya at his side. So many questions tumbled through her mind. They didn't have time for them at the moment. "How do I find any strands of hair I've left behind?"

"When you've taken everything else from the room, I can find them if you give me a strand from your head." He moved out of the doorway.

She gathered up her backpack and satchel and stepped out of the room, Gideon following. Plucking a strand of hair from her head, she handed it over to him and watched as he wrapped it around his finger and held his hand out. Strands of hair flew from the room to join the one he held. He did the same in the bathroom when she told him it was the only other room she'd used. When he gave her the strands of hair, she put them in the satchel, not sure what else to do with them.

"Is there anything else you need to do? We have to leave now. Finch can't look after Maya. Kaeder said he can have either the dog or the wolf, not both."

Relieved and annoyed, she nodded. Buddy would be in good hands. "I need to say goodbye." She strode over to Buddy, who lay across Finch's door and crouched down beside him. Opening his eyes, he sat up and she hugged him, smiling when he licked her cheek. She whispered in his ear. "I'll miss you. I'm glad you found somewhere you belong." He licked her cheek once more and she drew away from him. It took a moment before she could bring herself to rise to her feet and walk away.

Finch led Sweet Pea to Baenen. He turned to Quinn. "I'll take care of him."

"I know. That's the only reason I let him stay."

Gideon stepped forward and gave her a hug. "Take care."

Taking the packet of biscuits and orange from her backpack, she held them out to him. He probably needed them more than her. Or Grant might appreciate them if he was feeling homesick. "From home."

Gideon tried to smile. "Thanks."

She nodded before following Baenen to the courtyard. Once he was on Sweet Pea, she got up behind him. It was awkward with all her gear. When the mare started to move, she waved before wrapping her arms around Baenen. The moment she did, Sweet Pea picked up speed. Looking skywards she noticed how little of the day was left. Hopefully they'd reach the human world well before the Hunt was after them.

Chapter Thirty-Five

The entire ride Quinn wanted to urge Sweet Pea to go faster. They reached Ganat Castle as the sun set. In the distance she heard the sound of the Hunt, fear rising in her at the sound. Dismounting she slipped one of the rings onto her left hand, relieved the fear receded slightly.

The same boy as last time came forward and took Sweet Pea. Another servant came out of the castle and Baenen beckoned him over. Baenen took the backpack and satchel from her after she'd slipped the necklaces and other ring into her bag. "Put these in Quinn's room."

"Yes, my lord."

"If Mairwin should arrive she isn't allowed in the castle or to take anything she might use to send the Hunt after us."

With a nod, the servant took the bag and satchel inside with him.

Baenen turned to Maya. "I need you to stay here and look after the place for me." He rested his hand on the large creature's forehead. They stared at each other silently for a couple of minutes before the wolf trotted over to the castle and lay in front of the door.

"Were you talking to her? When you were both quiet."

"Yes." He held out his left hand. "We have to leave. The Hunt is getting close."

She didn't need to be told that, she could hear for herself. "What do we need to do?" She took his hand.

"Think of somewhere in your world. Somewhere you can picture clearly and you've been before. A place that isn't likely to have a crowd of people."

An image of her bedroom came to mind and she instantly discarded it. There was no way she could explain all this to her parents. She thought of her favourite beach, a large sandy expanse ending in one direction with rocks and a cliff face. She pictured the base of that cliff where she'd spent so much time standing with the wind tangling her hair as she looked out to sea, fascinated by what might be out there. It came to her then, she was like Scout. But where he'd done something about his desire to explore she'd remained at home, listening raptly to his many stories. Letting her one failure convince her it wasn't for her. No wonder she'd once thought she'd loved him. It hadn't been him she'd loved. It'd been the way he'd chosen to follow his own path. A path she'd only ever dreamt of. Maybe she was more herself here than she'd ever been at home. No wonder she hadn't been happy at the thought of leaving.

"Are you ready?" He opened his other hand, an autumn leaf in it.

The Hunt was close so she better be. Bringing the image to her mind again, she smiled. "Yes."

He crushed the autumn leaf and it scattered in the breeze as the world shimmered and reformed around them. The smell of rich earth clinging to them. "Why did you choose here?"

She breathed in deeply, the tang of salt filling her lungs. She had no idea what day or time it was other than to guess morning would be here soon from the greyness of the sky. "It's one of my favourite places."

He continued to hold her hand, walking towards the sandy part of the beach. "There are beaches in the realms of the Fae far more beautiful than this. Some of them it's hard to tell where the sky and the sea begin and end because both are as blue as each other."

"I'd like to see that one day."

"Once the Hunt no longer chases us, I can take you to visit as many of the beaches in my world as you want."

She didn't answer, not sure what would happen once they'd survived the seven nights. "It's so peaceful here." Even though she could hear the noise of traffic in the distance, the sounds of the waves on the beach made them seem insignificant.

"There are places in the realms of the Fae that are far more peaceful than this."

Stopping, she faced him. A smile slowly formed. "Is this your way of trying to convince me to stay in the realms of the Fae?"

He chuckled. "Obviously my social skills are a little rusty after being Gwyl for so long. I was trying to be subtle."

She laughed. "You were a long way from that." She fell silent, remembering the last time she'd been here. Daisy, Ted and Scout had been with her.

"What's the matter?"

"I wish I could see my family."

"Are they far from here? Even though the Hunt is quicker at finding the last Gwyl than any one else they track, we still have many hours before we have to return to the realms of the Fae."

She shook her head. "They wouldn't let me go. There's no way they could understand."

"I could make them understand." He grinned.

"How?"

"Eventually we'd have to leave and there's only one way I use to travel between the worlds." He held out an autumn leaf.

She couldn't see any difference between it and the one she'd used to call him. "Could I use it?"

"Only if you had Fae magic. Without your own magic I'd have to put too much of my own into it so you could use it on your own. I can't spare that much." He closed his hand and when he opened it again the leaf had disappeared. "Do you want to see your family?"

"Not today." She needed to think about it. "I wouldn't mind finding out if Scout is still here. He'd be able to tell me how my family are. But I don't have any money to use a public phone." She wasn't about to ask a stranger like last time. That hadn't worked out very well.

He drew a silver coin from his belt pouch, holding it out to her. "Your human machines are easily tricked with the help of a bit of magic."

"Will you still have enough magic left to take us

back to the realms of the Fae when the Hunt finds us?"

"Yes. I'd need to use very little to trick your machine."

She took the coin, grinning. "Let's find a phone box." She headed for the road. It took far longer than she'd expected to find one and the sun had risen by the time they had. She looked from the phone to Baenen. "Are you sure this'll work?"

"Should I be offended you think so little of my abilities?"

She smiled at the humour she could hear in his voice. Baenen was far different from Gwyl. She reached for him with her right hand. He was the one she'd glimpsed in his eyes. The one she'd been drawn to. "Do you remember it all? Being Gwyl?" When he nodded, she continued. "What was it like being someone so different from yourself?"

"We all have the potential within us to be Gwyl."

She shook her head.

He cupped her cheek, stopping the movement. "You might not think so, but you do. If your entire family were slaughtered and the one who did it continued on with their life as if they hadn't ripped your heart from you, what would you do? If you had no one but yourself to take care of things, would you let them live?"

She started to disagree, trying to tamp down the feelings his words evoked.

"You don't have to tell me. I can see it in your expression."

"Did it help? Did killing Tamek make you feel any better about their deaths?"

His eyes filled with sadness. Instead of answering, he gestured to the phone. "Are you going to ring Scout?"

She stared at him a moment longer before she nodded and slipped the coin into the slot. There was a faint smell of rich earth and then the phone registered five dollars. She dialled Scout's number.

He answered on the first ring. "Hello?" His voice was hesitant.

"Scout."

"It is you. I thought it might be since I don't get unknown calls. Where are you? Did you want me to pick you up? Are you home for good?"

She told him where she was. "But I don't want you to pick me up. I want to see you and find out how everyone is." She doubted Baenen would be able to travel in the car, not with how difficult he found being around iron. She was pretty sure steel was refined iron. "What day is it?"

"Monday the second of November. I guess I'll be skipping school today. I'll see you soon."

She hung up the phone, continuing to stare at it. She'd been in the realms of the Fae longer than last time and yet the same amount of days had passed in the human world. No wonder it was impossible to keep track of the days between the two worlds.

"Is something wrong?"

Facing Baenen, she shook her head. "No. Time is utterly confusing. How will we figure out when the seven days are up when time doesn't run the same between the two places?"

"It goes by sunrise of where we are."

"We only have five days left?"

"Yes."

If only the rest of the days could go so quickly. "That seemed too easy."

"Give them a chance. They'll get better at tracking us."

She was tempted to tell him she really hadn't wanted to know that. She guessed it was better that she did. Taking his hand, she drew him to a shady tree. "It looks like it's going to be a warm day."

"If you know of somewhere cooler, we can go there next time."

"No. I haven't done a lot of travelling."

Baenen stared at her, a slight frown forming between his brows. "You sound like you regret that."

She shrugged. "Not exactly regret, but I wouldn't mind visiting other places." When Baenen started telling her about some of the places she should visit in the realms of the Fae, she smiled.

His gaze was drawn to her lips. "I'd like you to stay in my world. I can't live very long in yours. Your modern world isn't good for Fae. We sicken and die if we stay here too long."

Her smile vanished and she reached for him. "How long does it take? Should we be here? What if we return now? I don't have to see Scout."

He wrapped his arms around her. "Your fear for my safety gives me hope."

She clung to him, no closer to a decision. They remained there, silently wrapped in each other's arms. After a while, the sound of a horn broke them apart. She turned to see Scout had arrived, Marley with him.

Marley started towards her, freezing when her gaze landed on Baenen. She grabbed hold of Scout, pulling him back towards her, whispering furiously to him.

"Wait here." Quinn strode over to her sister, not waiting for Baenen's answer. "He's no longer Gwyl."

"But-"

She interrupted her sister. "I broke his curse."

Marley grinned, throwing her arms around her. "You can come home?"

After returning the hug, she pulled away. "No. I have to survive seven nights of being hunted by the new Gwyl because I broke the curse of the old Gwyl."

Marley's grin vanished. "Oh."

"How long are you here for?" Scout asked.

Quinn shrugged before turning towards Baenen and beckoning him over.

Chapter Thirty-Six

When Baenen joined them, Quinn threaded her fingers through his, making sure to use her right hand. "This is Baenen." She faced him. "You know Marley and this is Scout."

Scout held out his hand, dropping it almost immediately. "Sorry. I forgot I was wearing iron rings."

"Why are you wearing them?" Baenen asked.

"So I can see through glamours."

"There are other ways."

"Really? Like what?" Scout asked.

Baenen met Quinn's gaze. "Is this the reason you wear iron?"

"No. It stops me from running from the Hunt."

The corner of Baenen's lips twitched. "Running is the sensible choice sometimes."

Her gaze narrowed. "Are you laughing at me?"

"I wouldn't dare." But his lips twitched at the corners again. "Would you like to be able to see through glamours without the use of iron?"

"How?"

"It involves magic. Not enough it would prevent you from returning to live in this world if you chose to do that."

"Of course she wants to come back here," Marley said.

"Do you?" Baenen held her gaze.

Quinn had no idea what to say. She wanted to disagree with Marley, but what if she decided she wanted to return here one day? "I want to be able to see through glamours without needing iron."

"And the other question?" Baenen asked.

When Quinn didn't answer immediately, Scout spoke. "I'd like to be able to see through glamours without needing iron too."

Baenen ignored Scout. "Quinn?"

"Stop hassling her. Of course the answer is no," Marley said.

Still meeting his green eyes, she finally spoke. "I don't know."

"What! No. Don't stay there." Marley tried to grab her arm.

Baenen stepped between Marley and Quinn.

Marley stumbled backwards. "Quinn?"

There was fear in her sister's voice. When she stepped to the side and looked up at Baenen, she could see why. He reminded her of the daytime Gwyl. She rested her hand on his arm. "Marley wouldn't hurt me."

When Baenen looked at Quinn, his expression softened, his voice quiet. "Wouldn't she? How many times has she put you in danger?"

Again Quinn had no idea how to answer. In the end, she said the only thing she could. "She's my sister. What haven't you done for your brothers?"

His expression lightened, a smile forming. "You're right. I've killed for mine."

Marley gasped, taking another step backwards.

Quinn sent a look towards her sister, about to tell her not to carry on. Her jaw dropped instead. When had she started thinking like the Fae? When had their actions started to seem normal and perfectly acceptable? It had happened so gradually she hadn't realised his world had become her world. She couldn't return home. She'd changed too much for that. And she liked the changes. She hadn't lost herself like she'd feared. No, she'd become herself.

Baenen grabbed her upper arms. "Quinn?"

At the fear in his voice, she met his gaze. Why had

she even been hesitating? She threw herself at him, pulling free from his grip to throw her arms around him. "Yes."

"No," Marley yelled. "Quinn! No."

Baenen held her equally tight. "You're staying in the realms of the Fae with me?" There was uncertainty in his voice.

"Yes."

"Even after everything?"

She thought about all their encounters. "You could have killed me numerous times. Especially when I refused to ask for the favour. Why didn't you?"

His arms tightened around her. "I kept focusing on the favour. Kept holding off the moment when I'd need to end the hunt."

Quinn continued to ignore Marley's pleas and demands, Scout trying to calm her. "Why?"

"You fascinated me from the moment the urge to hunt left me the next morning." He held her gaze a moment before he continued to speak. "No one else did during all the time I was Gwyl. At first I thought it was because of the challenge of our hunt and tried to focus on that. It didn't take me long to realise the hunt wasn't the reason you intrigued me."

She couldn't resist grinning. The grin faded when she heard the argument behind her. Remaining in

Baenen's arms, she faced her sister. "You can't tell Scout or me what to do."

"But I don't want to return there," Marley wailed.

"You don't need to," Quinn said.

"But-" Marley looked from Quinn to Scout and back again. "I'll be all alone."

"Stop being so dramatic, Marley." She couldn't keep the sharpness from her voice. "You have friends, Mum, Dad, other family. There's an entire world of people."

"But you and Scout won't be here."

"I'm not going forever," Scout said.

"It won't matter. By the time you get bored we'll all be dead and it'll be another world," Marley muttered.

Scout's eyes lit up. "I hadn't thought of that. How cool would that be? I'd get to see the future."

Quinn almost laughed at her sister's disgruntled expression. She turned her head so she could see Baenen. "Is it possible to give Marley one of those leaves so she can let you know when she needs me?"

"Of course." Baenen inclined his head.

She turned her attention to Marley. "You'd only be able to use it for important things. Not seeing me for a week or two doesn't count."

"What if I haven't seen you for several months?"

Quinn shook her head. "Not then either. Unless of course it's your birthday."

"Okay."

Baenen let go of Quinn, closing his hand for a moment and opening it again to reveal an autumn leaf, the scent of his magic in the air. "Speak my name against this when you want your sister and I'll bring her to you. Make sure you're in a place where no other people are. It takes far too much magic to make them forget someone stepping out of nowhere."

Marley took the leaf, pushing it into the pocket of her jeans. "What happens if it breaks?"

"It won't."

Quinn saw her sister didn't believe him. "It won't break. I carried one around for ages and it remained exactly the same." She thought of the flower in her pocket, hoping it was as durable.

"Okay," Marley said.

"Now that's sorted, what about being able to see a glamour without needing to wear iron?" Scout asked.

"Come and see me if you ever go to the realms of the Fae. Ask for me at Ganat Castle. Tell them you're Scout from the human world. I'll let them know you might turn up," Baenen said.

"I will turn up," Scout said. "Do you mind if I ask you about your world?"

Baenen shrugged, turning to Quinn with a question in his eyes.

"I don't mind." She looked at Scout. "Do you have a blanket in your car? We could sit on the beach."

Scout nodded. "I'll grab it."

Once Scout had the blanket, they wandered down to the beach. Before he started with his questions, Scout said he'd done a search online about Gideon.

"Why?"

Scout shrugged. "I was curious." He paused. "Everyone thinks he's dead. There was a fire at his friend's house and a body was found."

That hadn't been in the news clip she'd watched. "What happened to his friend?"

"He went looking for Gideon when he didn't turn up, forgetting he'd left food cooking on the stove."

"I wonder who the body was they found," Quinn said.

Scout shrugged again. "My theory is it was a burglar."

She smiled. Scout always had a theory about everything.

Scout turned to Baenen. "Mind if I ask some questions now?"

They spent several hours with Scout peppering them with questions until Quinn gazed longingly at the ocean. "If I had something dry to put on afterwards, I'd go for a swim."

Baenen squeezed her hand that he held. "Have you forgotten I can do magic?"

"Don't you need to conserve it to return home tonight?"

"It's nature magic. It'll take very little effort."

Quinn got to her feet, dragging Baenen with her. "Let's go swimming."

The rest of the day passed rapidly as they swam, then Scout went to buy lunch while Marley tried to convince her to come home once she was no longer the prey of the Wild Hunt. As the day drew to a close, Quinn kept listening for the sound she dreaded. When it came, it was barely after the sun had set.

Marley grabbed at her left hand, Baenen still holding her right. "I'm not ready for you to go."

"I have to." She drew her hand from Marley's.

"They want me to see someone who'll hypnotise me so they can learn where I was. They think it'll help them find you," Marley said.

"Who wants you to?"

"Mum and Dad."

"Why are you only telling me this now?" Quinn didn't bother keeping the annoyance from her voice. "Tell them no. Tell them…" She tried to think of an excuse, but the sound of the Hunt coming closer made it impossible. "I don't know. Tell them something. I'll see you next time I'm in this world." She hugged her sister with one arm, stepping back and turning to Baenen. "I'm ready."

He crushed an autumn leaf and the smell of his magic filled the air as the world shimmered and reformed. They arrived where they'd left, darkness having fallen. "Shall we find out how much time has passed?" He glanced skywards. "I have a feeling it's the early hours of the morning of the day after we left."

"How do you know?"

"The moon."

She walked beside him, as he strode inside the castle. A servant hurried forward the moment he saw them.

"Welcome home, my lord."

"When is it?"

"The early hours of the morning. You left yesterday at sunset, my lord."

"Thank you," Baenen said.

"Can I get you anything, my lord?"

"No, I'm fine for now." Baenen turned to Quinn. "Do you want anything?"

She shook her head.

He grinned. "Now it's my turn to show you some of my favourite places." With a nod for the servant, he headed back outside.

Chapter Thirty-Seven

They wandered around the grounds. Eventually they ended in a stone gazebo with a vine growing over it, covered in the dainty white flower Baenen had conjured for her. Glad for the rest, she sank onto one of the bench seats, resting her head against Baenen when he sat beside her.

She drifted off to sleep, waking with fear rushing through her, the sounds of the Hunt in the distance. It was still night. "What are we going to do?"

"Wait. Hopefully they won't arrive before sunrise."

"And if they do?"

"Then we haven't completed another day yet."

She clung to his hand as she listened to the Hunt come closer. Unable to sit, she strode outside, taking Baenen with her. She stared at the sky, willing the day to arrive. Was that light? She didn't know. It might have been wishful thinking. "How long until day?"

"Not long. Twenty minutes at the most."

Letting go of his hand, she began to pace, stepping around him when he tried to stop her.

"Quinn. We'll leave before they come that close. I won't let anything happen to you."

This time when Baenen stepped in front of her, she let him. "Why don't you feel the fear? You're not wearing any iron."

He wrapped his arms around her. "My magic does the same as your iron."

"Will enough magic to see through glamours help?"

"No. I'd need to give you far more than that. Too much to be able to give it to you before the hunt is ended. You do remember it will prevent you from returning to your human world for any length of time, don't you?"

"Yeah." She closed her eyes, trying to ignore the call of the Hunt. When the sound came close enough that she thought she'd be able to see them, she opened her eyes and tried to pull away from Baenen.

His arms tightened around her before he let go with one arm so she could see the autumn leaf he held. "If they come any closer I'll take us to your beach."

Her gaze was drawn from the leaf to the sky, which was starting to lighten. "How long now?"

"Minutes."

She continued to watch the sky, holding her breath as the sound of the Hunt came closer. When Baenen started to close his hand on the leaf, she placed her hand on his wrist. "Wait. Please wait."

"They're at the castle gate."

"Wait until you can see them."

"By then it might be too late. Some have bows."

"It's so close." Her gaze was drawn skyward again. "Give it-" She broke off when he tensed and started to close his hand. "No." Heart racing, she plucked the leaf from him, dragging him behind one of the stone columns. An arrow flew through the space they'd vacated. The sun rose and the sounds of the Hunt stopped. Her heart continued to race.

"How did you know?" He took the leaf from her. "How did you know about the arrow?" The leaf vanished from his hand.

"I didn't. But I remembered how far arrows could travel from when I ran from your castle."

"How did you know they were there?"

She smiled. "You told me." Her smile widened at

his confused look. "You said we'd go the moment you saw them. I saw you about to crush the leaf."

"Do you know how dangerous that was?"

"What if this kept happening? We could be stuck trying to avoid them for decades. I can't do this that long."

"I would keep-"

She drew away from him. "I can't do this that long."

He stared at her for a moment before he nodded. "I understand." He held out his hand again. "Would you join me for the morning meal?"

A reluctant smile formed and once again she thought of the first time he'd asked her. This time it was her that had nearly killed him. "Okay." She took his hand and walked with him to the castle.

After breakfast, she retired to her room and had a wash, dressing in a clean pair of jeans and shirt before she tumbled into bed. The flower was again in her pocket. She had no idea how long she slept before knocking on a door woke her. For a second she thought it was her door. Stumbling from bed she checked the hallway to see Baenen talking to a servant.

"What's going on?"

"Mairwin wishes to see us."

She closed her eyes, not wanting to put up with the arrogant woman. Opening her eyes, she looked from Baenen to the servant. "Why?"

Baenen answered. "She didn't say, but I'm guessing she's here to take you up on your offer."

"This is a good thing, right?"

Baenen shrugged, coming towards her. "Depends on if she likes what we have to say." He glanced over his shoulder to the servant. "Let her know we'll see her shortly. Put her in the drawing room and remain to watch that she doesn't steal anything that can be used against us."

"Yes, my lord."

Baenen took her hand. "Shall we?"

She wanted to protest. She was barely awake and probably looked a mess. Not that looking her best would help her in any way to compete with Mairwin. "Okay. Let's get it over and done with."

Baenen headed straight to the drawing room, pausing in the doorway. "Mairwin."

The woman stopped pacing to face him. "I don't need to talk to you. I want your pet to tell me how to break the curse."

"She isn't my pet." There was an edge to his voice.

Quinn let go of Baenen's hand, stepping into the

room before an argument broke out. "He has to take his revenge."

"You want him to kill someone?"

"Of course I don't want him to, but that's how it works. If he no longer needs revenge then he's not the one in the pack with the greatest need for it."

"He's too gentle to kill anyone."

Baenen stepped up beside Quinn. "There's nothing gentle about him once the sun sets. If the curse is broken there'll always be a part of him that remembers what it was like to lead the Hunt."

She wanted to ask him if that bothered him, but now wasn't the time. "He can't seek out his own revenge, only the revenge he's paid to take. You'll have to pay the Hunt to go after the one he seeks to kill."

"That's ridiculous. I can't do that. Their family is too powerful."

Quinn shrugged. "Then your brother will remain Gwyl."

"No."

"I didn't make the rules. Only followed them."

Mairwin gestured towards Baenen, her gaze remaining on Quinn. "You paid him to kill the person he wanted dead?"

"Yes. And now the Hunt is after us for seven nights."

Mairwin's eyes narrowed. "That's why you told me, isn't it? You want me dead."

"I couldn't care if you live or die. You want your brother back. I've told you how." Quinn glared at Mairwin.

"What do you want for the information?" Mairwin demanded.

"I don't-"

Baenen interrupted Quinn. "She doesn't know as yet. When she thinks of something of equal value she'll let you know." His lips twisted into a smile. "Providing you survive the Hunt." He eyed her up and down.

Quinn could almost hear him saying he had his doubts. She bit back her own smile. "They can't track you when you're completely submersed in water and when you shift between worlds it takes them some time to track you down again."

"Why would you tell me that?"

She shrugged.

Baenen answered. "You can't collect a favour from the dead."

"If this is some kind of trickery…" Mairwin let the threat hang.

"I'll send you word when you can approach your brother," Baenen said.

"Why can't I approach him now?"

"Because he won't take on any other hunts until he's completed his first one."

"How long until he's finished hunting you?" Mairwin asked.

Baenen shrugged. "That depends on how time shifts between the realms."

Mairwin strode towards them, stopping directly in front of Baenen. "My family will be informed. If this goes badly, you will be held responsible."

"If it goes badly it'll be your own fault. We've given you the truth. If you fail then it was your lack, not ours," Baenen said.

"I lack nothing." She pushed past them and swept down the hallway.

Baenen indicated for the servant to follow Mairwin.

"What will happen if she dies?"

"Nothing. That would be admitting she lacked something."

Quinn stared at him for a moment. "You Fae are strange."

Baenen laughed. "And yet you're willing to stay here in our realm. How strange does that make you?"

A smile escaped. "I never said I hated strange." She tried to sweep past him like Mairwin had done.

He caught her around the waist and drew her back. "I'm more than a little fond of strange myself." His lips met hers.

She wanted to ask him how fond, but words failed her. Instead she returned the kiss. When they finally broke apart, she stared up at him, grinning. "What now?"

"How about I show you some of the places I told you about?"

"You don't have to keep trying to convince me to stay. I've already said I would."

"I know, but you could leave any time. You haven't asked for magic of your own."

"You said you couldn't give it to me until the hunt was over."

"Does that mean you want it?"

She thought about it. There were so many things that would be good about it, but so many that would be worrying. Like the problem with iron. "I'm thinking about it."

"While you're thinking, I'll show you some more of the realm."

She couldn't resist laughing. He was definitely

trying to convince her. She liked the way he was going about it. "Okay."

"Are you ready?"

There wasn't anything she needed or that she had to do. "Yes."

Chapter Thirty-Eight

They spent the rest of the day on horseback, Quinn riding her own horse. When the sun set and the sounds of the Hunt filled the night they returned to the human world, Baenen first having told the horses to go home.

Quinn took them to a lookout, not wanting to listen to her sister's complaints after such a great afternoon. She'd see her the next time they returned. Or the time after. Luckily they arrived only an hour before sunrise, leaving them with three more nights to get through.

Quinn tried to convince Baenen they might be able to return to the realms of the Fae and get through another night quickly. He refused. Telling her it was too dangerous he made her wait until night and the arrival of the Hunt in the human world.

The next days were a blur of sleeping, changing

worlds, exploring and the sound of the Hunt. When the final night arrived, Quinn couldn't wait for it to end. Like previous nights they waited until they could hear the Hunt nearby.

Baenen held out an autumn leaf. "Where would you like to go tonight?"

"There's a national forest I'd love to show you."

"You don't want to see your sister?"

She shook her head, knowing she was only postponing the inevitable. There was already enough to deal with. She didn't want to put up with her sister's theatrics too. "After the hunt is over." There were things she needed to do in the human world. Decisions she'd made. She'd tell him after they beat the Hunt. Taking his hand, she brought to mind the forest. "I'm ready."

The scent of his magic rose around them and the world reformed. "I like this place."

She laughed. "I thought you would. Being a wood Fae."

He chuckled, starting to draw her close.

They both froze at the sound of the Hunt.

"How did they find us so fast?"

"We had to expect that. We've been coming to your world every time we hear them." He drew her close. "Ready to return?"

"Yeah."

Again his magic filled the air and they found themselves at Ganat Castle, the sound of the Hunt filling the night. "He's split the pack."

"He can do that?" When Baenen nodded in answer, she began to wish she hadn't asked. "What are we going to do?"

"Remember how I said that sometimes running is the sensible choice?"

It didn't sound very sensible to her. "On foot?"

He shook his head, smiling. "I'll have Sweet Pea saddled." He strode through the castle grounds, keeping hold of her hand.

"Do we have time?"

"Can you manage bareback?"

"Yes."

"Bareback it is." Reaching the stables, he brought Sweet Pea out with only a bridle on her. After jumping onto the horse's back, he held out his hand.

Quinn didn't hesitate, even though the sound of the Hunt had her wanting to freeze in terror. Clinging to Baenen, she once again found herself praying. She'd have to ask him about Fae gods, if they survived. She forced that thought from her mind. Of course they'd survive. It couldn't end like this. Not on their last night.

Sweet Pea raced through the night, taking to the forest. Baenen and Quinn remained low to avoid the whipping branches of trees. Behind them the Hunt followed, getting constantly closer. Ahead a single howl sounded.

She wanted to ask Baenen if it was a lone wolf, but fear raced through her and the sound caused her to shiver. Sweet Pea veered to the side. A howl came from that direction. Howls answered it, seeming to surround them.

"Please tell me it's nearly morning."

"It isn't even midnight."

His words made her want to beg him to say he'd lied. But the Fae couldn't. "Is there a river nearby that we could hide in?"

"It wouldn't help. It's more than scent when it comes to tracking the old Gwyl. We'd need a lake and have to keep moving."

She didn't bother asking him how he knew. With the certainty in his voice, he obviously remembered. "What can we do?"

"You're still owed a favour from Gwyl. No matter who holds that title."

"I won't leave you behind."

"He owes me no favour."

There had to be a way for both of them to benefit

from the favour if they were caught. Nothing came to mind. Panic raced through her when Sweet Pea reared, the Hunt coming out of the trees in front of her. She clung to Baenen and Sweet Pea, struggling to keep her seat. More of the Hunt closed in on them, brandishing weapons and flaming torches. She looked for the familiar antlers. For a moment she thought Gwyl might not be there.

He burst through the trees, a rider beside him carrying a flaming torch. Howling began at the sight of him, an eerie sound that filled the night. He pointed at them with the sword he carried. "Your lives are mine."

"Tell him," Baenen whispered.

There was nowhere for them to run. They were surrounded. "Not yet." Not until she could figure out a way to use it to save both of them.

"He doesn't know it exists. You have to tell him. Before it's too late."

Gwyl dismounted. "Face your death. Get off your horse."

Quinn slid off Sweet Pea, hitting Baenen's hands away when he tried to stop her.

"You wish to die first?" Gwyl stared at her, a glitter in his eyes.

Baenen dismounted, stepping in front of her. "No,

she doesn't." He lifted his hands. "Close your eyes." His words were quiet, meant only for her.

As she closed her eyes the wind whipped up around her, dirt stinging her arms and face. The scent of magic filled the air. Rich dirt and a second one. Rainforests. Another gust of wind rushed at them and she struggled to stay on her feet. When the wind died down and the ground rumbled, she opened her eyes. The Hunt struggled to reach them, the ground buckling and twisting beneath their feet. She stared at Baenen, who stood in front of her. He was doing this?

The ground in front of Gwyl smoothed out several times, buckling again almost instantly. Baenen and Gwyl remained still, facing each other, the glitter in Gwyl's eyes increasing. She shuffled to the side, wanting to stand beside Baenen. When she reached his side and saw his expression, she wondered if she'd have been better off remaining behind him. The glitter in his eyes reminded her of his words to Mairwin. It also reminded her of the old Gwyl she'd talked to in the Fringes. Baenen remembered the hunt clearly.

When a ripple ran through the ground from Gwyl towards her, she jumped behind Baenen again. How long could they keep this up? Would it count if they lasted until sunrise doing this? They might be surrounded, but they weren't caught yet.

A larger ripple came through the ground and she grabbed hold of Baenen when the dirt beneath their feet rose a metre upwards. The dirt collapsed like a wave crashing on the beach and they barely managed to keep their feet. They were now within reach of Gwyl.

He swung at them with his sword. A root snaked up out of the ground and grabbed hold of his wrist before he could connect. Continuing to hold Baenen with one hand, she covered her mouth with her other, holding back the scream she'd nearly let escape. She wanted her own magic. Wanted everything this world offered. And wanted to be able to stand at Baenen's side if they ever faced an enemy again, not cower behind him.

The sound of hoofbeats behind them drew her attention. Several Fae came in fast, members of the Hunt. Her heart sank. What if they used magic too? There was no way Baenen could fight against all of them. He was barely managing Gwyl.

The Fae didn't dismount. They joined Gwyl's attack on Baenen, the smell of their magic filling the air. The ground buckled and twisted, flinging Quinn and Baenen to the ground. The earth became still, rippling back into place, the roots sliding beneath it.

She struggled to her feet, coughing from the dust in the air. Baenen didn't move. Fear raced through her and she bent to help him. He staggered to his feet, looking drained.

"Who wishes to die first?" Gwyl asked.

"Tell him." Baenen whispered.

"How will I get far on foot?"

"Sweet Pea."

She looked around, spotting the horse that had retreated. An inkling of an idea came to her. She faced Gwyl. "You owe me a favour."

"I owe nothing."

"Gwyl owes me a favour. You're Gwyl."

"If as you say I owe you a favour then name it so I can check the truth of your words."

She tried to recall the exact words Baenen had used back when he'd been Gwyl. "You must let me go and give me a head start the first time you catch me."

Gwyl snarled. "Only you." He pointed his finger at Baenen. "He's mine."

"He also promised to let me ride his horse. I could take yours or he could tell his horse to let me ride her since he won't be needing her." It was more difficult to speak the last few words than she'd expected it to be, particularly with the startled look Baenen gave her.

"Take his. None ride mine except me," Gwyl said.

She tugged Baenen towards Sweet Pea, trying not to focus on all the weapons pointed in her direction. Stopping near the horse, she kept herself between Baenen and Sweet Pea. She looked towards Gwyl who'd followed, remaining several metres from her. "How long do you consider a head start?"

"You plan to haggle with me?"

She shrugged, trying to remain calm even though her heart raced uncontrollably. "The last Gwyl said an hour, but I was hoping you'd offer more."

"One hour is more than enough. Even with that much time you can't outrun us. Not with how far away sunrise is." His lips twisted into a smile. "All you'll do is give us the kind of hunt we like. No more of this changing worlds like you have been."

Chapter Thirty-Nine

Quinn stepped out of Baenen's way. "Can you ask her to let me ride?"

He reached for Sweet Pea, resting his hand against her forehead.

"You're wasting time," Gwyl said.

She nearly said good. When Baenen started to move away, she grabbed hold of his arm. "I need help getting on the horse. There's no saddle." When he cupped his hand to help her up, she pretended to stumble against him. "Join me." She glanced at Sweet Pea before meeting his gaze again and using his cupped hands to get on the horse. She looked towards Gwyl as she gathered the reins. "You can't follow me for one hour."

Gwyl nodded.

Baenen leapt onto Sweet Pea's back and the horse jumped forward, galloping through the trees. He leaned forward, forcing Quinn to lean too. "We haven't gained enough time."

"What if we change worlds? Maybe the rest of the pack came back here when we were caught."

"I don't have the magic to do so. I can lead them away from you. They want me more than they want you."

"No."

"If you-"

"Before you make any other suggestions, don't bother unless they're ones were we both live."

"There isn't-"

"Yes, there is. We've got to think, that's all." A possibility came to her. "When I was in the treasure room, would you have been able to find me if I'd still been there after sunset?"

"Yes, but it would have taken time. It's a maze down there." He changed the direction Sweet Pea was heading in. "We should make it to the castle with ten minutes to spare."

She fell silent, trying to recall all the diagrams. They needed to find the most confusing section. She had some ideas, but really needed to check the book. The moment they stopped at the castle door, she swung her leg over and slid off the horse. "I need to get the book."

"I'll tell everyone to leave. I don't want anyone else caught up in this hunt."

Nodding, she ran inside. It took her a few minutes to remember the way. She was headed back to the front door when Baenen came towards her. "Are they all leaving?"

"Yes. They'll be back at sunrise." He took her hand. "We'll use the inside entrance."

"What will we do for light?" She really hoped he didn't say the fireflies again.

"We can take a lantern from one of the corridors." He took the steps three at a time.

She struggled to keep up with him, but didn't dare ask him to slow down. When he stopped to take down a lantern, she flicked through the pages until she found the right sections, trying to ignore the sounds of the Hunt she could hear. "What do you think?"

He checked over the diagrams. "Good." He took her hand. "We should be there before they arrive." He strode through the corridors like he regularly used them.

She was relieved he knew where he was going so they weren't held up by frequent stops for her to consult the book. By the time they reached their destination, she could hear the Hunt was almost above them. She tightened her left hand into a fist, trying to focus on the iron ring. The fear continued to increase. She kept fighting against it. "How will we know it's sunrise?"

"We won't need to know. He will and that's all that matters."

"How long away do you think it is?"

"Maybe an hour."

That seemed far too long. How was she going to survive an hour of sitting here waiting for Gwyl? The fear came closer and she knew he must be searching for them. Would the maze-like corridors be enough to keep him busy for an hour? She could only hope. If she didn't take her mind off the approaching Hunt, she'd go crazy. "I want magic."

"Now?"

She laughed softly, surprised she was still capable of it. "No. As soon as possible. What you did was awesome."

"You can't do that straight away. First you might only be able to stir a puff of air."

"That's okay. I can work up to the 'stay out of my way or you're going to get it' stage."

"Is that why you want to stay?"

"No. I'd already decided. I was waiting until this

was over to tell you, but…" She didn't want to think they wouldn't make it let alone speak it.

"Do you want me to give you some magic now? It won't be much, but if something should happen and I can't give it to you tomorrow, at least you'll have some that will slowly increase over time."

"No. After everything is over. We also need to see my parents. I can't leave them wondering what happened to me. Or let them send Marley to someone to hypnotise her. I also want to let Gideon know everyone thinks he's dead so he can stop feeling guilty about not going back." She wished she could tell Daisy, but she knew her friend wouldn't understand. That she'd take it as an insult that she'd chosen a different world over her family and friends.

"When did you work everything out?"

"The day Mairwin arrived. Or at least I figured most of it out then."

"I–" His head turned in the direction of a noise. "I'm going to put the lantern out. It won't stop him from being able to track us, but it will slow him down. Lucky he isn't a Troll with their ability to see in the dark."

She wanted to argue against his whispered words. "Okay." She pressed closer to him, trying to ignore the rising fear. It was the worst she'd ever felt it.

Was being in narrow corridors making it worse? She heard frequent sounds, each one a little closer. How much longer did they have to wait? She wanted to run. Was that him? Close enough that she could hear him breathing. No, it was her own breath, harsh in her ears. She tried to slow it down, tried to be quiet. She didn't know how successful she was when the beat of her heart pounded in her ears.

If this took too much longer she might be tempted to run towards him, screaming out where she was. Another sound drew her attention. It was far too close. She guessed Baenen thought so too as he started easing away, drawing her with him. When there was a sound behind them, she nearly screamed. Baenen stopped moving. She stayed still with him.

"I hear you breathing, I can smell where you are. Did you think you could escape?"

His words sent a shiver through her. Yes. She'd thought they could escape.

"Run." Baenen whispered the word in her ear, breaking into a run, dragging her with him.

Behind she could hear footsteps as she regularly collided with walls. If she was lucky she'd feel all the new bruises later. Much later. After sunrise. They took another sharp turn and she gritted her teeth against the pain of hitting her shoulder against one more stone wall. The footsteps had nearly reached them, her legs and lungs burned and she was about to collapse on the floor. What had made her think she could do this? She was obviously insane.

"Hurry," Baenen whispered.

She couldn't go any faster. About to draw her hand from his and tell him to go on without her, she stumbled. The atmosphere changed. There was no fear. They slowed to a stop, standing still in the dark. "He's gone?"

"I would like to think so, but I believe it'll take him some time to get out of this maze."

"Can we have a light again?"

"I left the lantern behind."

She momentarily closed her eyes. Not that it made any difference opening them. "How about some fireflies?"

"If there were any down here, I'd call them."

"Do you know the way out?"

"It'll be quicker to use the exit you entered through last time."

By the time they found their way outside, standing at the rear wall of the castle, Quinn had begun to think they were lost. She turned her face to the sky, soaking in the morning sunlight. "We're alive."

Baenen crushed her to him. "I'm not sure how we managed. Several times it didn't seem possible."

She stared at him in disbelief. "You're Fae. How can you think anything is impossible when you're an impossibility yourself."

He laughed, keeping his arms around her. "You will be an impossibility soon too."

Her grin matched his. "I can't wait." Ignoring Daisy and jumping through the reflection of the moon after her sister was one of the smartest things she'd ever done. "After that, you have more places to show me."

"I can't wait."

She laughed at his choice of words, throwing her head back to watch the colours filling the sky. This was her world. A world full of locations to explore, magic and possibilities. It felt like home.

Chapter Forty

She stared at the delicate white flower she held, her apprehension slowly increasing. It had to be done. Yet she'd kept finding excuses to put it off. Somehow two weeks had passed and who knew how long in the human world. But she'd wanted her magic to improve and in the meantime there'd been places to explore, things to do, discoveries to be made and of course magic to practice.

"There's a lovely little valley I haven't shown you."

Smiling, she looked towards Baenen. He sat in the chair she'd used to smash the window when she'd been trying to escape from the castle, what felt like such a long time ago. She stood by the window that had been repaired. "I have to do this. I have to let them know I'm okay."

Baenen rose to his feet and strode to her. "There's time."

She met his gaze, frowning at what she saw in his eyes. "You're scared?"

"They're your family."

"You're scared to meet them?"

He shook his head. "No, worried you'll regret your choice to cut ties with your world."

Her frown disappeared and she threw her arms around him, continuing to hold the flower. "Never. This is my world. No matter what happens. This is where I belong."

His arms tightened around her. "Then why are you scared to visit them?"

"I'm not scared." She tried to think how to explain how she felt. It was a confusing mix of emotions. "I know they can't keep me there." She half smiled. "Not now I know how to travel between the realms." She shrugged. "I guess I'm worried about how they'll take it. I won't be coming home and I know they're not going to like it. Especially since they won't be able to pick up a phone and talk to me whenever they want or come and visit when they feel like it."

"You can give them a flower so they can call for you directly now."

She still couldn't believe her magic was associated with his mother's favourite flower. Although she had to admit it had become her favourite the moment he'd given one to her. "I know." She sighed heavily. "I guess we should get this over and done with."

"I'm ready to go whenever you are."

Keeping one arm around him, she let go with the other one and stared at the flower a moment before she crushed it, picturing her room. The delicate scent of the flower filled the air and the world shimmered before reforming. Darkness pressed in on them and for a moment panic flared. Had she done something wrong?

"Where are we?" Baenen asked.

"We should be in my room."

He let go with one arm and a moment later tiny fireflies landed on his palm, giving off a soft glow. Relief rushed through her. "It must be night." Letting go of him, she crossed the room to the window and drew the curtains back. Light filtered into the room. The familiar surroundings of her room looked almost alien to her.

Baenen came to stand beside her, the fireflies now on his shoulder. "Are you going to wake your parents?"

She shrugged. "I guess it depends on what time it is." She glanced towards the closed door of her room. "Wait here. I'll go and check." When he nodded, she left the room, leaving her door open and walking silently through the house.

In the lounge room, she stared at the electronic calendar. Wednesday the twenty-third of December. 3:57 a.m. It was nearly Christmas Day and daylight was about an hour away. A glance around the room showed there were no decorations. Guilt hit her at the same time as a scream rang through the house.

Running for her bedroom, she squinted when the hallway light came on. Her mum stood in front of her bedroom doorway, her hand pressed to her mouth and her dad stood near the hallway light switch, blinking sleepily.

Marley opened her bedroom door. "What's wrong?" She shielded her eyes from the glare of the hallway light.

"Mum." Quinn had no idea what to say when her mum looked towards her and burst into tears.

"Quinn?"

More guilt hit her at the uncertainty in her dad's voice. She should have come back sooner. No matter how hard it was going to be to tell them everything, she shouldn't have left it so long. Shouldn't have waited until her magic was strong enough to use. "I'm sorry."

"About time you got here," Marley said.

"Marley!"

Quinn almost smiled at the shocked tone of her mum's voice. She wouldn't be talking like that if she knew. As she walked towards her mum, she tried to think of what to say. Instead of speaking, she hugged her. "I'm so sorry. I didn't know so much time had passed." She glanced towards Baenen who was still in her room where she'd left him, the fireflies now gone.

Her mum's arms tightened around her. "You have nothing to be sorry about. We do. We lost your dog."

"She has a lot to be sorry about," Marley muttered.

"Marley-"

Drawing away from her mum, Quinn interrupted her dad. "I do. I need to talk to you." Again she glanced towards Baenen. "And I want you to meet someone."

"He's with you?" her mum asked.

Quinn nodded.

"Who are you talking about?" Her dad strode towards them, stopping behind them to stare at Baenen. "Who is this?" He turned to Quinn. "And how did you both get inside?"

"Mum, Dad, this is Baenen." She took a deep breath. "We might want to sit in the lounge room. This could take a while."

It took far longer than she'd expected to tell them

all the main details. There were things she didn't bother mentioning. Like the times when she'd thought she was about to die. The sun was long up before she became annoyed with her parents telling her she couldn't return. That she belonged here. Rising to her feet, she held out her hand. As soon as they could see it was empty, she closed it and the scent of her magic rose around her. Opening her hand again, she showed them the delicate white flower. "Don't you understand?"

Her mum kept shaking her head. "This isn't possible."

Her dad turned to Marley. "Why didn't you tell us?"

Quinn interrupted before Marley could get in trouble. "I told her not to. What would you have done? Send her to see someone because you thought she'd gone crazy?"

"This isn't possible."

Quinn opened her mouth to snap at her mum, but closed it instead. "I'm sorry I didn't come straight home. I'm sorry I let you wonder about what had happened to me for so long." She'd wanted her magic. Wanted to know that she had a way to return if anyone had tried to stop her. She guessed she'd been right to worry.

"I was going to call you tomorrow night anyway," Marley said. "So you could be here Christmas Eve and Christmas Day."

She held out the flower to Marley, who'd been sitting beside her. "You can call me directly now."

"I can't believe you chose that place over here. Fae don't think much of us humans." Marley took the flower.

She glanced towards Baenen, a smile slowly forming. "Some Fae like humans." Some Fae liked humans very much.

"I'll keep her safe if that's what you are worried about." Baenen stood near the window, well away from many of the metal objects in the room.

She knew exactly how he felt. The longer she remained in the room, the more ill she felt. "I can't stay here anymore. Not now I have Fae magic. This world will make me sick."

"You never should have made that choice. You're too young to know if that's where you want to spend the rest of your life."

She shook her head at her dad's words. "I'll probably never be able to convince you. And I'm sorry you don't like my choices, but this is my life and the realms of the Fae are where I want to spend it." She closed her hand and summoned another flower, taking the few steps separating her from her mum. "You can call me when you want to see me." She grinned. "Just not too often. Time doesn't pass as quickly in the realms of the Fae."

Her mum cautiously took the flower. "How does it work?"

"Speak my name against it."

"You could speak other words too. Quinn will hear them," Baenen said. "If you need her urgently speak her name against the flower then crush it."

Quinn watched her mum raise the flower to her lips and whisper against it. She smiled when she heard the words, 'you're not going'. "I have to go. I can't stay here. This world will kill me if I stay in it for too long."

Her mum rose, wrapping her arms around her. "We thought we'd lost you. That you were dead. And Marley couldn't tell us anything." She pulled away enough to glare at Marley, her look promising they would talk later.

"That's not my fault," Marley grumbled.

Quinn pulled away from her mum. "I'll be back Christmas Day. But someone needs to call me the moment you wake up because I won't know when it is. Time runs differently between the realms."

"You're going already?" Her mum reached for her.

Quinn stepped back. "I have to. I don't want to end up with iron sickness. I also won't be able to stay long on Christmas Day either."

Her dad rose to his feet. "I should build that entertainment area out the back that I've been talking about for a few years."

"Why?" She felt Baenen stop behind her and leaned back against him, one of his arms going around her waist.

"I can make it without iron. That way when you visit us you'll have somewhere to stay that won't make you sick."

Pulling away from Baenen, she threw herself into her dad's arms. "I love you." She reached for her mum who joined them. "Both of you."

"Then why did you choose this?"

She tried to think of an answer for her mum that wouldn't hurt her. There was none. "Because this isn't my world anymore. As much as I'll miss you, I'd miss the realms of the Fae more." She pulled away from them. "And miss Baenen." She took another step back. "I have to go." She conjured a flower, holding it up. "But I will be back."

Baenen stepped up beside her, wrapping an arm around her waist. "You're welcome to visit us in the realms of the Fae, but time goes slower there and you'd need someone to call you back before you're missed here."

"I'm not going back there. Once was more than enough for me," Marley said.

"We can?" Her mum smiled. "Why didn't you say earlier?"

Quinn shrugged. She hadn't thought of it.

"You better not expect me to go there," Marley said.

"You can stay home and call them back," Quinn said.

Marley's expression brightened. "Really? You'd leave me here on my own?"

"Not until you're older," her dad said.

"Much older," her mum added.

The last of Quinn's worries faded. "I'll see you Christmas morning." She turned her head to look at Baenen. "Are you ready?"

"Yes." His arm tightened around her waist. "Let's go home."

Smiling, she nodded. Home. That sounded like a plan. Closing her hand she crushed the flower and the scent of her magic filled the air as the world shimmered and reformed. She scanned her surroundings. She couldn't wait to show her parents her home. Her smiled widened. If her mum had thought everything she'd learned so far was an impossibility, she couldn't wait to see what she thought of the castle.

"About that valley."

Quinn laughed softly at Baenen's words. "That sounds-" She broke off as something else occurred to her.

"Is something wrong?"

"I haven't got Christmas presents for my family."

"Is that all? You had me worried for a moment."

"I have no idea how to find presents here. Do you have shops?"

Baenen gestured vaguely in the direction of the stairs that led to the area beneath the castle. "We have a treasure room you can choose things from. What do you think that is for?"

She slowly shook her head. Last year she'd spent fifty dollars on her parents combined. "Not quite what I was thinking."

Baenen lifted his hand, opening it to show an autumn leaf. "I know a little village with several craftsmen. It's on a cliff overlooking a lake. What do you say? We can explore the area afterwards." He held out his empty hand to her.

No wonder she loved it here. Even shopping was an adventure. She took his hand. There was only one thing she could say. "Let's go." She smiled. She was definitely far more like Scout than she'd ever realised. "There are places to explore."

Free Ebook

Sign up to Avril's newsletter to receive a free ebook. This ebook is exclusive to those on her mailing list. To find out more about this offer visit: http://www.avrilsabine.com/free-ebook/

*

Acknowledgements

As always, many thanks to all the usual crew. I couldn't manage without your help. And like last time, I absolutely love the cover of this book, Cat.

To The Reader

If you enjoyed this book, why not consider leaving a review to help other readers discover it too? Reader engagement is one of the few ways that lets an author know readers want more books in a particular series or genre. So leave a review and tell friends, not only about this book but also about other ones you've enjoyed, so you can continue to enjoy books by your favourite authors for years to come.

Dreams are meant to be lived,

Avril.

About The Author

Avril is an Australian fiction writer who lives with her family on acreage in South East Queensland. She writes mostly young adult speculative fiction, but has been known to dabble in other genres. You can find more information about her at her website www.avrilsabine.com where you can also sign up for her newsletter to be kept informed about new releases, current projects, blog posts and exclusive news.

Titles By Avril Sabine

Stories about strong characters and characters who discover their strengths.

SERIES

Assassins Of The Dead- Young Adult Fantasy/ Paranormal

Book 1: Dark Blade

Book 2: Dragon Touched

Book 3: Society Against Vampires

Book 4: King's Request

Dragon Blood- Young Adult Urban Fantasy (with elements of romance)

(5 book series)

Book 1: Pliethin

Book 2: Wyvern

Book 3: Surety

Book 4: Knight

Book 5: Mage

Dragon Mage- Young Adult Urban Fantasy (with elements of romance)

(Series two of Dragon Blood series)

Book 1: Promise

Dragon Blood Chronicles- Young Adult Urban Fantasy (with elements of romance)

(Companion stand alone series to Dragon Blood)

Book 1: Oath

Book 2: Betrayed

Guardians Of The Round Table- Young Adult Fantasy LitRPG

(Co-written with Storm and Rhys Petersen)

Book 1: Dexterity Fail

Book 2: Goblin Boots

Book 3: Singed Feathers

Book 4: Frog Mage

Book 5: Crystal Mine

Book 6: Cursed Harp

Rosie's Rangers- Young Adult Western Steampunk

(6 book series)

Book 1: Justice

Book 2: Vengeance

Book 3: Treachery

Book 4: Accused

Book 5: Wanted

Book 6: Corruption

Mark Of Kings- Children's Fantasy

(Upper middle grade/preteen)

(4 book series)

Book 1: The Arena

Book 2: The Island

Book 3: The Assassin

Book 4: The King

STAND ALONE SERIES

Demon Hunters- Young Adult Urban Fantasy/ Horror (with elements of romance)

Book 1: Blood Sacrifice

Book 2: Retribution

Book 3: Tainted

Book 4: Premonition

Book 5: Cursed

Book 6: Feud

Book 7: Extrication

Plea Of The Damned- Young Adult Urban Fantasy/Paranormal

(6 book series)

Book 1: Forgive Me Lucy

Book 2: Forgive Me Aiden

Book 3: Forgive Me Jena

Book 4: Forgive Me Kobe

Book 5: Forgive Me Marti

Book 6: Forgive Me Dawson

Realms Of The Fae- Young Adult Urban Fantasy (with elements of romance)

The Sword (short story in Like A Girl Anthology)

Heart Of Stone

Book 1: A Debt Owed

Book 2: Marked By The Hunt

Book 3: The Magic Collector

Book 4: An Unexpected Betrayal

Book 5: Imprisoned By Iron

Fairytales Retold (Short Stories)

Snow-White And Rose-Red

The Twelve Brothers

The Light Princess

Beauty And The Beast

Sleeping Beauty

Aschenputtel

The Golden Bird

The Frog Prince

The Death Of Koshchei The Deathless

Myths And Legends Retold (Short Stories)

Ion, Son Of Apollo

Sir Gawain And The Maid With The Narrow Sleeves

Princess Ilse, The Giant's Daughter

YOUNG ADULT NOVELS

Young Adult Fantasy (with elements of romance)

Elf Sight

Earth Bound

Young Adult Urban Fantasy

Stone Warrior (with elements of romance)

The Jungle Inside

Young Adult Contemporary (with elements of romance)

Through Your Eyes

The Ugly Stepsister

Perfect Little Princess

Young Adult Contemporary/Paranormal

Whispers In The Dark (with elements of romance and same sex relationships)

Over Too Soon (with elements of romance)

Young Adult Sci-Fi

Experiment X-One-Six (Urban Sci-Fi/Superheroes)

An Endless Dawn (Post Apocalyptic Sci-Fi)

CHILDREN'S BOOKS

Dragon Lord (Preteen/early teens) (Fantasy)

The Irish Wizard (Upper middle grade) (Urban Fantasy)

SHORT STORIES

Urban Fantasy

Eternally Late

Dealings With Joe

Glimpses (short story in That Moment When Anthology)

Contemporary

The Brat Next Door

Fantasy LitRPG

(Set in the same world as Guardians Of The Round Table Series)

Tales Of Inadon 1: The Disc (Co-written with Storm and Rhys Petersen) (short story in Game On! Anthology)

Post Apocalyptic Sci-Fi

Compulsive Directive

NONFICTION

A Year Of Weekly Writing Exercises (Creative Writing)

Cooking For Families With Allergies (Cooking) (Co-written with Storm Petersen)

Tell Me A Story, Grandma (Memoir)

For the most up to date details on available titles visit:

www.avrilsabine.com/books/bibliography

Realms Of The Fae Series

To learn more about this series visit:

www.avrilsabine.com/series/rotf

BOOKS AVAILABLE IN THE REALMS OF THE FAE SERIES

The Sword (short story in Like A Girl Anthology)

Heart Of Stone

Book 1: A Debt Owed

Book 2: Marked By The Hunt

Book 3: The Magic Collector

Book 4: An Unexpected Betrayal

Book 5: Imprisoned By Iron

Disclaimer

This is a work of fiction. Names, characters, businesses, places, events and incidents are either the products of the author's imagination or used in a fictitious manner. Any resemblance to actual persons, living or dead, or actual events is purely coincidental.